"This is not a good idea," Shannon murmured.

"Feels pretty good to me." Reece's thumbs rubbed distracting little circles on the points of her shoulders. His smile was wicked. "Maybe my technique is rusty. You could help me polish it up."

"There's nothing wrong with your technique." With an effort, she planted her hands against his chest. "It's just…it's too fast…this isn't what I want." Honesty and nerves compelled her to add, "Well, I *do* want it, but I'm not going to do it."

Reece opened his mouth but was cut off by the chime of the doorbell. "Saved by the bell," he murmured.

His hands dropped away from her shoulders as he stepped back, and Shannon told herself that the little pang she felt was relief, not regret.

And if she tried hard enough, she might be able to make herself believe it.

Dear Reader,

Things are cooling down outside—at least here in the Northeast—but inside this month's six Silhouette Intimate Moments titles the heat is still on high. After too long an absence, bestselling author Dallas Schulze is back to complete her beloved miniseries A FAMILY CIRCLE with *Lovers and Other Strangers*. Shannon Deveraux has come home to Serenity and lost her heart to travelin' man Reece Morgan.

Our ROMANCING THE CROWN continuity is almost over, so join award winner Ingrid Weaver in *Under the King's Command*. I think you'll find Navy SEAL hero Sam Coburn irresistible. Ever-exciting Lindsay McKenna concludes her cross-line miniseries, MORGAN'S MERCENARIES: ULTIMATE RESCUE, with *Protecting His Own*. You'll be breathless from the first page to the last. Linda Castillo's *A Cry in the Night* features another of her "High Country Heroes," while relative newcomer Catherine Mann presents the second of her WINGMEN WARRIORS, in *Taking Cover*. Finally, welcome historical author Debra Lee Brown to the line with *On Thin Ice*, a romantic adventure set against an Alaskan background.

Enjoy them all, and come back again next month, when the roller-coaster ride of love and excitement continues right here in Silhouette Intimate Moments, home of the best romance reading around.

Yours,

Leslie J. Wainger
Executive Senior Editor

Please address questions and book requests to:
Silhouette Reader Service
U.S.: 3010 Walden Ave., P.O. Box 1325, Buffalo, NY 14269
Canadian: P.O. Box 609, Fort Erie, Ont. L2A 5X3

DALLAS SCHULZE

Lovers and Other Strangers

Silhouette®

INTIMATE MOMENTS™

Published by Silhouette Books

America's Publisher of Contemporary Romance

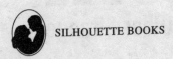 SILHOUETTE BOOKS

ISBN 0-373-27253-7

LOVERS AND OTHER STRANGERS

This edition published by arrangement with Harlequin Books S.A.

® and TM are trademarks of Harlequin Books S.A., used under license. Trademarks indicated with ® are registered in the United States Patent and Trademark Office, the Canadian Trade Marks Office and in other countries.

Visit Silhouette at www.eHarlequin.com

Printed in U.S.A.

DALLAS SCHULZE

loves books, old movies, her husband and her cat, not necessarily in that order. A sucker for a happy ending, her writing has given her an outlet for her imagination. Dallas hopes that readers have half as much fun with her books as she does! She has more hobbies than there is space to list them, but is currently working on a doll collection. Dallas loves to hear from her readers, and you can write to her at her Web site at www.dallasschulze.com.

For Mary Anne, Kathleen and Denise
for all the laughter, the quilting fun and the friendship.

Chapter 1

For the first one hundred years or so of its existence, the town of Serenity Falls had managed to live up to its name. It had been founded in the 1870s by a gentleman of uncertain background but considerable charisma. He liked to say he'd been called to California by a force from the stars, though there were those who suggested that the only stars involved had most likely been worn by members of a posse chasing him out of town. Whatever the reason, there was no question but that he'd ended up exactly where he was meant to be. Where else but California could a man adopt the name of Jonathan Everlasting Reconciliation and not find himself incarcerated in the nearest asylum?

Whatever his background, Brother Rec knew what he was doing when it came to laying out a new town, though there were complaints at the time about the amount of open space he insisted be incorporated into the town's design. What was the point of leaving empty fields sitting cheek by jowl with the houses? Didn't do anything but encourage mice and coyotes. Brother Rec spoke grandly of the need to retain a connection with nature, a close-up view of the good Lord's work here on earth. Folks shook their heads over this foolishness, bought mousetraps and took potshots at any coyotes foolish enough to come within rifle range. As time passed, the mice and the coyotes moved on to less hostile environs and the fields became parks, giving the town a rural quality that was considered one of its biggest charms.

In the early 1890s, Brother Rec left Serenity Falls, taking with him five thousand dollars in town funds and the mayor's sixteen-year-old daughter. The scandal rocked the community, not least of all because the mayor was more upset by the loss of the team of racing mules taken by the eloping couple than he was by the loss of his daughter. Then again, they *were* the finest mules in the county, if not in the state, and Millie Ann had been a pretty girl but not exceptionally bright so perhaps his reaction was understandable.

The town survived Brother Rec's betrayal and, over the next ninety years or so, it also survived two world wars, a depression, earthquakes both major and minor and the advent of cars, television and rap music. Through it all, it remained pretty much what it had started out to be—a smallish town with an unusually strong sense of community.

There had, of course, been crises over the years. There was the flood of '32, when boulders the size of small cars washed down out of the foothills and came to rest in the middle of town. In the midfifties, two lions escaped from a visiting circus, and citizens huddled inside their homes in fear of the ravening beasts.

The lions, possibly confused by the lack of an audience, wandered the streets for a couple of hours before allowing themselves to be recaptured.

The sixties had brought the requisite amount of turmoil—long hair, blue jeans, even a sit-in or two. But all in all, Serenity Falls had weathered the years well.

Of course, there was a time, more than twenty years back, when some citizens had thought the town might be brought to rack and ruin through the efforts of a single individual. Reece Morgan had been a newly orphaned ten-year-old when he came to live with his grandfather. For the next eight years, Serenity Falls had been considerably less serene than usual. If there was trouble, he was bound to be in the midst of it, and if he wasn't actually caught in the act, it was only because he'd just left the scene.

When he left town the day after getting his high school diploma, there was a general sigh of relief. Most folks agreed that he was bound to come to a bad end and they'd just as soon he did it somewhere else. With his departure, Serenity Falls settled back into its usual sleepy contentment.

But, small towns, like elephants, have long memories. When old Joe Morgan died and left his house to his erring grandson, transgressions more than twenty years old were suddenly news again. Those who had known Reece recalled his wild ways and shook their heads over the possibility of his return, but it was generally assumed that he would put the place up for sale as soon as the ink was dry on the title transfer.

Weeks passed. The lawn gradually turned brown under the heat of the summer sun, and the house took on a dusty, unlived-in look, but the expected For Sale sign did not materialize. Neighbors speculated on the possibility that the lawyers hadn't been able to find Reece.

As summer crept toward autumn, the speculation grew more lurid. Reece was dead. He was in prison. He was an underworld drug lord and the Feds were waiting to nab him if he came forward to claim his grandfather's house. Level-headed sorts pointed out that, according to the news and made-for-TV movies, drugs were a highly profitable business. If Reece was head of some sort of drug cartel, it didn't seem likely that he'd risk capture in order to claim a slightly shabby two-bedroom house on a medium-size lot in Serenity Falls. California real estate wasn't what it had been, after all. Besides, if the DEA or the FBI or any other set of initials was staking out the house, their presence would be known. Edith Hacklemeyer lived directly across from the Morgan place and there wasn't a secret agent living who could slip past her sharp eyes.

Eventually the speculation began to die down. There were complaints about the way the house was being let go, comments that its unkempt condition might affect property values. Edith commented acidly that it would be just like Reece to let the place go to rack and ruin out of sheer spite. He never did have any respect for property. Hadn't he once ridden his bicycle right through a bed of her best petunias? No one could tell her *that* had been an accident! No one tried. And no one offered much argument to her assertion that Reece Morgan was trouble—always had been, always would be.

By October, having the old Morgan house sitting empty had begun to seem almost normal, and most of the speculation had died down due to lack of information. But it revived quickly when Sam Larrabee's brother, who worked for the electric company, told Sam that the power was being turned on again.

The word spread quickly. Ex-con, drug lord or walking dead, it seemed that Reece Morgan was finally coming home.

Shannon Devereux frowned at the calendars laid out in front of her. She sighed and then shuffled through the stack of index cards that held information on the classes she was supposed to be scheduling and then looked at the calendars again, seeking inspiration. Finding none, she shuffled the cards a little more before resolutely picking one out.

When she bought the quilt shop four years ago, she hadn't known a thing about running her own business. She'd been looking for a focus in her life, something to fill her days and make the nights seem a little shorter. Patchwork Heaven had proven to be exactly what she needed. She felt a surge of pride as she looked around the shop. Shelves along two walls held bolts of fabric in a rainbow array of colors. Patterns and books were displayed in racks in the center of the shop. The front of the building was almost all glass, letting in sunlight and giving a pleasant view of the tree-lined street outside. At the back of the shop, where Shannon was sitting, were tables for classes, and every spare inch of wall was covered by class samples—a warm, multicolored wallpaper to entice potential students. The arrangement was both efficient and inviting.

She'd done a good job, she thought. Business had increased nicely. For the past two years, the shop had been making a small but steady profit. She wasn't likely to make it into the Fortune 500, but she was solvent and that was more than most small businesses

could say. Even better, she loved her work. Most of it,
anyway. She looked down at the calendars and the
stack of cards and sighed. Where was a scheduling
fairy when you needed one?

"You know, there are easier ways to do that." Kelly
McKinnon paused next to the table, a stack of bolts in
her arms.

"If you tell me that a computer would make this
easier, I'm going to fire you." Shannon fingered the
edge of an index card, debating whether to slot the
hand quilting class on a Saturday morning or Thursday
evening. And should it be January or February?

"A computer would make that a lot easier," Kelly
said, ignoring the warning.

"You're fired," Shannon said without looking up.

"You can't fire me."

"Why not? You're insubordinate. That's a good reason to fire someone."

"Insubordinate?" Kelly considered the accusation
for a moment and then shook her head. "I think insubordination applies only to the military."

"I don't see why they should get to hog all the best
words," Shannon said, frowning.

"They're selfish pigs, aren't they?" Kelly said sym-
pathetically.

Shannon sighed and sat back in her chair, looking
up at her friend and employee. At five feet one inch
tall—if she stretched a bit—with a mop of pale-blond
hair and brown eyes that always seemed to hold a
smile, Kelly made her think of the illustrations of pixies in old children's books. "You're sure I can't fire
you for insubordination?"

"I think you'd have to court martial me instead."

"Too much trouble. You'll have to stay."

"Thanks, boss." Her job security confirmed, Kelly nodded toward the calendars. "You want me to do that for you? It's a lot easier when you can just click and drag the class names from place to place. Saves a lot of wear and tear on erasers. Why did you buy a computer for the office if you're not going to use it?"

"People have been scheduling classes for centuries without using a computer."

"You're afraid of the computer." Kelly's tone made it a statement rather than question.

"I am not," Shannon said defensively. "I just don't see the point in using it to do something that I'm perfectly capable of doing by hand. People are too dependent on computers these days."

"Well, you certainly don't have to worry about that," Kelly said dryly. She set the bolts she'd been carrying on the edge of the table and lifted the top one—a midnight-blue fabric printed with a scattering of tiny gold stars. "You never even turn it on."

"I run it at least once a week," Shannon said. "I figure that will keep its pistons clean."

Kelly slid the bolt of fabric in amongst the other blues, turning her head to grin at Shannon. "Computers don't have pistons. I'll get that," she added as the phone began to ring.

"Maybe I'd like them more if they did," Shannon muttered as she walked away.

She could put away the rest of the fabric, she thought, eyeing the bolts on the edge of the table. It wouldn't really be procrastinating if she was doing something productive, would it? She allowed herself a brief, wistful moment of self-delusion and then resolutely picked up the first index card. If she didn't get this done soon, the winter class schedule was going to be going out next spring.

She heard Kelly say, "You're kidding!" in a tone of breathless surprise and then tuned out the rest of the conversation. Kelly McKinnon was one of the kindest, most generous-hearted people you could ever hope to meet. She also happened to be hopelessly addicted to gossip. As near as Shannon could tell, she was the unofficial clearing house for information for the entire town.

It could have been an intolerable character flaw but Kelly's interest came without a trace of malice. She was genuinely interested in everyone—not just what they were doing and with whom but what they were thinking and feeling. Which was probably why people were so willing to tell her things they wouldn't even share with their hairdresser. Besides, Kelly was quite capable of keeping a secret. She might know where all the bodies were buried, but she rarely told anyone where to find them.

With an effort Shannon forced her attention back to the schedules. A strand of strawberry-blond hair fell forward and she tucked it absently back behind her ear. She penciled in the beginning quilt-making class on Tuesday night. Esther McIlroy was teaching that. Esther didn't mind running the cash register to handle any purchases her students made, which meant that Shannon didn't have to be here.

"You'll believe what Rhonda Whittaker just told me!" Kelly said as she hung up the phone.

"Don't tell me." Without looking up, Shannon sensed the other woman approaching from the front of the shop.

"Don't you want to know?" Kelly asked impatiently.

"Know what?" Shannon went over the penciled line a little more heavily. Tuesday was a good night to learn how to make quilts, she decided. She'd double-check with Esther to make sure it was okay.

"What Rhonda just told me," Kelly said. "Don't you want to know what she said?"

Shannon set the pencil down and looked up, her blue eyes mock solemn. "You've already told me I won't believe it, so why bother to tell me? If I want to hear things I'm not going to believe, I can watch the news."

"This is firsthand information."

"What makes you think Rhonda Whittaker is more trustworthy than Tom Brokaw? Isn't she the one who says she saw Elvis going into a room at that motel on the edge of town?"

"That was Tricia Porter," Kelly corrected her. "And it wasn't Elvis she saw, it was Paul McCartney. And she saw him at the natural foods store, buying organic barley."

"That's sooo much more believable than seeing Elvis," Shannon drawled.

"Well, I think he's a vegetarian."

"Elvis?"

"Paul McCartney," Kelly said impatiently. "I think he's a vegetarian so I guess it's not totally beyond the realm of possibility to see him in a health food store."

"Oh sure." Shannon nodded agreeably. "I bet he flies over from England on a regular basis to buy barley at Finlay's Flourishing Foods for Fitness. The name is probably known all over the world. Or maybe it's that sign out front, the one that says Authentic Foods. I mean, how could Paul resist a chance to get 'authentic' food?''

"I never have known what that means," Kelly admitted, momentarily diverted. "It sort of implies that other stores are selling fake food, doesn't it?"

"I'm surprised they haven't sued for defamation of inventory or something."

"Defamation of inventory?" Kelly's eyebrows rose in question.

"If it's not already on the books, I'm sure there's a lawyer somewhere who could make a case for it," Shannon assured her.

"Probably. But that's not the point."

"What point?"

"Precisely! We've gotten away from the point."

Laughing, Shannon dropped her pencil and leaned back in her chair. "I feel like I've fallen into an Abbott and Costello routine. You're not going to ask me who's on first, are you?"

"I'm trying to tell you what Rhonda Whittaker told me," Kelly said sternly. "And you're not making it easy."

"Sorry." Shannon did her best to look meek, but there was a suspicious tuck in her cheek and her eyes were bright with humor. "What did Rhonda tell you?"

"Reece Morgan is here."

"In the shop?" Shannon's eyes widened in surprise.

"No, you idiot. In Serenity Falls. Rhonda saw him herself. He stopped at the '76 gas station on the north end of town. Rhonda was getting gas there when this mean-looking black pickup truck pulled in."

"How does a truck look mean?" Shannon interrupted. "Did it lift its front bumper in a sneer?"

"Do you want to hear the story or do you want to ask irrelevant questions?" Kelly asked, exasperated.

"I'll be quiet," Shannon promised meekly.

"Thank you." Kelly cleared her throat. "As I was saying, a black pickup pulled in."

"A mean-looking black pickup," Shannon reminded her helpfully.

"And a man got out of it."

"Elvis?"

"Rhonda recognized him right away," Kelly continued, ignoring the interruptions.

"If he was wearing one of those spangled jumpsuits, I wouldn't think that would be very hard."

"It was Reece Morgan."

"In a spangled jumpsuit?"

"He was wearing jeans, a black T-shirt and black boots."

"No sequins?" Shannon asked, disappointed.

"Rhonda said he looked mean."

"She thought his truck looked mean, too." Shannon reminded her.

"Rhonda does sometimes let her imagination run wild," Kelly admitted. "But however he looked, we at least know he's back in town."

"Unless it's really Elvis or Paul McCartney," Shannon murmured wickedly.

Kelly shook her head. "Rhonda wouldn't have been nearly as interested in one of them. She said it was definitely Reece Morgan. They were in the same class. She said she'd have known him anywhere."

Shannon shook her head, her soft mouth twisting in a half smile. Until she moved to Serenity Falls, she'd never lived in the same place for more than two or three years. She couldn't imagine what it felt like to have lived in the same town your whole life, to be able to recognize a classmate from twenty years before.

"I never really thought Reece would come back here," Kelly said.

"His grandfather left the house to him. It seems reasonable that he'd want to go through everything himself."

"From what I've heard of his relationship with the old man, it doesn't seem likely that Reece would come back looking for mementos," Kelly said, shaking her head. "Everyone says they were pretty much oil and water."

"Is this the same 'everyone' who saw Paul McCartney eating oats at the health food store?" Shannon asked dryly.

"It was barley, and even Frank says they didn't get along." Frank was Kelly's husband. "He was a couple of years younger than Reece, but he knew him pretty well since Reece and Frank's older brother were friends. He says Reece's grandfather was a flinty old bastard."

"I can't argue with that description," Shannon said, thinking of the old man who'd lived in the house next to hers. Tall and spare with a military bearing that made no concessions to age, he'd offered her a brief, rather formal welcome when she first moved in. For the next four years, their contact had been limited to an exchange of hellos if their paths happened to cross at the mailboxes. In all that time she couldn't ever remember seeing him smile or even look as if he knew how.

"If Reece has come back to stay, you're going to be living next door to him," Kelly said, giving her a speculative look.

Shannon had no trouble reading the expression in her friend's eyes. She shook her head. "Forget it. I am not going to spy on the man just to satisfy your curiosity."

"No one said anything about spying," Kelly said, all injured innocence. "But living next door to him, you're bound to get to know him."

"I lived next door to his grandfather for four years and the only thing I know about him was that he put out the neatest piles of trash I've ever seen. I think they were color coordinated."

"Reece doesn't sound like the type to color coordinate his trash."

"It's been twenty years since anyone in this town has seen him. He could have changed."

"From hellion to neatnik?" Kelly wrinkled her nose. "Doesn't sound likely."

"Anything's possible." Shannon dropped the index cards on top of the calendars, scooped them all into a haphazard stack and thrust them at Kelly. "Here. Make yourself useful. Feed these into your magic machine and give me back a schedule."

"Aren't you in the least bit curious about Reece?" Kelly asked as she took the papers. "I mean, what if he's an escaped felon or something?"

"Right." Shannon's tone was dry as dust. "If I were an escaped felon, I'd make it a point to hide out in the one place where everyone knew me, in the one place the police would be sure to look for me, in the one place where I couldn't possibly hide my presence. And I'd drive into town, in broad daylight, driving a mean-looking truck, wearing a spangled jumpsuit and buying barley at the natural food store."

"You're getting your celebrities mixed up," Kelly

pointed out, grinning. "Reece was driving the truck but he wasn't wearing a jumpsuit and no one has seen him eating barley."

"It's only a matter of time." Shannon waved one hand. "By the end of the day, the rumor mill will probably have him arriving in a spaceship complete with bug-eyed aliens for escort."

Kelly laughed. "We haven't had any alien sightings around here since Milt Farmer gave up corn liquor and found religion."

"With Reece Morgan returning, can aliens be far behind?" Shannon's smile lingered as she moved toward the front of the shop to wait on the customer who had just entered.

Despite herself, she couldn't help but wonder about her new neighbor. After everything she'd heard about him, she was more than a little curious to actually meet the man in the flesh. The image in her mind was a cross between a young Marlon Brando and the Terminator. What a disappointment it was going to be if he turned out to be a plump, balding accountant.

Chapter 2

Groaning, Reece rolled over and opened his eyes. This must be what it felt like to spend a night on the rack, he thought, as he inventoried an assortment of aches and pains. The last time he could remember sleeping in a bed this uncomfortable, he'd been an unwilling guest in a South American prison.

Blinking the sleep from his eyes, he stared up at the water stain on the ceiling directly over the bed. If he squinted a little, it was a dead ringer for the outline of Australia. He contemplated it with some regret, thinking of wide beaches, cold beer and tall, tanned Aussie girls in very small bikinis. Now *there* was the perfect place for working through a midlife crisis. What on earth had made him decide to come back here—where he'd spent the most miserable years of his childhood?

It was all a matter of timing, he thought as he rolled out of bed and slowly straightened his aching spine. The news of his grandfather's death had come at a time when he was reevaluating his life. A rainy night, a slick road, and he had regained consciousness in time to hear the paramedics weighing his odds of making it to the hospital alive. With the distance provided by shock, he'd pondered the irony of dying in a car wreck. He'd lived with the possibility of his own death for a long time, but he'd always assumed it would come in a more spectacular form—a bullet, a knife sliding between his ribs, a car bomb maybe. It seemed supremely ironic that death should come in the form of something as mundane as having a tire blow out.

He eventually limped out of the hospital minus a spleen and fifteen pounds, neither of which he'd needed to lose but he wasn't complaining. As the doctor had told him several times, he should consider himself damned lucky to be alive at all. It wasn't the first time he'd scraped past death by the skin of his teeth. In his line of work, it was something of an occupational hazard, and he'd lived with the possibility for so long that he didn't even really think about it anymore. But there was something about nearly waking up dead because of a car wreck that had made him stop and take a long, hard look at his life. Maybe it was the mundanity of it—the reminder that his death could be just as meaningless as anyone else's. Or maybe it was spending his fortieth birthday alone in the hospital—the sudden realization that half his life was over that made him question what he was going to do with the rest of it.

It wasn't a real midlife crisis, Reece thought as he pulled clean clothes out of his duffel bag and walked, naked, to the bathroom down the hall. In a real midlife crisis, you did stupid things like quit the job you'd had for the past fifteen years, let go of the apartment where you'd lived for almost as long, and had an affair with a woman half your age. He met the eyes of his reflection in the dingy mirror over the bathroom sink.

Hell. Two out of three and the most boring two, at that. Maybe he should have kept the job and the apartment and just gone for the affair. His mouth twisted in a half smile as he pushed back the shower curtain. Midlife crisis or temporary insanity? Looking at the grudging trickle of tepid water that seemed to be the best the shower had to offer, Reece wasn't sure he wanted to know the answer.

Shannon knelt on the lawn next to the flower bed and tugged halfheartedly at a scraggly patch of dichondra that was matted around the base of a rosebush. Generally, she gardened on the "survival of the fittest" philosophy. Any plant that couldn't survive a little competition was welcome to move to someone else's flower bed. She had neither the time nor the inclination to pamper delicate plants, and she tackled the weeds only when it began to look as if they were going to overwhelm the flowers.

She sat back on her heels and eyed the patch of ground she'd cleared. The weeds weren't really all that bad but it was such a beautiful day that it seemed a shame to spend it indoors. In early November, summer's heat was gone and the winter rains had not yet begun. The air was dry and warm and the nights were cool enough to be refreshing. Closing her eyes, she turned her face up to the sun, savoring the warmth of it against her skin. No matter how long she lived in southern California, she didn't think she'd ever learn to take this kind of weather for granted.

"Good way to end up with skin cancer."

The tart comment made Shannon jump and she stifled a curse when she realized who had interrupted the peaceful morning. Edith Hacklemeyer lived across the street. A short, thin woman on the far side of sixty, she was a retired English teacher who filled her days with gardening, quilting and offering unwanted advice to anyone who crossed her path. She was an unimaginative gardener, a mediocre quilter and a tireless busybody. Since she was both a neighbor and a customer at the shop, Shannon felt obligated to remain on amicable terms with her.

"Beautiful day, isn't it?" She chose to ignore the remark about skin cancer. One of Edith's less appealing characteristics was her ability to find the bad in everything and everyone.

"We need rain," Edith said, frowning at the crystal-clear sky.

"The rain will get here," Shannon said easily. She leaned forward to smooth the soil around a marigold.

"Ought to pull those up and put in some pansies," Edith told her, eyeing the marigold with disfavor.

"It's still blooming, and I like the flowers."

"Never cared much for marigolds. They always seemed a bit tatty looking to me but, even if I liked them, I'd pull them up. Got to get the winter bloomers in early so they can get established with the first rains."

"Mmm." Shannon made a polite, interested noise and tucked a little more soil around the marigold. The bright little blossoms seemed to smile at her and she smiled back.

"I don't envy you." Edith's attention shifted away from the flowers and her pale-blue eyes settled on the dusty black truck parked in the driveway of the house next door.

"Oh, I don't mind waiting a while to plant winter flowers," Shannon said, deliberately misunderstanding.

"I was talking about *him*," Edith said darkly. "I don't envy you having to live right next door to *him*. No telling what sort of trouble *he'll* cause."

"I don't see why he should cause any trouble at all." Shannon let her gaze rest on the truck. She'd taught a class at the shop the night before and the truck had been there when she got home around ten o'clock. Obviously, the grapevine had worked with its usual efficiency and Reece Morgan really was home. After all she'd heard about him, she had to admit that she was more than a little curious to see him in the flesh.

"His kind doesn't need a reason. Trouble comes naturally to that sort."

"You haven't seen him in twenty years. He might have changed."

"A leopard can't change its spots." Edith's tone suggested that this observation was original to her. "Mark my words, things won't be the same now."

"Maybe things could use a little shaking up." Shannon said mildly.

"Not the sort of shaking up *he'll* give them. Can't imagine why he came back here. He wasn't wanted before, and he's certainly not wanted now."

Until that moment Shannon had been reserving her opinion about Reece Morgan. Aside from a mild curiosity, she really hadn't given much thought to the man. But Edith's firm pronouncement that he wasn't welcome set her back up instantly. She had a sudden image of the sort of welcome Edith might have given to a newly orphaned boy twenty years before. And his grandfather—just how welcoming had that stern old man been? She rose to her feet in one smooth movement.

"Actually, I was thinking that it would be neighborly to invite him for breakfast," she said as she dusted her hands off on the seat of her cutoffs.

"Invite him to breakfast?" Edith couldn't have looked more horrified if she'd just announced that she was going to tap dance naked through the center of town. "You can't be serious."

"Why not?" Shannon's smile held an edge that would have warned a more observant woman, but Edith was nothing if not unobservant.

"He's a hoodlum, that's why not. He rode his bicycle through my petunias." She offered the last triumphantly, as if no more profound evidence of wickedness could be given.

"I don't think a man should be judged by a childish prank. If you'll excuse me, I think I just saw someone moving around in the kitchen," she lied.

Shannon walked away without waiting for a response. Behind her, she heard Edith's horrified gasp and then the rapid patter of her sneakers as she scurried back across the street, seeking a protective distance from potential disaster. Shannon knew the other woman would go into her house and immediately go to the front window, which gave her a clear view of the street and everything that went on there. It was that knowledge that kept her walking toward the Morgan house, even as her brief spurt of temper cooled. The last thing she wanted to do was invite a total stranger to breakfast, but she was too stubborn to back down now.

"This is what you get for letting your temper get the best of you," she muttered as she climbed the steps to the porch. "The man is going to think you're a total lunatic."

Shannon jabbed her finger against the doorbell button and heard the faint sound of chimes through the door. She could practically feel Edith's eyes boring into her back. Briefly she considered turning and waving. Such a breach of protocol would probably be enough to get her classified as a hoodlum, right next to Reece Morgan, petunia killer. The thought of Edith's horrified reaction made her smile, and the last of her annoyance evaporated.

This wasn't exactly how she'd planned to spend her morning, but she couldn't deny that she was more than a bit curious about her new neighbor. After everything she'd heard about him, she was prepared for anything from a tattooed refugee from a motorcycle gang to a Milquetoast accountant, complete with pocket protector and taped glasses.

What she was not prepared for was the six feet four inches of damp, half-naked male who pulled open the door. He must have just gotten out of the shower, she thought, staring at an impressive width of muscled chest. A solid mat of dark hair swirled across his upper body and then tapered down to a narrow line that ran across an admirably flat stomach before disappearing into the waist of his jeans. She was astonished by the effort it took to look away from that intriguing line and lift her eyes to his face.

Oh my. It hardly seemed fair that the rest of him matched the body: thick dark hair, worn slightly shaggy and long enough to brush his collar, if he'd been wearing one; sharply defined cheekbones; a strong blade of a nose; and a chin that hinted at stubbornness. Twenty years ago he might have been almost *too* good-looking.

But age and experience had added an edge to his features, refining and sharpening them to something far more potent than mere handsomeness.

None of her imaginings had prepared her for the man standing in front of her. Nor had they prepared her for the way her stomach clenched sharply in sudden awareness—a deeply feminine response to his masculinity. It had been a long, long time since she'd felt anything like it, and the unexpectedness of it had her staring at him blankly.

Reece's first thought was that he'd never seen eyes of such a deep clear blue—pure sapphire fringed with long, dark lashes. His second was that he hoped she wasn't selling anything because he had a feeling that his sales resistance might reach an all-time low under the influence of those eyes.

She didn't *look* like someone who was selling something. She was wearing a faded blue T-shirt that clung in all the right places and a pair of denim cutoffs that revealed legs that went on forever. There was a smudge of dirt on one cheek, and her reddish-gold hair was pulled back in a plain, unadorned ponytail. The stark style emphasized the fine-boned beauty of her features. He caught himself straightening his shoulders and tightening his stomach muscles in an instinctive male response. The reaction both amused and irritated him.

"Can I help you?" he asked when it began to look like she wasn't going to break the silence.

Shannon flushed, suddenly aware that she'd been staring at him like a teenager gawking at a rock star. Completely thrown off balance, she blurted out the first words that came to mind. "Would you like some breakfast?"

"Breakfast?" he said, trying to sound as if he was

accustomed to having beautiful women show up on his doorstep and offer him a meal. What a shame, he thought. She looked perfectly normal, but she was apparently not rowing with both oars in the water.

"I live next door," Shannon said, aware that the invitation hadn't come out as smoothly as she might have liked and trying to salvage the situation. "I didn't mean to sound abrupt. It's just that I wasn't expecting you."

Reece's brows rose. She sounded flustered but sane. He leaned one shoulder against the doorjamb, starting to enjoy the situation. "You knocked on my door," he pointed out gently.

"I know. But I wasn't expecting…you." She waved one hand, the gesture encompassing the six feet four inches of male standing in front of her. His brows went higher and she caught the gleam of laughter in his dark eyes. Sighing, she grabbed for the tattered shreds of her dignity. "I bet you're wondering if you should call for the men with the butterfly nets."

"The thought had crossed my mind," he admitted, and she couldn't help but laugh.

"Can I start over?"

"Go ahead."

She drew a deep breath. "I'm Shannon Devereux. I live next door."

"Reece Morgan." He offered his hand, and she took it automatically, startled by the jolt of awareness that shot up her arm at the light touch.

"I know who you are," she said as she withdrew her hand. She rubbed her fingertips against her palm. "We were expecting you."

"We?" Reece threw a questioning look past her shoulder at the empty street and Shannon cursed the

easy way the color rose in her cheeks. This was what
she got for letting temper and curiosity get the better
of her, she thought. If she'd minded her own business
instead of listening to Edith Hacklemeyer, she would
still be pulling weeds and enjoying the weather. Instead, she was standing in front of the most attractive
man she'd seen in a very long time, confirming his
initial impression of her as a blithering idiot.

"I meant that everyone knew you were coming,"
she said.

"Did they?" Reece frowned uneasily. He'd spent
too many years keeping to the shadows to be comfortable with the idea, but he knew there were few secrets
in a small town. Besides, it didn't matter anymore, he
reminded himself. It was just that old habits were hard
to break. "I didn't exactly take an ad out in the local
paper."

"You didn't have to. Sam Larrabee's brother spread
the word." When Reece gave her a blank look, she
clarified. "He works for the electric company. He saw
the order to turn on the utilities."

"And *he* took out an ad in the paper?"

"No, he told Sam. And Sam told Alice—that's
Sam's wife. And Alice told Constance Lauderman,
who probably called—"

"Okay, I get the picture." He shook his head as he
interrupted her recitation of the local grapevine. "I'd
almost forgotten what this place was like," he said,
looking both irritated and reluctantly amused.

"Well, it's a small town, and news does tend to get
around."

"I guess it does." Reece slid the fingers of one hand
through his still-damp hair.

The movement drew Shannon's eyes back to the

solid width of his bare shoulders and chest, and she felt her stomach clench in helpless awareness. She didn't know what it was about him that brought on this deeply female response. The sight of a bare male chest had never caused this kind of reaction before. It would be nice to believe it was because she'd spent too much time in the sun this morning. With an effort, she dragged her gaze upward and met his eyes.

"Anyway, that's how I knew who you were. I thought you might not have taken the time to do any shopping when you got in yesterday and might like to have breakfast at my house."

Reece rubbed his hand absently across his bare chest. She'd guessed right about the shopping. As far as he knew, the only food in the house was a package of slightly squashed Twinkies he'd bought somewhere in Arizona the day before. On the other hand, he hadn't come back here to develop a social life. He just wanted to put the house in shape to sell and maybe get himself in shape—mentally and physically—while he was at it. No matter how attractive she was, he didn't want to—

"Coffee's already made," she added, as an afterthought.

"Let me get a shirt." The promise of caffeine was too great a temptation. He still wasn't sure his new neighbor was all there, but she was beautiful and she had coffee—the combination was more than he could resist.

He disappeared into the house, and Shannon drew a deep breath and then released it slowly. *Wow.* What on earth had happened to her? It wasn't as if Reece Morgan was the first attractive man she'd met. Kelly had made it her life's work to introduce her to every single, straight, attractive male who came within range—a rapidly shrinking pool, as Kelly reminded her tartly every time Shannon turned down a date. She'd never given any of those men a second thought, had barely noticed them even when they were standing right in front of her. But this man—*this* one made her very aware of the differences between male and female, something she hadn't paid much attention to lately.

By the time Reece returned, she'd regained her equilibrium and was able to give him a casually friendly smile. Whatever she'd felt earlier, it was gone now, and if she felt a slight tingle when his arm brushed against hers, it was probably only because she had a touch of sunburn.

"I thought you could go years without meeting your neighbors in California," he said as he pulled the door shut behind him and checked the knob to be sure the lock had caught.

"In California, maybe, but not in Serenity Falls." She caught his questioning look. "You see, the town is caught in some sort of space-time-continuum warp. You know, like the ones on *Star Trek?* I think we're actually somewhere in the Midwest right now. As near as I can tell, the change occurs just as you pass the town limit sign. If you pay attention, you can actually feel the shift as the very fabric of space folds and deposits you in...oh, Iowa maybe."

"Really? I didn't notice," Reece said politely but she caught the gleam of laughter in his eyes.

She liked the way he could smile with just his eyes, she thought. Of course, so far, there wasn't much about him that she *didn't* like. *Tall, dark and handsome.* The old cliché popped into her head, and she smiled a little at how perfectly it fit him. At five-eight, she was tall for a woman and was accustomed to looking most men in the eye, but walking next to him, she felt small and almost fragile.

As if sensing her gaze, he glanced at her, and Shannon looked away quickly, half-afraid of what her expression might reveal. Distracted, she tapped her fingers against the tailgate of his truck as they walked past.

"It doesn't look particularly mean to me." She immediately wished the words unsaid but it was too late. What was it about him that caused her to blurt out the first thing that popped into her head?

"What?" Reece gave her a look that combined wariness with curiosity, confirming her guess that he had doubts about her mental health. Not that she could blame him, she admitted with an inner sigh. She hadn't exactly been at her best this morning.

"Reports of your arrival spread around town yesterday afternoon. Someone mentioned that you were driving a mean-looking truck."

"Mean-looking?" Reece glanced back at his truck and shrugged. "It's never attacked anyone, that I know of." He frowned thoughtfully. "There was a woman at the gas station yesterday. Skinny, big teeth and a face sort of like a trout. She looked at me like I was an alien with green skin and antennae sticking out of my head."

"Or Elvis in a spangled jumpsuit," Shannon murmured, thinking of her conversation with Kelly.

"No, I think she'd have been less surprised to see him," Reece said thoughtfully.

Shannon's laughter was infectious, and Reece found himself smiling with her. He wouldn't be all that surprised if it turned out that she'd escaped from a mental ward, but he wasn't going to let that stop him from enjoying her company. Walking beside her, he was conscious of the long-legged ease of her stride, of the way the sunlight caught the red in her hair, drawing fire from it.

"That was Rhonda Whittaker at the gas station," she told him.

"Whittaker." His eyes narrowed thoughtfully as he repeated the name. "I think I went to school with her. She looked like a trout then, too."

Shannon laughed again. His description was wickedly accurate. Rhonda *did* look a great deal like a trout—a perpetually startled trout.

"Careful. That trout holds a key place on the local grapevine."

He shook his head. "I'd almost forgotten what this place was like. Everybody always knew everybody else's business, and what they didn't know, they made up."

"According to Edith Hacklemeyer, no one ever had to make up anything about you."

"Good God, is that old bat still around?" He stopped at the beginning of Shannon's walkway and looked at the neat white house across the street. A modest expanse of green lawn stretched from the house to the street, perfectly flat, perfectly rectangular, cut exactly in two by an arrow-straight length of concrete sidewalk. The only decorative element was a circular flower bed that sat to the left of the sidewalk. It contained a single rosebush, planted precisely in the center. The rest of the bed was planted in neat, concentric rows of young plants, bright-green leaves standing out against a dark layer of mulch.

"Of course she's still there," Reece answered his own question. "The place looked exactly the same twenty years ago. Every spring she planted red petunias, and in the fall, she planted pansies. It never changed.''

''It still hasn't.'' Shannon wondered if it was just her imagination that made her think she could see a shadowy figure through the lace curtains. She had to bite back a smile at the thought of Edith's reaction to having Reece boldly staring at her house. She touched him lightly on the arm.

''You're not supposed to do that.''

''Do what?'' He looked down at her, one brow cocked in inquiry.

''Look at her house.'' Shannon shook her head, pulling her mouth into a somber line.

''There's some law against looking at her house?'' Reece asked, but he turned obediently and followed her up the walkway.

''You're stepping out of your assigned place in the world order. It's Edith's job to watch you. It's your job to be watched.''

''I'll try to keep that in mind,'' he said, amused by her take on small-town life. ''I can't believe old Cacklemeyer is still around.''

''Cacklemeyer?'' Shannon's gurgle of laughter made him smile. ''Is that what you called her?''

''She wasn't real popular with her students,'' he said by way of answer. ''She's not still teaching, is she?''

''No. She retired a few years ago.''

''There are a lot of kids who should be grateful for that,'' he said with feeling.

''According to Edith, you committed petuniacide on at least one occasion,'' Shannon commented as she stepped around a small shrub that sprawled into the walkway. She glanced at him over her shoulder. ''She seemed to think it was a deliberate act of horticultural violence.''

"It was.'' His half smile was reminiscent. "She acted like that flower bed was the gardens at Versailles. If she was in the yard when I rode my bike past her place, she'd scuttle out and stand in front of it, glaring at me, like she expected me to whip out a tank of Agent Orange and lay waste to her precious flowers.''

"So you lived up to her expectations?''

"Or down to them.'' He shrugged. "Sounds stupid now.''

"Sounds human. Hang on a minute while I move the hose,'' she said as she stepped off the path and walked over to where a sprinkler was putting out a fine spray of water.

In an effort to avoid staring at her legs like a randy teenager, Reece focused his gaze on the house instead. It was a style that he thought of as Early Fake Spanish—white stucco walls and a border of red clay tile edging a flat roof, like a middle-aged man with a fringe of hair and a big bald spot. The style was ubiquitous in California, a tribute to the state's Spanish roots and its citizens' happy acceptance of facades. In this case, age had lent something approaching dignity to the neat building. The front yard consisted of a lawn that appeared to be composed mostly of mown weeds and edged by two large flower beds that held a jumble of plants of all shapes and sizes in no particular order. Reece was no horticulturist but he was fairly sure that Shannon was growing an astoundingly healthy crop of dandelions, among other things.

"I don't advise looking at my flower beds if you're a gardener,'' she said, following his glance as she rejoined him. "I'm told that the state of my gardens is enough to bring on palpitations in anyone who actually knows something about plants.''

''What I know about plants can be written on the head of a pin.''

''Good. I may call on you for backup when the garden police come around.'' For an instant, in her cutoffs and T-shirt, her hair dragged back from her face, her wide mouth curved in a smile, her eyes bright with laughter, she looked like a mischievous child. But she was definitely all grown up, Reece thought, his eyes skimming her body almost compulsively as she stepped onto the narrow porch and pushed open the front door. It took a conscious effort of will to drag his eyes from the way the worn denim of her shorts molded the soft curves of her bottom.

The last thing he wanted was to get involved with anyone, he reminded himself. He was here to clean out his grandfather's house and maybe, while he was at it, figure out what he was going to do with the rest of his life. He didn't need any complications. Breakfast was one thing, especially when it came with caffeine, but anything else was out of the question.

And if his new neighbor would be willing to start wearing baggy clothes and put a paper sack over her head, he just might be able to remember that.

The interior of the house continued the pseudo-Spanish theme of the exterior. The floor of the small entryway was covered with dark-red tiles, and archways led off in various directions. Through one, he could see a living room, which looked almost as uncoordinated as the flower beds out front. A sofa upholstered in fat pink roses sat at right angles to an overstuffed chair covered in blue plaid. Both faced a small fireplace. The end table next to the sofa was completely covered in magazines and books. In one corner of the room, there was a sewing machine in a cabinet. Heaped over and around it and trailing onto the floor, there were piles of brightly colored fabric. The comfortable clutter made it obvious that this was a room where someone actually lived, and he couldn't help but compare it to the painful neatness of his grandfather's house—everything in its place, everything organized with military precision. The whole place had a sterile feeling that made it hard to believe it had been someone's home for more than forty years. Pushing the thought aside, Reece followed Shannon through an archway on the left of the entryway.

The kitchen was in a similar state of comfortable disarray. It was not a large room but light colors and plenty of windows made it seem bigger than it was. White cupboards and a black-and-white, checkerboard-patterned floor created a crisp, modern edge, but the yellow floral curtains and brightly colored ceramic cups and canisters added a cheerfully eclectic touch.

"Have a seat," Shannon said, gesturing to the small maple table that sat under a window looking out onto the backyard.

Reece chose to lean against the counter instead, his eyes following her as she got out a cup and poured coffee into it.

"Cream or sugar?" she asked as she handed him the cup. "I don't actually have cream, but I think I've got milk."

"Black is fine." Reece lifted the cup and took a sip, risking a scalded tongue in his eagerness. But it was worth it, he thought as the smooth, rich taste filled his mouth. "This is terrific coffee," he said, sipping again.

"It's a blend of beans that I buy at a little coffee

shop downtown. They roast it themselves.'' She opened a cupboard, stared into it for a moment and then closed the door.

''You do your own grinding?''

''I haven't figured out yet whether or not it actually makes a difference but the guy who runs the shop sneers if you ask him to grind it for you.''

Shannon opened the refrigerator door, and Reece felt his stomach rumble inquiringly. It had been a long time since dinner last night, and if she cooked half as well as she made coffee, breakfast was bound to be special. Relaxing back against the counter, he sipped his coffee and allowed his eyes to linger on her legs with absentminded appreciation while he entertained fantasies of bacon and eggs or maybe waffles slathered in butter and maple syrup or—

''How do you feel about Froot Loops?''

Chapter 3

"I haven't really given them much thought," Reece admitted cautiously.

"I don't suppose you'd be interested in having them for breakfast?" she asked. "I have that and Pepsi."

"Pepsi?" An image of multicolored, sugar-coated bits of cereal floating in a sea of flat cola flashed through his mind, and his stomach lurched. "On the Froot Loops?" he asked faintly.

"Of course not!" Shannon's nose wrinkled in disgust. "*With* it, not poured over it."

It seemed a marginal improvement. Reece took another swallow of coffee and tried to decide just how polite he should be in turning down her offer. It seemed a pity to offend someone who made coffee this good.

Shannon sighed abruptly and pushed the refrigerator door shut with a thud. She turned to face him, her hands on her hips, her chin tilted upward. "The truth is, I don't cook." Her tone mixed apology and defiance. "In fact, I'm a complete disaster in the kitchen. I live on frozen dinners and junk food. Coffee is the only thing I can cook without destroying it, and that's only because it's an automatic pot."

"You invited me to breakfast," he reminded her mildly.

"I know." She sighed and spread her hands in a gesture that might have been apology. "It was Edith's idea."

"Cacklemeyer suggested you should ask me to breakfast?" His brows rose in disbelief.

Shannon shook her head. "She said I shouldn't. She came across the street while I was working in the garden."

Reece took a fortifying swallow of coffee and tried to sort out the conversation. "She walked across the street to tell you *not* to invite me to breakfast?"

"Not exactly." She scowled and shoved her hands in the back pockets of her cutoffs. His eyes dropped to the soft curves of her breasts, pure male appreciation momentarily distracting him from both the conversation and the emptiness of his stomach. "She came across the street to tell me to pull my marigolds and that you were sure to cause trouble. So, I told her I liked marigolds and that I was going to invite you to breakfast. I hadn't planned on it, obviously."

"The marigolds or breakfast?" he asked, fascinated by her circuitous conversational style.

"Breakfast," she said, her eyes starting to gleam with laughter. "I knew I liked marigolds but I *didn't* know I was going to invite you to breakfast until she annoyed me."

"So this was all part of a plot to irritate Cacklemeyer?" A more sensitive man would probably be offended, Reece thought.

"I don't think you could call it a plot." Shannon's tone was thoughtful. "If it had been a plot, I would have planned a little better and bought some decent food. Oh, wait!" Her eyes lit up suddenly. "There's a box of waffles in the freezer, but I don't think I have any syrup. I have grape jelly, though," she added hopefully.

Reece barely restrained a shudder. Her idea of "decent" and his were not quite the same. Nothing—not the best coffee he'd had in months, not five feet eight inches of long-legged, blue-eyed, dangerously attractive redhead—could make him eat toaster waffles spread with grape jelly.

Shannon must have read something of his thoughts, because her hopeful expression faded into vague suspicion. "Are you a health food nut? One of those people who only eats roots and berries and never lets a preservative touch their lips?"

Reece thought about the Twinkies lying on the seat of the truck. "No, I've got nothing against an occasional preservative." He finished off his coffee—no sense in letting it go to waste—and set the cup down, trying to think of a tactful way to make his escape.

Seeing his vaguely hunted expression, Shannon felt a twinge of amusement. Not everyone shared her casual attitude toward food. "Not a fan of grape jelly?"

Reece caught the gleam in her eye and relaxed. "Actually, I'm allergic."

"To grape jelly?" Shannon arched one brow in skeptical question.

"It's a rare allergy," he admitted.

"I bet." She told herself that she wasn't in the least

charmed by the way one corner of his mouth tilted in a half smile. "Fred and Wilma are on the jelly glass," she tempted.

"The Flintstones?" Reece shook his head, trying to look regretful. "That's tough to turn down, but my throat swells shut and then I turn blue."

"Really?" Her bright, interested look startled a smile from Reece.

"I hope you're not going to make me demonstrate."

"I guess not." Her mouth took on a faintly pouty look that turned Reece's thoughts in directions that had nothing to do with breakfast. He reined them in as he straightened away from the counter.

"Maybe I can take a rain check on breakfast?" he asked politely.

"I'll get an extra box of Cap'n Crunch next time I go shopping," she promised, and he tried not to shudder.

"You did what?" Her eyes wide with surprise, Kelly turned away from the pegboard full of sewing notions, a stack of chalk markers forgotten in her hand.

"I invited him to breakfast," Shannon repeated.

"That's what I thought you said." Kelly came over to the cutting table where Shannon was making up color-coordinated packets of fabric and leaned against its edge, her expression a mixture of disbelief and admiration. "You just sauntered up and offered him bacon and eggs?"

"Froot Loops," Shannon corrected her. She slid a cardboard price tag onto a length of lavender ribbon before tying it around a stack of half a dozen different pink fabrics. "I didn't have any bacon. Or eggs."

"Froot Loops? You invited Reece Morgan over for

Froot Loops? And you waited until now to tell me?''
It was difficult to say what Kelly found most shocking.

"Yesterday was your day off. And there's nothing
wrong with Froot Loops. I eat them all the time."

"You could have called me at home." Kelly grum-
bled. "And Froot Loops aren't exactly what I'd call
company fare." She shook her head, her dark eyes
starting to gleam with laughter. "I'd have given anything to see his face when you put the box on the
table."

"Actually, the box didn't get that far." Shannon began folding the next stack of fabric.

It was Tuesday morning, the sky was gray with the
promise of rain that probably wouldn't show up for
another month and there were no customers. It was a
perfect chance to catch up on a few things around the
shop. And to indulge in a little gossip. Glancing at
Kelly's stunned expression, Shannon couldn't deny that
she was enjoying being the one with astonishing news
to deliver.

"Apparently, Froot Loops and Pepsi are not among
his favorite breakfast combos."

"Who can blame him?" Kelly pulled her face into
a comical grimace. "If he really is a mob boss, he's
probably already put a contract out on your life just for
suggesting it."

"I thought he was supposed to be a vegetarian zombie."

"That's Paul McCartney." Kelly picked up the
chalk pencils and carried them over to the notions wall
to hang them up.

"Paul is a zombie?" Shannon looked surprised. "He
looks so normal."

"No, he's a vegetarian."

''Does that mean he can't be a zombie?''

''Zombies pretty much have to be carnivores, don't you think?'' Kelly wandered back to the cutting table and reached for the roll of ribbon and began snipping it into eighteen-inch lengths. ''I mean, how frightening would it be if a bunch of squash-eating undead were roaming the streets?''

''I guess it would be pretty frightening for the squash.'' Shannon tossed another fabric packet into the box.

''I suppose,'' Kelly agreed absently. ''What's he like?''

''Who?''

''Reece Morgan.'' Kelly's tone was exasperated. ''Who were we talking about? And if you mention Paul McCartney, I'm going to brain you with the nearest blunt object.''

''I wasn't going to mention him,'' Shannon lied meekly.

''Good.'' Kelly set the ribbon aside, lifted a bolt of fabric from the stack leaning against the side of the cutting table, clicked open a rotary cutter and began slicing off half-yard chunks. ''You're the first eye witness I've talked to, so tell me what the infamous Reece Morgan is really like. Did he send shivers up your spine?'' she asked, grinning.

''Not that I noticed.'' At least not the kind of shivers Kelly was talking about. If there had been a small—practically infinitesimal—shiver of awareness, she was keeping it to herself. The last thing she needed was for Kelly to turn her matchmaking eye in Reece Morgan's direction.

''Is he mean looking? Does he have a patch over one eye? Antennae growing out the top of his head? A nose ring? Wear three-inch lifts and a girdle? Tell me all.''

"He doesn't need a girdle," Shannon said, remembering the muscled flatness of his stomach. "Or lifts. He's tall. No eye patch, nose ring or antennae that I noticed. And I didn't think he was mean looking, though I imagine he could be. He has dark hair, dark eyes.''

"Good-looking?" Kelly asked, folding the end of the fabric and pinning it to the bolt.

"I think most women would say so," Shannon offered, careful to sound neither too interested or suspiciously indifferent.

"Well, who cares what men think? Unless…" The bolt of fabric hit the table with a thud as a possibility occurred to her. "Do you think he's gay?"

"No," Shannon answered without hesitation.

"Are you sure?" Kelly shook her head as she began folding the fabric she'd just cut. "Because it seems like every good-looking, single man in the state of California is these days."

Shannon could have told her that Reece Morgan was more likely to turn out to be the world's first squash-eating zombie, but she settled for a half shrug and mild reassurance. "I'm pretty sure."

Kelly folded in silence for a moment then sighed abruptly. "Well, it's certainly going to disappoint a lot of people."

"People are going to be disappointed that he's not gay?" Shannon asked, startled.

"Not that." Kelly grinned. "They're going to be disappointed if he's normal. I mean, what's the point of having a bad boy come back to town if he's not bad anymore?"

"I see what you mean. I hadn't thought of it that way." Shannon shook her head sadly. "When you think of it, it was pretty inconsiderate of him. The least he could have done was get his nose pierced or maybe file his teeth."

"Exactly." Kelly looked wistful. "I was really hoping for black leather and chains."

Shannon's brows rose. "Does Frank know about this?"

"Not for me, silly. For Reece Morgan. He could at least have worn a black leather jacket and maybe an earring. For heaven's sake, even stockbrokers are wearing earrings these days!" She shook her head at the unfairness of it.

"The man's an inconsiderate lout." Shannon looped a ribbon around the next stack of fabric.

"So, what did you do about breakfast?" Kelly asked.

"Well, I offered him toaster waffles and grape jelly but he said he was allergic to grape jelly and took a rain check." Shannon dropped the fabric packet into the basket and waited for Kelly's reaction. She wasn't disappointed.

"Toaster waffles and jelly?" Kelly stared at her in horror. "You actually eat that?"

"Not voluntarily, but there wasn't anything else in the house."

"What did he do?"

"Actually, I think he turned a little pale."

"Who can blame him?" Kelly muttered and then giggled. "I'd love to have seen his face."

"It was...interesting," Shannon admitted, grinning at the memory of Reece's poorly concealed revulsion. "But he managed to remain polite."

"I'm almost sorry to hear that," Kelly said.

"I suppose you'd rather he'd threatened me with bodily harm?"

"Well, you have to admit that the man is starting to sound depressingly normal. In fact, he sounds downright dull."

The bell over the door jangled, saving Shannon the necessity of a response. *Dull?* she thought as she turned to greet the customer who'd entered. That was just about the last word she could imagine applying to Reece Morgan.

There was nothing like a small town to make you appreciate the joys of living in a city, Reece thought as he rolled his shopping cart into place behind a middle-aged woman wearing a hot-pink jumpsuit and purple sneakers. In the fifteen years he'd lived in D.C., no one had ever gawked at him over a pile of bananas or waylaid him in the dairy aisle to offer condolences on his loss and, in the next breath, ask what he planned to do about the condition of his lawn. He'd been discreetly eyed by a young woman pushing a cart full of baby food and disposable diapers, blatantly stared at by an old man carrying a six-pack of Coors and a bag of pretzels and nearly mowed over by a toddler trying to escape parental supervision.

Obviously, shopping at Jim & Earl's Super Food Mart had been a mistake. It was just a few blocks from his grandfather's house, which meant it was convenient, not only for him but for his neighbors, who apparently found his presence a source of endless fascination. He didn't even have to turn his head to know that the skinny blonde in the next checkout line was studying the contents of his cart as if trying to commit a complete inventory to memory. If only he'd thought of it sooner, he could have thrown in half a dozen boxes of neon-colored, fruit-flavored condoms and a couple cases of tequila so the local grapevine would have something really interesting to talk about. As it was, he doubted they were going to be able to do much with the news that he'd been seen buying boneless chicken breasts and bok choy.

He listened with leashed impatience as the cashier quizzed the woman in the pink jumpsuit about the health of every member of her family, clicking her tongue in sympathy or exclaiming with delight, as necessary. If only her hands moved as fast as her mouth, she could win the grocery-checking Olympics, Reece thought acidly. She paused, a box of bagels in her hand, her mouth forming an *O* of amazement as the customer detailed the results of her niece's breast reduction surgery and he bit back a groan. At the rate she was going, he stood in real danger of growing old and dying before he made it up to the register. He turned his head to see if there was a shorter line—or a longer one with a deaf and dumb cashier—and forgot all about his irritation.

His coffee-making, Froot Loop-eating neighbor was walking toward him, though he might not have recognized her if it hadn't been for the unmistakable reddish-gold gleam of her hair, which was caught up in a soft twist at the back of her head. The T-shirt and shorts had been replaced by a silky-gold blouse and a calf-length skirt in shades of rust and moss green. He couldn't help but feel a pang of regret that those incredible legs were covered, but he had to admit that there was something tantalizing about knowing just what that flowing skirt was hiding. She looked older, more sophisticated and just as delicious, he admitted, letting his gaze skim over the soft curves and angles of her.

He hadn't set eyes on her since their not-quite-breakfast encounter a little more than a week ago, but he'd thought about her more than he liked to admit. More than was smart for a man who wanted no entanglements, because, even on a short acquaintance, he was fairly sure that Shannon Devereux was not the sort of woman to fall into a casual affair with a currently unemployed ex-government agent who just happened to be living next door to her for a few weeks.

Shannon looked up and saw him. Her eyes widened in surprise and then she smiled and Reece found himself thinking that maybe Serenity Falls wasn't such a bad place after all. She walked over to him, a mesh basket hanging over her arm.

"You know, recent studies indicate that people who eat large quantities of fresh vegetables are twice as likely to develop cauliflower ears."

"I didn't know cauliflowers had ears," he said, responding to the unconventional greeting without missing a beat.

She widened her eyes in surprise. "Of course they have ears. How else could they know what's being said on the grapevine?"

His smile widened into a quick grin that made Shannon's breath catch. Over the past week, she'd almost convinced herself that her new neighbor couldn't possibly be as attractive as she'd thought. Her imagination, fueled by months of whispered speculation about the mysterious Reece Morgan, had exaggerated his looks, created an image to suit his two-decade-old reputation. But the way her pulse stuttered when she looked up and saw him forced her to admit that no exaggeration had been necessary. Not when you had six feet four inches of dark-haired, dark-eyed, solidly muscled male standing right in front of you. Even on its best days, her imagination couldn't improve on that reality.

With an effort she pulled her eyes away from his face and glanced at the contents of his shopping cart. Clicking her tongue, she shook her head in disapproval. "You don't plan on buying that stuff, do you?"

Reece's expression shifted to wary amusement. "You're not going to tell me that they've decided that vegetables are carcinogenic, are you?"

"Not yet, though I'm fairly sure that further research will eventually prove Brussels sprouts were never intended to touch human lips," she said darkly. "But that's not the point now." Shannon flicked her fingers at the bags of vegetables and the package of boneless chicken breasts. "You actually have fresh ginger in there."

"And that's a bad thing?" Reece wondered if he should worry that her circuitous conversational style was starting to seem almost normal. The skinny blonde in the next line was craning her neck in what she probably thought was a subtle attempt to eavesdrop on their conversation. Reece ignored her.

"It hardly suits your image." Her soft mouth primmed into a disapproving line. "Think about it. Bad boy returns home and buys vegetables? What kind of a message does that send?"

"Bad boy?" Reece repeated, not entirely pleased. "Is that what I'm supposed to be?"

"Of course." She seemed surprised that he had to ask. "According to local myth, you were the scourge of Serenity Falls."

"Scourge?" He was caught between irritation and

amusement. "I think that's overstating things a little. I may have raised a little hell, but I didn't exactly pillage and burn the town."

"You're forgetting the petunias," she pointed out.

"One flower bed and I'm a scourge?" How did she manage to pull him into these conversations?

Shannon looked regretful. "In a town this size, it doesn't take much." She shifted her shopping basket from her right hand to her left, and her voice took on a self-consciously pedantic tone that, for some reason he couldn't fathom, made Reece wonder if her mouth could possibly be as soft as it looked. And wouldn't *that* set the grapevine humming—news that that Morgan boy had kissed his very attractive neighbor right in the middle of the food mart with God and half the town looking on. With an effort, he dragged his attention back to what Shannon was saying.

"Actually, the Bad Boy is a classic figure in Western mythology. An important character in both film and literature. Think of James Dean."

"James Dean?" Reece's upper lip curled. "Kind of a skinny little twerp, wasn't he?"

Shannon's eyes widened in horror, and she pressed her free hand to her chest as if to protect her heart from the shock. "James Dean? The king of cool? You're calling him a twerp?"

"Couldn't have weighed more than one-fifty soaking wet and with his shoes on. Maybe if he'd eaten his vegetables, he'd have bulked up a little."

Shannon's mouth twitched and was sternly controlled. "Don't you think that would have spoiled his lean and hungry look? It's hard to seem tragically misunderstood when you look like you could eat hay with a fork."

"So only the scrawny get sympathy?" Reece shook his head. "Doesn't seem quite fair to me."

"I'm told that life isn't always fair."

"I've heard that rumor."

"Do you have plans for Thursday?" she asked, changing the subject abruptly.

"Thursday?" he repeated blankly.

"Thanksgiving?" Shannon arched her brows. "You know, turkey, dressing, pumpkin pie. Pilgrims shaking hands with the Indians they're eventually going to wipe out. The fourth Thursday in November when we all get together and eat too much? This coming Thursday? Do you have plans?"

"Not that I know of," Reece admitted cautiously.

"Well, you're welcome to join the crowd at my house," she offered. "It's nothing formal. People just drop by."

"Are you cooking?" he asked involuntarily, visions of freeze-dried turkey flashing before his eyes.

Shannon's quick, throaty laugh made the skinny blonde sidle closer in an attempt to overhear what was being said. "Don't worry, it's potluck. Everyone brings something, and I've been strictly forbidden to set foot in the kitchen."

"No Froot Loops?"

"Only in the stuffing," she promised solemnly. Looking past him, she nodded toward the checkout counter. "Looks like you're up next."

Turning, Reece saw that the woman in the pink jumpsuit was paying for her purchases and the cashier was giving him a distinctly ominous look of bright-eyed interest.

"Watch out for Agatha," Shannon said, confirming his concern. "She can wring information out of granite.

If the Inquisition had had her, they wouldn't have needed the rack.''

"Great, a full-service store," Reece muttered as he pushed his cart forward. "They bag your groceries while they pump you for information.''

"Just say no," Shannon advised solemnly but she was grinning as she turned away without waiting for a reply. "See you Thursday, maybe.''

Not likely, Reece thought as he began loading his groceries onto the conveyer belt. He didn't want any involvement and, while attending a potluck Thanksgiving dinner along with half the town wasn't exactly a prelude to a passionate love affair, it was too…neighborly. Too friendly. It suggested that he had a place here, which he didn't—not now, not twenty years ago.

He glanced over his shoulder in time to see Shannon disappear down the frozen food aisle. It was nice of her to invite him, but he was perfectly content with his own company, on Thanksgiving or any other day. Still, he had to admit that it would be interesting to see if she really did manage to slip Froot Loops into the stuffing.

Chapter 4

For the past few years, the fourth Thursday in November had been just another number on the calendar to Reece, and he was perfectly content to keep it that way. So what was he doing standing on Shannon Devereux's doorstep holding a spinach salad?

The door opened, saving him the necessity of having to come up with a satisfactory answer to his own question. He'd been expecting Shannon and had to adjust his gaze five inches lower and his thinking fifty years older. Suspiciously black hair topped a thin, wrinkled face. Reece had heard of someone applying makeup with a trowel, but he'd never seen anyone who looked as if they might actually have done just that until now. Foundation, blusher, concealer and possibly a bit of spackle coated every inch of skin from forehead to chin. False eyelashes, black eyeliner and royal-purple eyeshadow were balanced, more or less, by stoplight-red lipstick that had bled into the fine lines around her mouth.

Her clothing was no less colorful. A purple sweat-shirt with a design of teddy bears at a picnic topped a pair of hot-pink pedal pushers. Her calves were bare and colored a streaky orangey brown that suggested either a severe nutritional problem or a badly applied tan-in-a-bottle. Purple sneakers with pink glitter and black laces completed the ensemble.

"What is that?" Her voice, surprisingly deep for a woman, brought Reece's dazzled eyes back to her face. She was staring at the bowl in his hands, dark eyes full of suspicion.

"Spinach salad."

"Does it have meat in it?"

"No."

Her dark eyes flickered suspiciously from the bowl to his face. Reece half expected her to insist on an inspection, but she must have decided he had an honest face or maybe it just occurred to her that spinach salad was an unlikely place for meat to lurk. Whichever it was, she shuffled back into the entryway, letting the door open wide, spilling laughter and voices out into the warm afternoon.

His first impression was of wall-to-wall people. His second and third impressions pretty much confirmed the first. There were people standing in the entryway, clutching plastic cups holding liquid of assorted colors. There were more people in the living room, sitting on the sofa, the chairs, perched on the hearth, leaning against the wall next to the front windows. Yet more people standing in the hallway, which he assumed led back to the bedrooms. Everywhere he looked, there was someone standing or sitting. Fat people, skinny people, old, young, enough variations of skin tone to make a liberal cheer or a conservative weep. Male, female and...well, he wasn't willing to hazard a guess about the one wearing the leather pants and a pink Mohawk.

"You can take that out to the patio."

Reece blinked and focused his attention on the woman who'd let him in. Compared to the Mohawk wearer, she looked downright conservative. "Patio?"

"Go through the kitchen," she said, reading the question he hadn't asked.

Reece nodded his thanks and made his way across the entryway. He exchanged greetings with three total strangers and one woman who looked vaguely familiar before ducking through the doorway into the kitchen. More people. Food smells. Voices raised in argument over the correct way to make gravy. He had enough experience in hand-to-hand combat to lay odds on the skinny woman. Her opponent was male and outweighed her by a good forty pounds, but size wasn't everything, and the way she was gripping the wooden spoon suggested she meant business. He was willing to bet that roux was going to win out over slurry, whatever the hell that meant.

And then he was outside and there were more people but they were scattered across the surprisingly spacious patio and out onto the lawn, still dull and mostly brown from summer drought. The weather was typical of a southern California autumn—clear blue skies and warm enough to qualify as summer in some parts of the country. Not exactly your traditional crisp Thanksgiving weather but nostalgic in its own way. Not so much for the years spent with his grandfather—holidays with the old man had generally been long on tradition, short on feeling—but for the years when his parents were alive. They'd been very short on any recognizable traditions—dinner was as likely to be McDonald's as it was turkey—but there had always been plenty of love and laughter.

"You *did* come."

Reece turned to greet his hostess, feeling that now-familiar little kick of awareness when he saw her. Shannon was wearing a long, soft skirt in some bluey, greeny shade and a simple scoop-necked top that hovered between rust and gold. The color brought out the red in her hair, which was drawn back from her face with a pair of gold clips and left to tumble on her shoulders. Her eyes sparkled, bluer than the sky, sapphire bright and warm. Her mouth was warm coral, and he wondered what she'd do if he kissed her, right here in front of God and half the populace of Serenity Falls.

"How could I resist the possibility of a turkey stuffed with Froot Loops?" he asked, reining in his suddenly raging libido.

Her smile widened into a grin, her eyes laughing at him. "Sorry, I couldn't get near the stuffing. Sally actually held up a cross when I got too close to the oven."

"So, it's safe to eat the stuffing?" he asked, raising one eyebrow.

"Coward. Froot Loops provide an important assortment of vitamins and minerals."

"Not to mention artificial colorings and preservatives," he murmured, following her to the long table, set up on one side of the patio and already groaning under a vast array of bowls and platters.

"I think we can wedge this in here," Shannon said, turning to take the bowl from him. She found a space between a bowl of iceberg lettuce and carrot shreds and an elaborate, layered vegetable aspic. "The turkey came out of the oven a few minutes ago. Sally says it has to rest for half an hour, which seems ridiculous. How much rest can a dead bird need?"

"It's to let the juices settle back into the meat," Reece said absently. She really had the most amazingly kissable mouth.

Shannon gave him a look that mixed surprise and faint disapproval. "You know how to cook."

Reece shrugged. "I'm no Wolfgang Puck, but I've lived alone for a long time. I got tired of going out to eat."

"You can buy a gourmet meal in a box, like any other civilized human being."

"Depends on your definition of gourmet, I suppose," he said mildly. She shook her head in apparent despair.

"Be sure and take some of the aspic," she said, gesturing to it.

"Good?" Reece asked, eyeing it with interest.

"Probably not." Shannon frowned down at the aspic. "Last year, Vangie brought a coffee cake that was so hard someone suggested selling it to NASA to replace the ceramic tile on the shuttle."

"And that's supposed to encourage me to eat the aspic?" Reece asked.

"Oh, I didn't say you had to *eat* it. I just said you should take some." She saw his raised eyebrow and shrugged. "Vangie has sensibilities," she said, as if that explained everything and it probably did.

Reece cleared his throat and tried to look regretful. "Actually, I'm allergic to aspic."

"Aspic *and* grape jelly?" Shannon's eyes widened in surprise.

"Grape—" He caught himself, remembering that first morning when she'd offered him toaster waffles and grape jelly and he'd claimed allergies. He coughed a little. "Not many people know that one of the primary ingredients of aspic is grape jelly."

"Really?" Shannon cast a doubting look at the shimmering aspic. "Wouldn't grape jelly make it purple?"

"The, um, baking soda in the aspic neutralizes the, uh, chemical additives that give grape jelly its characteristic color."

"Wow." Shannon shook her head in amazement. "Have you always been such a good liar?"

"Always. It's a gift." He said it with such simple pride that it startled a quick, choked laugh from her.

His eyes flickered from her eyes to her mouth. She couldn't possibly taste as good as she looked. Could she? He couldn't possibly be thinking about finding out. Could he? Maybe she read something of what he was thinking because her smile faded abruptly and her breath caught a little. Reece dragged his gaze from her mouth, saw the awareness in those clear blue eyes. Did he lean down? Did she sway toward him?

The screen door banged behind him, and Reece straightened, abruptly aware of where he was—standing on a sun-splashed patio with a dozen people in plain sight. Shannon threw him a quick, uncertain smile, a murmured—and unheard—comment and moved past him toward the kitchen door. Reece turned to watch her walk away. The phrase, "Danger, Will Robinson" drifted irresistibly—ridiculously—through his mind.

What the hell had just happened? Nothing. That's
what had happened. Absolutely nothing. And nothing
would have happened, even if they hadn't been interrupted. Right. Nothing would have happened.

Oh, hell. Who was he kidding? If they hadn't been
standing right here in front of God and half of Serenity
Falls, he'd probably be trying to give her a tonsillec-
tomy with his tongue right about now. And the fact
that he was fairly sure she wouldn't have objected did
nothing to alleviate the sudden snugness of his jeans.
Reece shifted uncomfortably, moving away from the
table to lean against one of the redwood support posts,
one that happened to be in shadow. Forty freaking
years old and he was showing all the self-control of a
sixteen-year-old. No, come to think of it, he hadn't
made a habit of getting erections in public when he
was sixteen.

He wasn't here to start an affair, he reminded himself. The last thing he wanted was any kind of involvement. He had enough to do with cleaning out his grandfather's house and figuring out what to do with the rest
of his life. Beautiful neighbors with gorgeous red hair
and legs that went on forever did not fit into his plans.

The only way the aspic could have tasted worse was
if it had actually been made with grape jelly and baking
soda. Reece managed to swallow the single bite he'd
taken and then pushed the remainder of it to one side
of his plate, concealing it under a slightly wilted piece
of iceberg lettuce. The unknown Vangie might have
sensibilities but she apparently lacked taste buds.

The food was as eclectic as the guests. Tofu and
turkey. Couscous and three-bean salad. Pearls and blue
jeans. Retired professors and born-again hippies. It was

a guest list right out of a hostess's nightmare or maybe a Marx Brothers movie. Potential disaster lurked around every slice of jellied cranberry sauce and dollop of…what exactly was the brown stuff with the little orange bits in it? Reece poked it cautiously to the side of his plate, hiding it under the lettuce leaf with the aspic.

"Darva Torkelson's family secret rice pilaf," someone said, and Reece looked up guiltily. "The secret is that no one knows what the orange things are, and I haven't found anyone brave enough to actually try tasting it to find out. I'm voting for M&Ms."

A stocky man with stoplight-red hair was standing just to his left, his blue eyes bright with amusement and…expectation? It only took a moment for the memory to snap into place.

"Frank? Frank McKinnon?"

"You know anyone else who looks like Howdy Doody on steroids?" Frank grinned and held out his hand. Reece felt memories flood over him as he shook it.

"How are you, man?"

"Good. I'm good. Is Rich here?" Reece scanned the crowd around the buffet table, looking for more of that bright-red hair. Rich McKinnon had been his best friend during the years he lived in Serenity Falls. The two of them had gone through football, detention, first dates and first cars together. They'd kept in touch for a while after Reece left town—Christmas cards, a few phone calls, but they'd gradually lost touch.

Frank shook his head. "Rich lives in Montana now. He's a gen-u-ine cowboy." He drew out the words with a thick Western drawl. "Got hisself a little ranch with horses and cows and all that good stuff."

"A ranch, huh?" Reece grinned and shook his head. "What happened to becoming a world-famous wildlife photographer?"

"He found out that wildlife photographers spend a lot of time sitting in huts, freezing their privates off, waiting for a ring-necked wallaby to wander into camera range and hoping a hungry grizzly bear doesn't wander by first."

"I can see how that would take some of the fun out of things. How are your parents?"

Ruth and Daryl McKinnon had always treated him as if he were one of their own. They'd had a rambling old house where everything was always covered in a fine layer of plaster dust from the ongoing series of remodeling jobs that were never quite finished. Dogs, cats and kids wandered in and out in an ever-changing parade of fur and faces. It had taken him a while to figure out that only three of the kids actually belonged to the McKinnons, and he never had figured out which of the animals were theirs.

"Dad retired three years ago, and he and Mom bought an RV. They spend most of the year on the road. Kate is married and has a couple of kids. She lives in Boston now, and Rich married a woman with three kids and then they had two more so Mom and Dad divide their time among the grandchildren. They spend a couple of months here in the spring so Mom can catch up on the local gossip and Dad can make sure I'm not running the hardware store into the ground, and then they take off again."

"Did your dad ever finish remodeling the house?" Reece asked.

Frank laughed and shook his head. "Hell, no. When we moved in, three out of four bathrooms were torn apart and the back hall was halfway through a wall-papering job.''

"And three years later, two bathrooms are still without tile and the wallpaper is up but the floor is only half-refinished," a new voice said.

"What can I say? It's genetic," Frank said, his smile softening as he turned to slide one arm around the woman who'd joined them. She was small, not just short but slim, with the kind of delicate build that made Reece think of pixies. Big brown eyes set in a heart-shaped face and a tousled cap of blond hair reinforced the impression. He had the fanciful thought that if she turned he might see wings on her back. But her bright, interested expression was human and familiar. The first few times he'd seen that particular expression, he'd had the urge to check to make sure his fly was zipped or look in a mirror to see if a third eye had appeared in the middle of his forehead, but it hadn't taken long to figure out that it wasn't the possibility of imminent indecent exposure or extra body parts, it was just him. His mere presence was enough to elicit interest.

Reece Morgan, walking, talking scenic wonder.

But unlike the elderly man who'd gaped at him while he was buying cleaning supplies or the trout-faced woman at the gas station that first day, Kelly McKinnon didn't stare at him as if he was a two-headed calf at the county fair. The curiosity was there but banked, about what you'd expect from a woman meeting someone who'd known her husband twenty years ago.

She said the town must have changed a lot since he'd lived here before and Reece agreed that it had. She asked where he lived and he told her he'd been living in D.C. and added that he'd given up his apartment and wasn't sure where he was going to settle when he left Serenity Falls.

"Maybe you'll decide to settle here," she said, taking a bite of dinner roll.

"I don't think so." The statement left room for doubt, and he frowned. "I'm just here to clean out my grandfather's house," he added firmly. "Get it in shape to sell, then I'll move on."

"Got a place in mind?" Frank asked. He used the side of his fork to cut a mushroom-soup-covered green bean in two. "Somewhere to settle?"

"Nowhere in particular," Reece admitted. He poked another bit of the brown stuff under the lettuce leaf with the aspic.

"Just going to travel?" Frank asked. "The romance of the open road, huh?"

Reece mumbled something around a bite of really excellent scalloped oysters and hoped Frank would take it as agreement. In his experience, the open road offered little by way of romance, unless you happened to *like* lumpy mattresses and bad food.

"So, you're running the hardware store now," he said, steering the conversation away from his possible future plans.

Frank was willing to go along with the change of topic and, for the next few minutes the conversation moved easily from hardware stores to the housing development that was going up on the west edge of town, to old acquaintances. Reece was surprised at how many of the names he remembered and even more surprised to feel a twinge of nostalgia at some of the memories Frank evoked. He hadn't exactly been brimming over with warm and fuzzy feelings when he left here but maybe there had been more good times than he'd realized.

"Well, all I can say is that it's a crime to use the word *Thanksgiving* in connection with such a barbaric display." The raspy comment preceded the arrival of the old woman who had answered the door for him earlier. She stomped to a halt next to Kelly, every scrawny, makeup- and glitter-covered inch quivering with indignation.

"Hello, Mavis," Frank said. Reece caught a glint of mischief in his blue eyes before he added, "Happy holiday."

The innocuous greeting had an immediate and startling affect. Mavis drew herself up, her eyes narrowing in a glare that should have withered Frank on the spot. "Happy? *Happy?*" she repeated, her deep voice lending resonance to the word. "What's happy about a day on which millions of innocent creatures are slaughtered in the name of celebration? Death and destruction. *That's* what you're celebrating. Death and destruction."

Kelly gave her husband an exasperated look before putting her hand on Mavis's arm. "No one is celebrating death and destruction. People have to eat, and you know that not everyone feels the way you do about—"

"You." Reece tensed as those dark eyes pinned him to the pillar behind him. "Do you know what you're eating?"

Reece thought of the alleged rice pilaf and the inedible aspic and thought he could answer, with some truth, that he *didn't* know, but he had a feeling that pleading ignorance wasn't going to do him any good.

He was almost relieved when Mavis continued without waiting for a response.

"Turkey." She fired the word at him. "You're eating turkey."

"Umm, yes," Reece admitted cautiously. He shot Frank a questioning look, but the other man just shook his head, eyes bright with laughter.

"Are you aware that that was once a living, breathing animal with hopes and dreams?"

"Dreams?" Reece repeated, looking at the half-eaten slice of turkey on his plate.

"A future," Mavis continued ruthlessly.

"He coulda been a contenda," Frank murmured. His Brando imitation was not the best Reece had ever heard, but it was good enough to startle a snort of laughter from him. Mavis swelled up like a pouter pigeon, narrow chest expanding, dark eyes flashing beneath their awning of false eyelashes. Kelly shot her husband a look of mixed amusement and annoyance and thrust her plate at him before setting her hand on Mavis's sinewy arm.

"Ignore him," she told the other woman. "He just doesn't understand." Head bent in attentive sympathy, she led the other woman away from the turkey-laden table.

"*I* don't understand?" Frank muttered, staring down at the plate she'd handed him. "This from the woman with a turkey haunch the size of a small pony on her plate?"

"I think it was the bit from *On the Waterfront* that showed a certain lack of sensitivity," Reece suggested.

"Hell, I was just trying to show that I understood the sacrifice this turkey had made." Frank managed to balance his wife's plate on a nearby planter and cheerfully transferred the rest of her lunch to his plate. "Mavis is a vegetarian."

"Yeah, I kind of gathered as much. Either that or she's got a thing for turkeys." Reece chewed thoughtfully on piece of turkey. "What do you think a turkey dreams of?"

"Thanksgiving being canceled," Frank said promptly, and the two men snickered.

They ate in companionable silence for a while. Reece's eyes drifted over the guests, thinking again that they were an unlikely mixture. He saw Shannon standing on the summer-browned lawn, talking to a skinny young man with a prominent Adam's apple and thinning hair. As he watched, the guest with the pink Mohawk and indeterminate sex approached, and the three of them stood talking together.

"She certainly does believe in mixing her guest list." Reece was hardly aware of speaking the thought out loud until Frank answered.

"Shannon?" He followed Reece's gaze, grinning at the eclectic little group. "It's not exactly a guest list. It's more a case of Shannon collecting stray puppies. Pretty much anyone who doesn't have somewhere else to go is welcome."

Stray puppies? Stray puppies? Was that how she thought of him? As a stray with nowhere else to go? The idea stung, all the more so because there was an element of truth to it. He hadn't exactly been overwhelmed with invitations for the holiday. But that didn't make him a stray, for god's sake. It wasn't as if he hadn't had anywhere else to go. He had options.

He had a standing invitation to spend the holiday with his ex-wife and her family. Never mind that it had been left standing for the past ten years because he and

Caroline liked each other best when they were a few thousand miles apart. The point wasn't whether or not he'd *wanted* to go. The point was he *could* have gone. He could have gone back to Virginia, admired the fall foliage, thrown a football with his son. He hadn't seen Kyle since the beginning of summer. Almost six months ago. Too long.

And if he didn't want to go back to Virginia, he could have stayed home, could have fixed himself a steak dinner and eaten it while he watched football on his grandfather's ancient television.

Frank had shifted from updating him on old acquaintances to giving him a running commentary on the other guests. The one with the pink Mohawk was female, if you could judge by the name, which you couldn't always these days, but Becky seemed an unlikely name for a boy. Then again, it seemed an unlikely name for someone dressed like that. Spike maybe or Squeaky, but Becky conjured up images of pinafores and ankle socks, not pink Mohawks and skin-tight leather. Maybe she was another one of his neighbor's "strays," Reece thought, feeling a quick little pinch of irritation.

The irritation lingered in the back of his mind, niggling at him as he let Frank pull him into a conversation with a balding man who bore no resemblance to the quarterback who'd made all the girls swoon when they were in high school together. It tugged for his attention as he watched Shannon chat with an elderly woman with blue hair and a sweet smile, and it was still there when he saw her laughing with a group of children who were playing tag in the backyard.

Strays, he thought as he watched her head off a potential brawl between Mavis and a heavyset man who looked prepared to use lethal force in defense of the turkey leg he was clutching.

Stray puppies. The phrase echoed in his mind as he helped clear the tables and then break them down for storage. Well, maybe some of the guests were lost souls but he wasn't. It hadn't been loneliness or an excess of holiday spirit that had brought him here. It had been something a little more basic. His eyes followed Shannon as she and another woman wrapped the leftovers. She'd taken her shoes off at some point and, barefoot, with the soft skirt swishing around her calves and her hair tumbling down her back, she looked both earthy and elegant—a gypsy in silk.

Lust, Reece thought. Not turkey, not the chance to mingle with a guest list right out of central casting for eccentrics, not a desire to give thanks for anything, except maybe the soft curves of the female body and the bright glint of laughter in a pair of blue eyes. Okay, so lust *and* liking. It was a scary combination. Lust was simple. You either acted on it or you didn't and, one way or another, you were done with it. Liking was more complex. Liking suggested friendship, and friendship meant ties, connections, things he wasn't looking to add to his life right now.

Then again, maybe he was making a bigger production out of it than it really should be. His eyes on Shannon, Reece folded one metal leg against the underside of the table. Really, did it have to be a big deal? Like. Lust. Not a bad combination. It didn't have to lead to anything more than say, oh, maybe a blazing hot affair. The thought rolled through his head, creating a sudden, potentially embarrassing pressure against his zipper, making him grateful for the solid screen of the table as he carried it to the side gate and out to Frank McKinnon's truck.

By the time he'd loaded the table into the bed of the pickup and promised Frank that he'd stop by the hardware store and promised Frank's pretty wife that he'd come to dinner soon, the excess pressure in his jeans had subsided, but the thought of having an affair with his Froot Loops-eating neighbor remained.

Why not? The attraction was mutual. He might not have done much dating in recent years, but he hadn't forgotten the way a woman looked when she was interested. They were both consenting adults. There was no reason they couldn't act on that attraction.

He made his way back through the side gate, stepping around a teary five-year-old who'd thrown herself down in the middle of the walkway and was refusing to move, despite her father's strained pleas for reason. The scene in the backyard was one of controlled chaos. Cleanup, like the meal itself, was apparently a cooperative effort. Well, it was mostly cooperative, he amended as he watched Mavis and a tall, thin man with a goatee and painfully plaid trousers square off over the leftover turkey. He was too far away to hear what they were saying but it seemed likely that Mavis was thinking burial with honors and the guy in the loud pants was thinking sandwiches. They were locked in an apparent stalemate until Shannon touched Mavis on the shoulder. A few words, a smile, and the older woman relinquished the platter to Mr. Plaid Pants, who wasted no time in carrying his prize into the relative safety of the kitchen.

Shannon stayed with Mavis, her head bent attentively to listen to what the other woman was saying. Her hair swung forward in a tumble of red-gold curls.

Reece's fingers curled into his palm in a reflexive urge
to touch, to see if her hair was as soft as it looked.

Maybe he'd get a chance to find out.

Shannon waved goodbye to Lillian and Hector Gon-
zalez, waiting until the elderly couple had tottered their
way down the walkway and into their car before she
shut the door with a sigh of relief. She leaned back
against the door and listened to the quiet. When she
was growing up, holidays had meant her and her father
eating in a restaurant, listening to perky, piped-in music
and trying to think of something to say to each other.
Well, *she'd* tried to think of something to say to him.
She'd never been sure that the silences bothered him,
not then, not at any other time.

There had been a lot of silence when she was growing up, which was probably why she enjoyed the noise
and controlled chaos that went along with opening up
her home to so many people, but that moment when
the last guest left and silence descended again...

"Breathing a sigh of relief?"

Shannon's eyes flew open. Reece Morgan was leaning in the archway that led to the kitchen. Well, not
quite the last guest, she amended, looking at him. She'd
known he was still here. She known where he was at
any given moment all afternoon. A fine thread of
awareness had spun between them, a faint line of
warmth that had tugged at her senses. She was fairly
sure that should bother her, and maybe it would. Later.
When she wasn't alone with him. When she couldn't
feel this low, electric hum of interest.

It was nearly dark outside and the entryway was dim,
lit only by the soft yellow glow that spilled in from the

living-room lamp and the sharper white glow of the kitchen light that silhouetted Reece's tall figure.

"No food fights. No medical emergencies and everyone went home smiling," she said, answering his question. "I think a sigh of relief is warranted."

Reece's brows rose. "Are food fights and medical emergencies a usual part of the day?"

"Not usual, exactly, but last year Professor Durshwitz thought he was having a heart attack and we had to call the paramedics but it turned out to be indigestion, and the year before that, one of the Brinkman boys threw a dinner roll at his sister. She retaliated and there was a brief flurry of flying rolls. Pretty harmless really until someone hit Edith Hacklemeyer in the forehead with a buttered roll."

Reece's sharp bark of laughter echoed in the tiled hall, and Shannon's mouth curved in response. "I don't imagine Cacklemeyer was particularly gracious about it."

"Well...no, I don't think you could use the term *gracious*. She seemed to think that everyone involved should be drawn and quartered. When no one offered to at least lock Bobby Brinkman in a closet somewhere, she left in a huff." Shannon frowned a little, remembering. "The thing was, it was really hard to take her seriously with this big blotch of butter right between her eyes. She hasn't been back since."

"I'm not surprised. Cacklemeyer was never big on forgive and forget." Reece straightened away from the door and started toward her, and Shannon felt her heart begin to beat a little faster. "I'm surprised she was here at all since she doesn't seem to be a friend of yours."

"She doesn't have anywhere else to go, really." Shannon watched him approach. The door at her back suddenly seemed like a very good idea, because her knees weren't 100 percent sure they wanted to support her.

"A stray puppy?" Reece murmured, stopping in front of her.

"What?" She tilted her head to look at him. She wished the light was better so she could see his expression, but maybe it was better this way because she wasn't at all sure she wanted him to see what must be in her face, in her eyes. Pressing her palms flat against the door on either side of her hips, she tried to steady her breathing, tried to swallow against the excitement that was swelling in her chest.

"Cacklemeyer." Reece set one hand on the door near her head and leaned toward her. "Is she one of your strays? Frank said you collect strays."

"He did?" She was having a hard time following the conversation.

"Do you think *I'm* one of your strays?" he asked, his voice low, husky, a little dangerous.

His free hand came up, long fingers tracing the line of her jaw. There was nothing particularly sexual about that light touch but she felt it like a thin line of fire running down her body. She stared up at him, searching his expression in the fading light, reading hunger mixed with humor and a trace of distinctly masculine irritation.

"Is that what you think?" he whispered, his head dipping toward hers.

Think? Shannon closed her eyes, her mouth parting in anticipation. She wasn't sure she remembered what thinking was, not with his mouth so close that she could feel his breath on her skin, smell the faint crisp scent of aftershave.

"I'm not a stray puppy," he said against her mouth.

Not a puppy, she thought hazily. A wolf, maybe, all sleek muscle and power but definitely not a puppy, stray or otherwise. Shannon's hands came up, her fingers curling into the solid muscles of his upper arms, holding on to him, holding him. Her breath left her on a sigh as his tongue flickered across the seam of her lips, asking—demanding—entrance. She gave it to him willingly, hunger and need fluttering in the pit of her stomach.

She'd been waiting for this, wanting it since that first moment, when he'd opened the door and stood there bare-chested and damp from the shower. It was everything she could have imagined, everything she hadn't let herself think about. His mouth was warm and firm, shaping and molding hers. He tasted of chocolate cream pie and coffee, of desire and hunger.

There was no slow buildup, no soft, coaxing kisses. Just this…need…that washed over her like the ocean, a warm wet wave that overwhelmed with gentle strength, pulling her under, rolling her, leaving her dizzy and clinging to Reece as if he were the only steady thing in the universe. It was too much, she thought. It shouldn't happen this soon, shouldn't be this much this soon. There should be uncertainty, hesitation, fumbling. Instead, they fit together as if they'd known each other forever. As if they were already lovers.

Reece's hand slid behind her, fingers splayed wide across her lower back, drawing her away from the door and up against his body. Solid, she thought, letting her fingers slide into the thick dark hair at his nape and tilting her head to deepen the kiss. He was so solid and it had been so long, so very long since she'd been held like this. A lifetime since she'd been wrapped in some-one's arms, held close and safe. Not that *safe* was ex-actly the word that came to mind at the moment. Not with her heart hammering in her chest and her knees threatening to give out.

It had never been like this, she thought hazily, tilting her head back into the support of Reece's hand, her breath leaving her on something that was almost a whimper as his mouth slid down her throat in a series of biting kisses. She'd never felt this kind of urgency, this kind of hunger, not even with… Her breath caught again, not with pleasure but with a quick little pinch of fear. It was too much. Too much heat, too much need, too much everything. She didn't want… Reece's tongue stroked across the pulse that beat at the base of her throat and Shannon moaned softly, her fingers dig-ging into his shoulders. Okay, obviously she *did* want. Her body wanted, anyway, but that didn't mean she had to give in to— Oh, my…why hadn't anyone told her that her collarbone was an erogenous zone?

Reece was working his way back up her throat, and Shannon shuddered as he caught her earlobe between his teeth, worrying it gently before releasing it to taste the soft skin behind her ear. It was difficult to remem-ber why this was a bad thing, when long-dormant hor-mones were stirring, humming a chorus of how good this was, of how much better it could be if she'd just stop thinking, if she'd just give in and let the pleasure take her where it would.

It took a conscious effort to slide her fingers from his hair, to brace her hands on his shoulders—those very wide, very attractive shoulders—and push back from him.

"This is not a good idea," she managed, wishing she sounded more definite.

"Feels pretty good to me." Reece's thumbs rubbed distracting little circles on the points of her shoulders. His smile was crooked, inviting, a little wicked. "Maybe my technique is a little rusty. You could help me polish it up."

"There's nothing wrong with your technique." Shannon turned her head, and the kiss he'd aimed for her mouth landed on her cheek. Making the best of it, Reece slid his mouth a little farther to the right and nibbled on her earlobe. Shannon's knees and her resolve weakened. With an effort, she stiffened both and planted her hands against his chest. "Your technique is just fine," she assured him breathlessly. "I just… It's too fast… This isn't what I want." Honesty and nerves compelled her to add, "Well, I *do* want it but I'm not going to do it."

Reece gave her a speculative look, and she knew he was debating whether or not to try and change her mind. She sternly suppressed the urge to flex her fingers against his chest, to explore—just a little—the solid wall of muscle and tried to look like a woman whose mind was unchangeable. Maybe she overdid it a little, because she saw a glint of humor edge out the speculation. He opened his mouth but whatever he'd intended to say was cut off by the mellow chime of the doorbell. He hesitated a moment and then one corner of his mouth kicked up in a rueful smile.

"Saved by the bell," he murmured.

His hands dropped away from her shoulders as he stepped back, and Shannon told herself that the little pang she felt was relief, not regret. And if she tried hard enough, she might be able to make herself believe it.

Chapter 5

Conscious of the rather obvious bulge in his jeans, Reece retreated through the nearest archway, leaving Shannon to open the door. Standing in the middle of her cluttered living room, he stared blankly at the heap of fabric that nearly covered the sewing machine occupying the corner near the front window.

What the hell had just happened? A kiss. Right. He'd done that before. Not much in the last year or so, maybe, but that didn't mean he'd forgotten what it was like. There was a sort of unwritten protocol to first kisses. Two mouths, four lips, maybe a bit of tongue, a little body heat, some polite groping, a sort of unspoken inquiry about whether or not both parties wanted this to go any further. This had broken all the rules.

Too fast, she'd said. That was an understatement. He'd barely wrapped his mind around the possibility of having an affair with his sexy neighbor before he found himself groping her up against her own front door. Too fast and too much. It was one thing to indulge in a few fantasies about his pretty neighbor with the legs that went on forever and that full lower lip that seemed made for tasting. It was something else to...*want* like this, this much, this fast. If she hadn't called a halt, he'd have taken her to bed or maybe, God help him, have just taken her up against the door.

Which maybe wasn't the best thing to be thinking right before meeting Shannon's older brother.

When the doorbell rang, Shannon assumed it was one of the guests, come back for some forgotten item. Keefe was just about the last person she expected to see standing on her doorstep. Her brother, she reminded herself. Not just Keefe Walker, near total stranger, but her brother. It didn't seem any more real now than it had months ago when she'd suddenly acquired an entire family she hadn't known existed. Four brothers, a mother she'd thought long since dead and an assortment of sisters-in-law and various children whose relationship to her and to each other she'd yet to sort out. It was more than a bit overwhelming to go from being an orphan to having more family than she could comfortably keep track of. She still hadn't quite managed the emotional shift.

"Keefe." It came out more stunned than welcoming, and Shannon felt herself flush when he raised one dark brow in silent comment.

"Shannon."

"I hope you don't mind us dropping by like this." Keefe's wife rushed to fill the silence, giving Shannon a welcome excuse to look away from her brother.

"Of course not." Her smile relaxed, grew warmer

as she looked at the other woman and the sturdy infant
straddling her hip. A small, quietly pretty blonde with
big blue-gray eyes and a shy smile, Tessa was one
member of Shannon's new family who seemed to understand just how overwhelming the Walkers could be
en masse.

Shannon made an effort to pull her scattered wits
together and stepped back into the hall, opening the
door wide in invitation. "Please come in. I'm sorry if
I seem a little scattered. The last of the guests just left
and I was..." Her voice trailed off as she remembered
just what she'd been doing right before they arrived.
She shot a glance toward the living room and wondered
what the odds were that Reece was still there. Pretty
good unless he'd climbed out a window, she admitted
with a sigh.

She pushed the front door shut and turned to smile
at her unexpected company, suddenly conscious of her
bare feet and tousled hair. Not that there was anything
about those things that suggested she'd been doing anything...well, anything in particular just before they arrived. Bare feet were just bare feet, and her hair could
be tousled for any number of reasons. Feeling a quick
spurt of irritation at her own self-consciousness, she
quashed the urge to smooth her hair. It wasn't any of
Keefe's business what she'd been doing or with whom.
Just because he was her brother, it didn't mean he was
her...brother. And maybe, in an alternate dimension,
that would make sense.

Sighing at her own tangled thoughts, Shannon led
the way into the living room. She hoped Reece had
strong nerves.

Reece had always considered his nerves to be better
than average. It had been pretty much a job require-

ment since nervous people didn't last long in his line of work. But he had to admit that he could think of a whole list of things he'd rather be doing than trying to exchange light conversation with Shannon's rather large older brother. He fought the urge to smooth his hair where Shannon's fingers had been buried in it and hoped that her mouth didn't look as kiss swollen to everyone else as it did to him. Looking at Keefe Walker, he had an uneasy feeling that not much got past those dark eyes.

Keefe's eyes slid from Reece's hair to Shannon's mouth and then back. Reece met his look calmly, but there was nothing he could do to stop the heat he could feel rising in his face. Blushing like a damned schoolboy, he thought, caught between irritation and amusement. Then again, the last time he'd dealt with a hostile older brother, he'd been sixteen and Lisa Ann Palmerston's brother, home on leave from the air force, had caught the two of them red-handed in the back of Reece's beat-up Corvair. Ritchie Palmerston had threatened him with the loss of several treasured body parts. Something told him Keefe Walker was not much for threats but would probably head straight for dismemberment.

"We were on our way home from Los Olivos," Tessa was saying. "Everyone got together at Rachel's for the…" She looked at Shannon and flushed. "Well, *almost* everyone," she said, flustered. "You, um, weren't there, of course, and Gage is in South America or some such place."

"Africa," Keefe said, the first word he'd spoken since the introductions.

"Africa. South America." Tessa waved one hand to

indicate her indifference to the exact location. The baby—David—chortled and clapped his hands together, pleased with the entertainment. Reece grinned, remembering Kyle at that age. God, how many years ago had that been?

"Either way, he couldn't make it home for Thanksgiving but he'll be back for Christmas." She paused and drew a deep breath, sending Shannon a shy smile. "Anyway, we were on our way home and we thought we'd drop in, since you couldn't make it home for Thanksgiving and this is on the way. More or less."

She looked uncomfortable, and Reece wondered just how far out of the way they'd come for this casual visit. And wasn't it interesting that Shannon had missed out on a family get-together, choosing to stay here and fill her home with a mixed bag of misfits and strays for the holiday? Couldn't be a major breach with her family, or Tessa and Keefe wouldn't be here. On the other hand, the tension in the atmosphere made it pretty plain that there was a problem of some sort.

"I'm glad you stopped by," Shannon said, and Reece gave her points for sincerity. He wondered if anyone else noticed the fine lines of tension bracketing that full mouth. Maybe he should come to her rescue? But short of setting fire to the sofa or faking a seizure, he didn't see a way to cut this visit short. Besides, rescuing her suggested that they were…involved, which they weren't. Never mind that not ten minutes ago he'd had her pressed so close against him that she probably had the imprint of his shirt buttons on her breasts. And this was definitely not the time to be thinking about her breasts, not with her brother standing there looking at him with those dark eyes that saw way too much for comfort.

"Shannon said you're a neighbor?" Keefe asked.

"More or less." Reece leaned against the back of the sofa. Might as well *look* relaxed, even if he didn't *feel* relaxed. "My grandfather owned the house next door. He died a few months ago, and I'm staying there while I clean the place out, get it ready to put on the market."

"So you're not staying on permanently?" There was nothing but polite interest in Keefe's tone, but Reece didn't think it was his imagination that put a hopeful note in the question. There was only one possible response, of course. Never mind that rattling the other man's cage was a testosterone-laden cliché. It was just irresistible.

"Hard to say," he murmured. "The place sort of…grows on you." A glance in Shannon's direction would have overplayed his hand so he kept his eyes on the other man, his expression easy, open, as innocent as he could make it. There was a quick flash of humor in those dark eyes, acknowledgment of the hit, maybe, and Reece let his mouth curve in a half smile. It was practically bonding, guy style.

When he looked at Shannon, she gave him that look of mingled irritation and amusement that was unique to females witnessing obscure male territorial rituals. There was only one possible response to that look. Reece widened his eyes in mock innocence, and her mouth twitched before being sternly controlled.

"Why don't I make a pot of coffee?" she said, apparently deciding to ignore the whole exchange.

"Sounds good," Keefe said. "I'll help you with it."

Reece saw a quick flare of something that might have been panic in Shannon's eyes at the thought of being alone with her older brother, and he had the impulse to offer to help with the coffee, too, but judging from Keefe's expression, it wouldn't be anything more than a temporary stay of execution. Whatever he wanted to say to his sister, he looked determined to get it said. If it wasn't over a coffeemaker now, it might end up being over a midnight snack hours from now. Might as well let him get it out.

He watched them leave and then turned to meet Tessa's shy smile. The baby bounced against her hip, looking at Reece with a bright, interested expression that made him grin.

"So, how old is David?"

Shannon was painfully aware of Keefe's rather large presence in her kitchen as she went through the familiar motions of getting out the coffee grinder and taking the beans out of the freezer. Of her four newly acquired brothers, Keefe was the quietest, the one she found hardest to know. Not that she knew any of them, really. She'd made sure of that, she thought, with a twinge of guilt. She'd been careful to keep her distance from them for reasons she'd been equally careful not to examine too closely.

"You grind your own beans?" he asked.

It was the first thing either of them had said since leaving Reece and Tessa in the living room. Though that had only been a few minutes ago, Shannon's voice felt rusty, as if she hadn't used it in weeks.

"It's supposed to taste better." She shrugged as she twisted the lid on the grinder. "I'm not sure I can tell the difference, really."

The high-pitched whir of the grinder cut off any reply he might have made, and she allowed herself a moment of wistful regret that grinding coffee only took a few seconds. When she shut the machine off, the silence seemed painfully loud. Well, he could just say something, she told herself. She dumped the freshly ground coffee into the filter, inhaling deeply at the rich, brown smell of it. *She* wasn't the one who'd shown up on *his* doorstep with some sort of agenda in mind. If the silence didn't bother him, it certainly didn't bother her. It didn't bother her at all.

She hadn't turned on the overhead light, turning on the milk-glass lamp that sat on the table and one of the fluorescent lamps that were mounted under the upper cabinets instead. She usually found the soft glow of the smaller lights restful, but it would take more than cozy lighting to soothe the tension in the room tonight.

Keefe was leaning back against the counter, hands braced on either side of his hips. The body language was relaxed but his eyes were watchful, still. Shannon fussed with the coffee cups she'd taken from the cupboard, arranging them just so on the Holstein patterned tray.

"So, how was your holiday?" she said, and barely managed to restrain a wince at her own perky tone. Apparently, he had a higher tolerance for uncomfortable silence than she did.

"It was good," he said. "Too much food, too many people for the space. Lots of noise. Gets noisier as the kids get older."

"Sounds nice," Shannon said, trying to remember how many nieces and nephews she had. Three? Four? She felt an unpleasant little pinch of shame that she didn't even know that much.

"We were all sorry you couldn't join us," Keefe said. One corner of his mouth kicked up in a half smile.

"It's been a very long time since we were all together for the holidays."

"I already had other plans," she said, hating the defensive note that crept into her voice. She wanted to sound assured, mature with just a hint of none-of-your-business. Instead, she sounded as if she was making excuses. God, was there some genetic thing about older brothers that made her feel guilty even when she didn't have anything to feel guilty about? Well, not much to feel guilty about.

"It was…I've had this sort of potluck for the last couple of years," she said, even as she told herself that she didn't owe him any explanations. "I, ah, didn't want to disappoint people."

Keefe nodded in apparent acceptance. Shannon looked desperately at the coffeemaker but the carafe was still less than half-full.

"Mom's hoping you'll join us for Christmas."

Mom. Shannon winced away from the word. The small, dark-haired woman with the warm brown eyes was *his* mother but, no matter how much she wished otherwise, she couldn't quite see Rachel Walker as *her* mother. *Her* mother was the ghostly figure in her childhood imaginings, a not-quite-remembered presence. She'd grown up telling herself how things would have been if her mother were alive. *They wouldn't move so often if her mother were alive. They'd have a real home if her mother were alive. Her father would care about her if her mother were alive.* She couldn't help but appreciate the irony when she found out that it wasn't her mother's *death* that had made her life what it was, it was, in an odd way, the fact that she was alive.

"I-I'm not sure what my plans are for Christmas,"

she said finally, unwilling to say yes, not quite able to say no.

A muscle flexed in Keefe's jaw, and Shannon had to look away from the sudden sharpness in his eyes. She stared at the coffeemaker, willing it to drip faster. Out of the corner of her eye, she could see him. He was still leaning against the counter but, where his fingers curled around the edge, the knuckles showed white through his tanned skin. She swallowed and kept her eyes on the coffee, which was still dripping with glacial slowness into the glass carafe.

"You know, for someone who went to a fair amount of trouble to find her long-lost family, you sure don't show much interest in getting to know us." He didn't raise his voice. He didn't need to, not when he could put razor-sharp anger into that easy tone.

"Of course I want to…" He arched one dark brow, and she stumbled to a halt, color flooding her cheeks. No, she couldn't really expect him to believe that, not when she'd turned down most of their invitations and offered none of her own. "I've been really busy," she said, hating the weak sound of the excuse. Shame fueled a jagged little spurt of anger. What right did he have to come into her home and chastise her? She tilted her chin and met his eyes. "I have a business to run. It doesn't allow me much time for a social life."

"Social life?" Keefe repeated the phrase with a deadly lack of emphasis. "Funny, I never thought to put family in the category of a social life."

Shannon flushed and looked away. "You know what I mean."

"No, I don't." He straightened away from the counter. There was nothing threatening about the move but he suddenly seemed to be *looming* over her, and she had to resist the urge to step back, to put more space between them. "I'll tell you what I *do* know. I know *you* came looking for *us*. I know you waltzed into our lives—into our mother's life—waved hello and then waltzed back out again. I know she looked like she'd been kicked in the gut when she said you weren't coming for the holiday." His voice was low and even, but the words hit with the impact of bullets. "And I know I don't ever want to see that look in her eyes again. Maybe you've got a reason for keeping your distance, but just in case it hasn't occurred to you yet, let me point out that you're not the only one involved here."

Shannon wanted to hold on to her anger, wanted to wrap herself in a blanket of righteous indignation, but she couldn't quite manage it because, beneath the anger in his eyes, there was something that told her Rachel Walker wasn't the only one she'd hurt. She opened her mouth to tell him…to tell him— She wasn't sure what she wanted to tell him. That he was wrong, that she did know she wasn't the only one involved, that the last thing she wanted to do was hurt anyone, that she didn't want to be hurt herself.

Before she could sort out her tangled thoughts and come up with actual words, the coffeemaker pinged. Startled, Shannon jumped and jerked toward the counter, staring blankly at the full carafe.

"Coffee's ready," she said stupidly.

Keefe sighed and lifted one hand, running his fingers through his dark hair. "You know, maybe we'd better head home," he said, looking suddenly tired and older. "It's getting late and we've still got a long drive ahead of us. Sorry I put you to the trouble of making coffee."

"No trouble," she murmured.

He started toward the door and, as if it belonged to someone else, she saw her hand come out, her fingers curling into the sleeve of his chambray shirt. "Keefe, I...I didn't..."

He waited, his expression unrevealing as he looked down at her. Shannon bit her lip, fumbling for the right words.

"I-I'll try to be there for Christmas," she said at last. It seemed pathetically inadequate, but maybe it was enough because his eyes were suddenly warm.

"Good." One corner of his mouth curved up in an oddly endearing half smile. "You know, if you give us a chance, you might even end up liking us."

He didn't seem to expect an answer, which was just as well because she could hardly tell him that that was what she was afraid of, that she'd like them, that she'd more than like them.

Feeling as if she'd been through an emotional wringer, Shannon followed him out of the kitchen. She could hear Reece talking, the low rumble of his voice in response to Tessa's lighter, softer tones. When she stepped into the living room, she saw that he was standing in front of the fireplace, the baby was perched on his hip, chewing happily on Reece's knuckle. Tessa was sitting on the sofa, smiling as she watched the two of them. The smile faded when she looked at her husband, her eyes concerned and questioning. Whatever she read in his face must have reassured her because the smile returned, her softly pretty features lighting up with an expression so full of love that Shannon looked away, feeling her heart twist a little with something that wasn't—couldn't be—envy.

Not that looking at Reece was much better. He held the baby with a casual ease that spoke of experience.

It was an unexpected side of her tall, dark and handsome neighbor and made her realize how little she really knew about him. Her skin still tingled with the imprint of his hands, but she didn't know if he had children or if he was—horrible thought—married.

David stopped chewing on Reece's knuckle and pulled back to study his hand with solemn intensity that hinted at deep, philosophical questions.

"Gonna read my palm?" Reece asked, grinning.

"He's probably trying to decide where to chew next," Keefe said, his tone dry. "It's worse than having a puppy in the house."

At the sound of his father's voice, David's head jerked around, his face breaking into a wide, mostly toothless grin. Squealing with delight, he threw himself toward Keefe, heedless of the five-foot gap between him and his goal. Reece caught him easily, fingers splayed across the baby's chest. Grinning, he handed the squirming bundle off to Keefe.

"Looks like he's aiming for a career as an acrobat."

"I think his main goal in life is to see if he can turn all my hair gray before he learns to walk," Keefe said dryly. He shifted his gaze to his wife and raised his eyebrows. "I was thinking maybe we ought to skip coffee and hit the road. It's getting pretty late."

"I was just thinking the same thing," Tessa said, standing up. She gave Shannon an apologetic look. "I hope you don't mind."

Mind? When the alternative was the four of them sitting here, trying to make conversation over coffee that none of them wanted? Shannon just hoped she didn't look as relieved as she felt, because she really did like Tessa.

Goodbyes were mercifully brief, and it was easy to

pretend she didn't see the look that passed between the two men, one of those annoying male exchanges that managed to convey ridiculous testosterone-driven concepts of territorial warnings and responses to same, all with just a glance.

She closed the door behind Keefe and Tessa and, for the second time in less than an hour, breathed a sigh of relief. This had, without question, been the strangest Thanksgiving of her life. An afternoon spent preventing a pitched battle between Mavis and just about every other turkey-eating guest, followed by a kiss that had threatened to leave her toes in a permanent curl and then this visit from Keefe, who'd made her see things about herself that she didn't particularly like. And it was still only seven o'clock.

"You want some help drinking that coffee?" Reece asked, and she turned to look at him, resting her shoulders back against the door. He was standing in the living room doorway, one shoulder braced against the frame.

"Help would be good," she said, surprised to find she meant it. She was generally content with her own company, but for some reason she wasn't particularly anxious to be alone tonight. She pushed away from the door and headed for the kitchen, aware of Reece following her, trying not to think of how good it felt not to be alone with her thoughts right now.

The Holstein-patterned tray was still sitting on the counter, holding four cups and a blue-flowered sugar bowl that didn't match the red spatterware creamer. She'd bought most of her dishes at garage sales and flea markets and, if any two pieces matched, it was purely by coincidence. While she was putting two of the cups away, Reece was lifting the carafe out of the coffeemaker and filling the remaining cups.

"Maybe this will kill the taste of the aspic," he said, lifting his cup—a thick white china mug decorated with a bright-red chicken on one side and a neon-yellow sun on the other.

Shannon grinned as she stirred two spoonfuls of sugar into her own cup. "Poor Vangie."

"Poor Vangie?" Reece arched one dark brow and shook his head. "How about some sympathy for the victims? I think that stuff softened the enamel on my teeth."

Laughing, Shannon picked up her cup and tilted her head toward the door. "I've been on my feet most of the day, and I think I hear the sofa calling my name."

If the sofa hadn't been actually sending out signals, it certainly seemed to welcome her. Shannon sighed as she sank into the yielding comfort of the plump cushions. Reece settled in the blue-plaid chair, one ankle propped on the opposite knee. He looked relaxed, at ease in her home, comfortable with the silence between them. She heard the barely audible whoosh as the old gravity-fed heater kicked on. The sound made her realize that the room was on the cool side, not uncomfortably so but enough to provide a reminder that summer was well and truly gone.

Reece took a drink of coffee, the silly chicken mug all but hidden in his big hand. It reminded her of the easy way he'd held Keefe's son.

"Are you married?"

He looked at her, brows raised in a look of mild surprise. "Not anymore. Why?"

"I thought bachelors were supposed to run in terror

at the mere sight of an infant, but you seemed pretty comfortable with David.''

''I have a son,'' he said easily. ''It's been a while since he was that size, but I guess there are some things you don't forget.''

''I guess not.'' She wondered how long he'd been divorced and if he saw much of his son, but couldn't think of a way to ask without sounding nosy.

''We got divorced when Kyle was eight,'' he said, as if reading her thoughts. Or maybe it was just the obvious next question when someone said they were divorced. ''It was an amicable divorce, or as close as you can come when you're talking divorce. Caroline remarried a couple years later, and she and her second husband have two children together. They live in Virginia. Her husband's a lawyer with a big D.C. law firm, and Caroline sells overpriced antiques to people with more money than sense. Charles, her husband, is a decent guy.''

''It's great that you were able to stay on good terms.''

''We worked at it.'' Reece took a sip of his coffee, now tepid and slightly bitter, just like his marriage had ended up, he thought, and then wondered if it was a sign of encroaching middle age when he started finding metaphors in a coffee cup. ''Neither of us wanted Kyle to get caught in the middle of the mess we'd made. Kyle's nineteen now and still speaking to both of us, so I guess we did okay.''

''It's too bad more people don't work at it,'' Shannon murmured. ''Especially when children are involved.''

Reece nodded and wondered what had put the distant look in her eyes. Curled up in the corner of the sofa, those distracting legs curled up under the long folds of her skirt, her hair tumbling around her shoulders in red-gold waves, her expression soft and almost wistful, she looked simultaneously tempting and untouchable. Less than an hour ago he'd been holding her, his fingers buried in her hair, her mouth sweet and warm beneath his. It hardly seemed possible, yet the memory of it was so real he could almost reach out and touch it. It was, in fact, oddly more touchable than the woman herself was at the moment.

"You want to talk about it?" He caught her quick, startled look.

"Talk about what?"

Definitely not cut out for undercover work, Reece thought. Couldn't lie worth a damn. Those big blue eyes slid away from his as if afraid of what he might read there. He debated letting the subject drop. Whatever was bothering her, it was none of his business. He was just passing through, not planning to stay, not planning to get involved. Except he already was involved. Maybe he had been from the moment he'd opened his door to a leggy redhead of dubious sanity. Or maybe it had been the offer of toaster waffles and grape jelly that had done it. Or maybe it was those eyes, looking so…lost. With a sigh for best-laid plans that seemed to be agleying all over the place, he gave up the whole idea of noninvolvement.

"You want to talk about whatever it was that had your big brother all tight-jawed?" he asked. "Feel free to tell me to butt out."

Shannon opened her mouth to tell him—politely— to do just that, but she closed it again without speaking, startled to realize that she *did* want to talk about it. Sort of. Given a choice she would have liked to forget about the whole tangled mess but, since selective amnesia wasn't an option, maybe talking about it would help sort things out in her mind.

"It's a long story," she said, half hoping Reece would grab the excuse to end the conversation. When he arched one brow and looked expectant, she sighed, half relieved, half irritated.

"It sounds like something out of a Dickens novel. Or a soap opera." Shannon paused to take a sip of her coffee. The tepid liquid made her grimace, and she leaned forward to set the cup on the edge of the coffee table. The small delay had given her a chance to sort her thoughts a little and, when she continued, her tone was distant as if she were telling a story about something she'd seen on the news or a movie she'd watched.

"My parents split up before I was born. It was a second marriage for her and she already had four sons. Her first husband was a police officer in Los Angeles, and I guess they were very happy but he was killed in the line of duty. Maybe she was still grieving when she married my father. He was a cop, too, and maybe he reminded her of her first husband." She smoothed her fingers along a fold in her skirt, keeping her eyes on the aimless movement. "Maybe…maybe she really loved him." She released her breath on a long sigh and shrugged irritably. "Whatever. It didn't work out, and they split up before I was born. She got custody but he got visitation rights. I guess things worked out okay for a while, a few years anyway. Then, he showed up to pick me up one day and he just…didn't bring me back."

"Parental abduction," Reece murmured.

"That's what they call it." Shannon leaned her head against the back of the sofa and closed her eyes. "I don't remember much about it. Or about what it was like before he took me. I don't know if it's because I was so young or some sort of traumatic amnesia. I had a few memories of my...family but nothing clear. I grew up thinking my mother was dead. My father moved us around a lot. I suppose he was afraid someone would find out.''

''He must have loved you very much.''

She shrugged. ''I suppose.''

She wanted to believe that, but Shannon couldn't help but think of the lonely years of her childhood, of the silent man who'd seen that she was fed and clothed and educated but had seemed incapable of offering even the simplest gesture of affection. There was a part of her that thought it more likely he'd taken her out of spite and then, once the deed was done, he'd either been too stubborn or too frightened of the consequences to take her back.

Pushing aside the old questions, questions that could never have an answer, Shannon straightened away from the plush cushions and looked at Reece. ''You see before you an authentic milk-carton kid,'' she said, grinning crookedly. ''My face was plastered on dairy products all across America, smiling at people as they ate their breakfast cereal.''

Reece raised his brows and looked impressed. ''That might explain your obsession with Froot Loops.''

Shannon blinked in surprise and then gave a startled little giggle. The few people she'd told about her past had reacted with sympathy and concern. No one had ever *joked* about it.

''I've never met a real celebrity. Should I ask for your autograph?'' Reece asked. His smile widened when she choked on another laugh.

"Talk to my press agent." She'd always found this so difficult to talk about. All the angst and pain. It always seemed so...melodramatic. Never mind that it was all real—all the hurt, all the years lost. She didn't like to talk about it, tried not to think about it but this...this felt good. It felt good to laugh about it.

"Thanks," she said, relaxing back into the cushions, feeling a pleasant lethargy slipping over her. It had been a very long day. Morning seemed a century ago. "I think I needed that laugh."

"Laughter is the best medicine," he said, mock solemn.

"I've heard that rumor," Shannon admitted. She released her breath in a slow sigh. "So, you might as well hear the rest of the story. It's even more like something out of a Dickens plot. My father died when I was eighteen. We'd moved too much for either of us to collect a whole lot by way of household goods, but he had a few boxes that he'd left in storage in Des Moines. I didn't bother to send for the boxes until a couple of years ago, and—here's the part Dickens would have liked—I found these pictures of me with these people who looked vaguely familiar and papers that made it clear my mother hadn't really died when I was born. It was just a little bit of a shock."

Her tone was light but it didn't take much imagination to know what she must have felt, realizing that her father had lied to her, that her whole life had been based on a lie. Reece had had the rug pulled out from under him a time or two, had his entire life turned upside down in the space between one breath and the next. It was never a pleasant experience. The only words that came to mind sounded incredibly banal and meaningless so he said nothing, letting a surprisingly easy silence build between them.

"You know that thing about being careful what you wish for?" Shannon asked suddenly, smiling a little as she looked at him. "I'd spent my whole life wishing I had a big family, brothers and sisters, a mother, roots—every cliché you've ever seen on television. And then I found out I had four older brothers and a mother who wanted nothing more than to welcome me back into the fold."

"But you discovered the family business is white slavery?" he asked, and she grinned and shook her head.

"No. No, they're all really nice." She pleated the hem of her skirt between her fingers, her eyes on the aimless movement. "My...brothers even married nice women and their kids seem nice, too. They're all just..."

"Nice?" Reece finished, when she seemed at a loss for words. She gave a surprised little huff of laughter.

"Exactly. They're just...really nice. Not that I'd want them to be un-nice," she added, frowning a little as she groped for words to explain something she didn't completely understand herself. "I mean, it's great that they were so warm and welcoming. Really great."

"Must be hard, though, hard to wake up one morning and find yourself with a ready-made family, especially when you don't remember them but they remember you. Lot of expectations there."

"Yes." Shannon felt something tight and hard loosen inside her. "Yes, that's it exactly."

That was what she hadn't been able to articulate these past few months. The Walkers had opened their arms and their hearts to her and, when she couldn't do the same, she'd felt guilty and confused and lost. She'd found the warm, loving family of her childhood fantasies, but they were strangers to her. In retrospect, it seemed ridiculous that she could have expected them to be anything else, but there had been a part of her that half expected some mystical emotional connection to spring up the moment she saw them. Blood calling to blood like something out of a Victorian novel, she thought, with a twinge of sad amusement for her own naiveté. Instead what she'd felt was the weight of their expectations and the sharp bite of her own disappointment.

"Family," Reece said. "It's never as simple as it looks in the sitcoms." He lifted his empty cup from the coffee table and stood up. "Definitely a case of false advertising."

Following his lead, Shannon rose, too. "Maybe they should come with warning labels. Professional actors just pretending to be a family—don't try this at home, boys and girls."

He followed her out to the kitchen, setting his cup on the counter next to the sink before turning to look at her. His hand came up, fingers barely touching her lower lip.

"You know, it's been a long time since I've had a big brother interrupt a necking session."

"Necking session?" she arched one brow. "Is that what it was?"

Reece's smile was wicked. "If you have to ask, maybe I need to work on my technique."

"I don't think you need to worry about that," she said primly. She was fairly sure that if his technique got any better, she'd have melted into a puddle in the entryway, but she wasn't going to tell him that.

"I'll take that as a compliment." He brushed his thumb across her mouth and she knew, as surely as if he'd spoken out loud, that he was thinking about kissing her again. She waited, not sure what she'd do if he did. Kiss him back, that was pretty much a given. Based on her one-time experience, she didn't think it was possible to *not* respond when Reece Morgan kissed you.

He let his hand drop, and the moment was gone. Shannon told herself she was relieved. Well, mostly relieved.

"It's been a long day. I should go, let you unwind." He picked up the big glass bowl that had held spinach salad and moved toward the front door.

Shannon followed, suddenly aware of how tired she was. It really had been an incredibly long day. She wrapped her fingers around the edge of the door, leaning against it as he stepped out onto the porch. It was full dark out, and the air was cool and dry. It wasn't the crisp, maybe-it-will-snow weather of picture postcards but there was a feeling of autumn in the air. Maybe it was the collective panic rising from the home of every potential shopper, that humming awareness that there were only four more weeks until Christmas breaking through the post-Thanksgiving-dinner lassitude.

"Thanks for the dinner."

"Even the aspic?" she asked, biting her lip to hold back a smile.

"Don't push it," he said, and she laughed.

Leaning against the door, she watched him walk

down the cracked walkway, admiring the way the faded denim of his jeans hugged his narrow hips. Life was certainly more interesting since Reece Morgan had moved back to town.

Chapter 6

Reece stared glumly at the partially disassembled faucet. He picked up a washer, moved it from one side of an unidentifiable part to the other and looked at it some more.

He could break down an AK-47 in the pitch-dark, working solely by feel, and reassemble it again in a matter of minutes. He could rig a car bomb with not much more than a pocket knife and a wad of chewing gum, turn a tube of toothpaste and a couple of hairpins into a deadly weapon and build a fire in the middle of a blinding rainstorm. He was skilled in several forms of hand-to-hand combat, had fought his way through hostile jungles, the back alley of more than one foreign city and escaped from an enemy prison—twice. His body bore the scars of two bullet wounds, half a dozen close encounters with sharp-edged weapons and the more recent car wreck that had nearly killed him.

For the last twenty years or so, he'd felt justified in

considering himself a man of more than average competence, equipped for survival in even the most hostile of environs. Only now did he realize he had yet to face the ultimate challenge. It was one thing to look death in the eye; it was something else altogether to go head-to-head with a broken faucet.

Still frowning, Reece picked up a bottle of a surprisingly decent locally brewed beer and took a fortifying swallow. A man was supposed to be master of his environment. It was one of the things that separated man from beast, civilization from chaos. Technology—that was the problem. A few thousand years ago he could have just built a hut in the howling wilderness, killed a mastodon or two for dinner and felt pretty good about himself. Now a man needed to understand the intricacies of plumbing before he could be master of his own home.

He'd rather face a mastodon any day.

The sound of the doorbell offered the possibility of retreat with honor. No one could expect him to think about plumbing when there was someone at the door, anxious to either lighten his wallet or save his soul. At this point he didn't care which it was, as long as it didn't involve washers, wrenches or gaskets of any kind.

"Frank." Reece greeted the other man with real pleasure. In the week since Thanksgiving, he'd thought about calling several times and just hadn't gotten around to it. He was glad Frank had taken the initiative. "Come on in."

"Hope you don't mind me just dropping in," Frank said. "You can tell me to go away if you're busy."

"Actually, I had an appointment with destiny but it

was canceled.'' Reece shut the door and turned to see Frank studying the dimly lit living room.

"Love what you've done with the place," he said, looking at the pile of cardboard boxes that blocked access to the sofa and the mound of bulging black plastic trash bags that blocked half the front window.

"It's called Dumpster decor," Reece told him. "It's the latest thing on the East Coast."

Frank nodded. "I can see why. It's cheap and you can definitely do it yourself."

"Don't be fooled by the apparent simplicity," Reece warned him. "It took me three solid weeks of work to achieve this effect."

"I bet." Frank looked around again. "You got someone coming to get rid of this junk?"

"Tomorrow," Reece said immediately, and Frank chuckled.

"I helped my parents clean out my great-aunt Josephine's house a couple of years ago. I don't think she'd thrown anything out since Truman was in office."

"I think my grandfather has her beat," Reece said, thinking of the stacks of old envelopes saved to use for scratch paper, the balls of string and an entire drawer full of rubber bands that were so old they'd disintegrated at a touch.

"You want a beer?" he asked, leading the way into the kitchen.

"Thanks." Frank nodded approval at the label when Reece handed him an ice-cold bottle. "Good stuff. I know the guy who makes it, Larry Lebowitz. He was in my class in high school. Computer nerd, tape on his glasses, pocket protector, the whole nine yards. Figured he'd vanish into the bowels of some big company and never be heard from again. Went off to San Francisco for a few years then came back with a boyfriend who looks like a refrigerator with a head, bought an old commercial laundry and started a brewery. Everyone thought they were crazy but they've done okay. Won a prize at the State Fair a couple years back.'' He grinned. ''And Larry still looks like a computer nerd.'' He took a long pull from the bottle and, when he lowered it, his eyes settled on the pathetic pile of faucet parts on the counter. ''Need some help?''

Reece weighed his options. He could give a manly grunt and deny any need for assistance or he could abandon his pride and hope Frank actually knew what all those little parts did.

''You know anything about faucets?'' he asked, choosing a cautious middle ground between denial and shameless begging.

''I run a hardware store,'' Frank reminded him. ''There's not much I don't know about faucets. What's the problem?''

''The main problem seems to be that I don't know what the hell I'm doing,'' Reece admitted, tossing pride to the wind in hopes of actually having a working faucet again. ''I got it apart okay, but I know there weren't this many parts when I started and I think the repair kit I bought is actually for the carburetor on a '56 Chevy because none of this stuff looks like it goes in a faucet.''

Frank grinned. ''Not a do-it-yourselfer, I take it.''

''My idea of doing it myself is picking up the phone to call the manager of my apartment building.'' Reece eyed the other man speculatively. ''There's a case of beer in it for you if you can actually put it back together.''

"Bribery." Frank nodded his approval. "I like that, but I'd probably have done it for a six pack." He set the bottle on the counter and began rolling up the sleeves of his blue flannel shirt, eyeing the parts like a man who knew what he was looking at.

"I don't mind paying a fair price for a working faucet," Reece said graciously.

He leaned one hip against the counter and watched as Frank sorted through the parts, setting some aside, shaking his head a time or two as he disassembled some of Reece's tentative attempts to put the thing back together again.

"Man, you're a plumber's wet dream," he said, grinning as he pried apart two items that apparently didn't relate to each other.

"I bought the kit at your store. It was right under a sign that said it was a suitable project for home owners without much do-it-yourself experience," Reece pointed out.

"Yeah, but we didn't say it was suitable for people with severe parts-recognition impairment and a total inability to read a schematic." Frank's grin held cheerful malice.

"Bite me, McKinnon." Reece was too grateful for the help to put much force behind the words.

He finished the last of his beer, debated about getting another one, and then decided it was too early in the day for a second. He dropped the empty bottle in the recycle bin and leaned back against the counter while Frank worked.

Thin sunlight shone through the window over the sink. It had rained the day before and the sky was still overcast, defying the weather reports that had promised clear skies and sunshine. The window faced Shannon's house, and Reece found his thoughts drifting in that direction.

He'd seen her several times in the last week but not to talk to. He was usually halfway through his second cup of coffee about the time she was leaving in the morning. From the front porch he could watch her back out of her driveway. She drove a fire-engine-red Miata that clashed so magnificently with her hair that it was a sort of fashion statement all on its own. She intrigued him, he admitted, and not just because she did interesting things to his libido.

"Have you known Shannon long?"

If Frank was surprised by the abrupt question, he didn't say so. "About as long as anyone, I guess. I was friends with Johnny Devereux before they got married."

"Married!" Reece was too startled to conceal his reaction. "She's married?"

"Widowed," Frank said. "Johnny died three years ago this past August."

Reece stared at him blankly, trying to slot this new information into the image he had of his pretty neighbor with the long, lazy stride and easy smile. "She's awfully young to be widowed," he said at last, the first clear thought to surface out of the tangle.

"Yeah, it was a real tragedy." Frank nodded as he reached for two parts that bore no apparent relation to each other and put them together with a quick twist of his fingers. "She and Johnny had only been married a few months. Johnny was a firefighter and she was working as a receptionist in a dentist's office. A bunch of the local guys got called out to help with a big brush fire in Los Angeles, one of those where they had to call in units from all over the state. It looked like they might be getting it under control then the Santa Ana winds kicked up and they were right back where they started. Johnny and another firefighter were trapped in a wash when the winds shifted. The fire went right over them, not a damned thing anyone could do to get to them.''

Imagining it, Reece felt sick to his stomach. He'd seen what burns could do to the human body. ''Hell of a way to die.''

''Yeah.'' Frank nodded, his round face uncharacteristically somber. ''The other guy made it a couple of days but he was so badly burned that...'' He stopped and shook his head and, after a moment, went back to work on the faucet while Reece stared blankly out the window at the house next door, his mind spinning with the effort of trying to shuffle all this new information into what he knew—or thought he knew—of his neighbor.

''I was a little surprised Shannon stayed on,'' Frank said as he reached for a wrench. ''She'd only lived here a few months and, with Johnny gone, I thought she might sell the house and move away from the memories, but a couple months after he died, she bought the shop.'' He glanced up, saw Reece's blank look and clarified. ''Quilter's Haven over on Sycamore.''

''She owns a store that sells quilts?'' Reece asked, feeling his mental image shift yet again.

''Not the actual quilts. Fabric and stuff to make quilts,'' Frank clarified.

''People make quilts?'' Reece asked blankly. He had a vague image of little old ladies in long dresses hunched over a cloth-covered frame, gossiping while they wielded their needles. ''Enough of them to support a whole shop just for that?''

"Oh, yeah." Frank laughed. "I heard Shannon tell someone once that a quilt shop is a destination business, and she sure was right. Quilters drive all the way from Los Angeles to go to her shop. It's weird because there are plenty of quilt shops in L.A. but they'll drive all the way out here, anyway, like some sort of religious trek.

"I thought she was crazy when she bought the place and I told her so, but she just gave me this little smile and said it would give her something to do, so Kelly and I pitched in and helped her get the place in shape. Kelly went to work for her from day one, and I'll be damned if she hasn't made a success out of it. She's not getting rich but she's turning a profit, which is more than most small businesses manage."

So, his long-legged neighbor was a successful businesswoman. It was difficult to reconcile that with the woman who let a coffee-shop employee intimidate her into grinding her own coffee or the one who would invite a stranger to breakfast to spite her nosy neighbor. On the other hand she certainly had people skills, he thought, remembering the way she'd managed to avert a war over the turkey leftovers last week. That kind of diplomacy came in handy for working with the public.

When he'd seen her going off to work in the mornings, he'd pictured her working in an office somewhere, not running her own business.

Obviously, he had a lot to learn about his temporary neighbor.

"Ohmmm. Ohmmm."

Shannon grinned as Kelly chanted under her breath. "You know, you sound like you're set on fast-forward. I think you're supposed to try for a sort of slow, rhythmic pace. The monks aren't actually racing each other to the finish line.''

''They've never had to deal with Edith Hackle-meyer,'' Kelly muttered darkly. ''The woman has the taste of a-an aardvark and all the finesse of a water buffalo.''

''Actually, there are very few aardvark quilters. I think it's the opposable-thumb problem.'' Shannon un-rolled the last yard of fabric from a bolt and set the empty cardboard insert aside. The fabric was a leafy print with brightly colored frogs scattered across it, and they'd sold the whole bolt in two days, so she'd reor-dered in hopes that the sudden frog frenzy would last until the new bolt arrived.

''Well, I'd rather deal with an aardvark than deal with that woman,'' Kelly said, casting a dark look to-ward the back of the shop where Edith was looking at fabrics. ''Do you know what she said to me?''

''With Edith, almost anything is possible.''

''She said that bleached blond hair tended to make a woman look hard and cheap.'' Kelly smoothed her hand over her streaky blond hair, her eyes bright with annoyance. ''I *don't* bleach my hair.''

Shannon choked on a laugh. It was so typically Edith. She hadn't actually said that Kelly's hair was bleached so no one could accuse her of making a per-sonal remark. If Kelly *chose* to take an apparently ran-dom remark personally, well, that was hardly Edith's fault.

''I *don't* bleach my hair,'' Kelly whispered fiercely, apparently objecting to Shannon's obvious amusement.

''I believe you.'' Shannon assured her. ''I just can't help but admire the way she manages to deliver an insult without ever actually saying anything insulting. You've got to admit, it's a real talent."

"It's the only one she has," Kelly muttered, moving away from the cutting table as Edith approached with half a dozen bolts of fabric stacked in her skinny arms.

Shannon put on her best, friendly shop-owner smile. "Did you find what you wanted?"

"Eventually." Edith pursed her lips in discontent. "Most of the fabrics are so bright and garish. I don't understand why you don't stock a better selection of quieter, more tasteful prints. *You* wouldn't remember, of course, but those of us who were quilting in the seventies remember the charming little calicos that were available then."

Shannon kept her smile in place, ignoring Kelly's muted growl from behind her. Most of the long-time quilters she knew were grateful for the wide selection of fabrics available to them now and referred to the seventies as the dark ages of quilting.

"There are fashions in quilt fabric, just like everything else. Right now the fashion is for cheerful prints and colors."

"Garish," Edith said, sniffing her contempt.

"Well, I'm glad you found something to your taste," Shannon said, ignoring the comment as she lifted the first bolt off the stack and unrolled the fabric onto the table. "How much of this one would you like?"

"Two yards of each," Edith said. "Whatever I don't need for the top I'll use to piece the back."

Kelly was looking at the stack of fabric and rolling her eyes in disgust, and Shannon bit the inside of her lip to hold back a laugh. She generally tried to appreciate her customers' choices. It was both good manners

and good business, but she had to admit that Edith
made it difficult. She must have looked long and hard
to find six fabrics so dull and washed-out. Paired with
something more vivid, they would have provided the
eye with a resting place and added richness to a quilt.
Mixed together, they looked old and worn-out, even
before they were cut from the bolt. Still, the old rule
about the customer always being right held true, even
when they had no taste.

"Another log cabin quilt?" Shannon asked as she
measured off the fabric. As far as she knew, log cabin
was the only pattern Edith ever made. She turned out
half a dozen log cabin quilts a year, each as uninspired
as the one before it, and donated them all to a woman's
shelter. Shannon tried hard to admire her for the charitable work but it wasn't easy.

"Yes. For those poor, unfortunate women. I feel it's
important to do what I can for those less fortunate than
myself. You do still offer a discount on fabric bought
for charitable purposes, don't you?"

"Of course."

Kelly gave a disgusted snort, or maybe she was just
clearing her throat. Shannon decided to give her the
benefit of the doubt, but to be safe she kept her attention on the fabric. Laughter and rotary cutters were not
a good mix.

"Two yards of the green, too." Edith tapped the bolt
with one finger as if Shannon might need guidance in
telling green from pink. "I understand you've spent
some time with the Morgan boy," Edith said and, between the abrupt change of topic and the word *boy,* it
took Shannon a moment to figure out who she was
talking about.

"He came over for Thanksgiving dinner," she admitted.

"I generally don't interfere in other people's business," Edith said, and Shannon shot an involuntary look at the older woman's nose to see if it had grown. In her experience Edith Hacklemeyer *lived* to interfere. "But I feel it's my duty to offer you some advice."

"Really, it's not necessary." Even as she spoke, Shannon knew it was futile. Nothing could stop Edith when she was on a roll.

"You're too young to remember Reece Morgan from the first time he lived here. Of course, you didn't even live in Serenity Falls, but if you *had* lived here, you would have been too young to remember him."

From somewhere behind a wooden display full of books, Shannon heard Kelly choking back a laugh. Ignoring her, she concentrated on cutting a straight line.

"But I certainly remember him," Edith announced, verbally shrugging off the muddled beginning of her speech. "And let me tell you, he's trouble."

Shannon was surprised to feel a twinge of real annoyance. Usually Edith's pompous pronouncements rolled off her back. The woman loved to complain, especially about things that were none of her business. But this time she found herself remembering the gentle way Reece had handled Keefe's baby son, the way he could smile with just his eyes, and her patience thinned.

"He's been very pleasant," she said mildly. "Very pleasant" seemed like an odd thing to say about a man she'd almost had sex with up against her own front door but it would have to do.

"The devil can charm when he wants to," Edith said, pressing her lips together.

More choking sounds came from behind the books.

Edith cast a frowning look in that direction, but Kelly was either crouched down straightening out the fabric below the book rack or she was rolling on the floor trying to control her laughter. Shannon kept her attention focused strictly on the task in front of her, folding the cut end of fabric neatly over the bolt and pinning it in place.

"As the twig is bent, so grows the tree," Edith continued, dismissing the noise.

Had she memorized an entire book of homilies? Shannon reached for the next bolt and tried to block out the other woman's voice.

"Not that Joe Morgan didn't do his best, but you can't make a silk purse out of a sow's ear."

The bell over the door rang and Shannon looked up eagerly, hoping for an entire busload of quilters to come spilling through the door or even a frazzled mother with sticky-fingered children in tow, anything to provide a distraction.

What she got was Reece Morgan, all six feet four inches of him. He was wearing black jeans that hugged his narrow hips in a way that was probably illegal in more conservative parts of the country and a heavy gray cable-knit sweater that emphasized the width of his shoulders. Droplets of water sparkled against the thick darkness of his hair, courtesy of the light mist falling outside.

His eyes skimmed the shop, one dark brow arching when he saw Edith, and then his gaze settled on Shannon, his mouth curving in a smile that made her knees go weak. She smiled back helplessly. Edith was still droning on, something about troublemakers and spots that couldn't be changed, but it was background noise. Somewhere in the back of her mind she wondered if she should be worried about that, about the way everything else just faded away except Reece—his eyes, his smile, the subtle smell of wet sidewalks and damp wool that came in with him.

The multicolored striped awning sparkling against the white stucco storefront had caught his eye and, on an impulse, he'd turned into the small parking lot across the street. Impulse didn't explain why he'd been driving down that particular street to start with, but Reece decided to cut himself some slack and not insist on an explanation.

Stepping out of the drifting mist into the bright warmth of Quilter's Haven, Reece was reminded of the scene in the *Wizard of Oz* where Dorothy opens the door of the hurricane-tumbled house and steps out of the black-and-white world of Kansas into the technicolor sprawl of Oz. The walls were lined with bolts of fabric in every color of the rainbow. Books with colorful covers were displayed in a low wooden rack. The space between the shelves of fabric and the ceiling were covered by a dizzying variety of what he assumed must be quilts, though they weren't the somber geometric designs of his vague imaginings. Plaid chickens jostled for space with floral teacups and a penguin carrying a bouquet of daisies. The geometric patterns were there, too, but there was nothing somber about them. So much for little old ladies wielding their needles and discussing the latest doings at the Grange Hall.

He pulled his eyes away from the display and found himself staring at the back of Edith Hacklemeyer's head. He'd seen her several times since he moved back. She spent time in her yard each day, probably using tweezers to eradicate any weeds foolish enough to lift their heads in her lawn. But even if he hadn't seen her, he would have recognized that nasal voice. God knew, he'd spent enough hours listening to it as she droned on about dangling participles and the importance of proper punctuation. She was saying something about leopards not being able to change their spots, no matter how much they tried and no one could tell her that *he* had tried all that hard. It wasn't hard to guess who the leopard in question was and Reece felt a quick little spurt of amusement. You had to give the old bat points for consistency. Uproot a few petunias and twenty years later, he was still the spawn of the devil.

He looked past her and met Shannon's eyes and felt his mouth curve in a smile. She was wearing a thin, soft sweater in a warm shade of blue that reflected the color of her eyes. Trim black jeans clung to her hips and those illegally long legs. She'd pulled her hair back from her face with a pair of clips shaped like bright-blue butterflies and let the rest of it tumble onto her shoulders. She looked young and vibrant and ridiculously attractive.

It was getting easier and easier to forget that he was only staying in Serenity Falls long enough to clean out his grandfather's house. Harder to remember that he wasn't looking to get involved with anyone at this point in his life.

With an effort he looked away from Shannon, hearing Cacklemeyer's voice still droning on.

"I always try to take a charitable point of view," she said, a portrait of self-delusion. "But one must face facts, after all, and the fact is that some people are just born to trouble. That's all there is to it. I don't—"

She broke off abruptly as Reece stepped into her field of vision.

"Ms. Hacklemeyer. It's been a long time, hasn't it?"

"Yes, it has, um, been a long time." Her expression made it clear that it hadn't been nearly long enough, and Reece let his smile widen, showing the maximum number of teeth.

"Your flowers look very nice this year."

He heard Shannon choke back a laugh as Edith's eyes widened in a look that mixed indignation with just a touch of fear. Before she could say anything, Kelly McKinnon popped up from behind the book display.

"I'll finish cutting Edith's fabric," she said, moving over to the cutting table and nudging Shannon away from the stack of fabrics there. "I'll take care of business while you talk."

Smiling and prodding, she edged the two of them toward the back of the store and the illusion, at least, of privacy.

"Let me guess," Shannon said. "You've always wanted to make a quilt."

"Actually, I didn't know you *could* make a quilt," he admitted. "Frank dropped by this morning and mentioned that you owned a quilt shop. I was in the neighborhood so…" He let a shrug finish the sentence. No point in mentioning that being "in the neighborhood" had taken him fifteen minutes out of his way. "I wasn't sure what to expect."

"Gray-haired ladies in granny gowns?" she guessed, giving him a shrewd look.

"Pretty much," he admitted sheepishly.

She clicked her tongue and gave him a disapproving look. "Stereotypes. That's not at all politically correct of you. I could give you my standard lecture on the diversity of quilters in America today, but I've got a meeting with a fabric rep in half an hour so I'd only have time to hit the high points.''

Reece tried to look both chastened and disappointed but, from her sudden laugh, guessed that he'd managed to look more relieved than anything else. Her laugh was infectious, low and warm, inviting, and he had a sudden, fierce urge to lean in and see if he could taste that warmth. It took a conscious effort to pull his eyes away.

''Nice place,'' he said, seeking a distraction.

''Thanks. We do pretty well.'' Shannon glanced around the shop with obvious pride. ''When I first started, it seemed like there weren't enough hours in the day to do everything that needed to be done, but I've got half a dozen women who work part-time now so I don't have to be here every minute of the day. It still takes a lot of time but it's not quite twenty-four hours a day anymore.''

''Not many small businesses make it past the first year.''

''I wasn't sure I would, either,'' she said, grimacing at the memory of those first, lean months. ''It's taken a while but we're finally showing a profit. I'm not ready for the Fortune 500 but we're in the black and that's more than most small businesses manage.'' She gestured to the colorful quilts hanging on the walls. ''We run a schedule of about forty classes per quarter and most of them fill up. When we bring in a big-name teacher, we sometimes get students from as far away as San Diego, and we've got several block-of-the-month programs that are—''

Shannon stopped abruptly, suddenly aware that she'd been all but lecturing him. She felt herself flush and gave him an apologetic look. "Sorry, I didn't mean to ramble on like that."

"I don't mind. It's interesting."

"Yeah, right." Her eyebrows rose in disbelief. "And I suppose your idea of light entertainment is reading the stock market report."

"Insurance," he said solemnly. "Actuarial tables drive me wild." He waggled his eyebrows up and down, grinning when she gave a strangled little chuckle.

"You must be a laugh riot on a date."

"See for yourself. Have dinner with me tonight."

Shannon's laugh ended on a gasp. "What?" Had he just asked her for a date?

"Have dinner with me," Reece repeated calmly, but there was something in his eyes that made her wonder if he wasn't as surprised by the invitation as she was. "Frank mentioned a new restaurant that opened up where the old library used to be."

"Emilio's," Shannon said. Frank had taken Kelly there for their anniversary a couple of months ago and Kelly had raved about the food.

"That's the one. It's a weeknight so I should be able to get a reservation on short notice."

A date. He'd just asked her out on a date. She hadn't gone on a date in…well, years. She wasn't sure she even knew *how* to date anymore. Food, conversation. She was pretty sure she remembered how to do that part of it. And afterward? A kiss good-night or… It was the "or" that made her hesitate. That wasn't surprising—women had been hesitating over that particular "or" since at least the beginning of the sexual revolution. No, it wasn't the "or" itself that worried her, it was what her answer might be if the question of "or" came up.

Chapter 7

The food at Emilio's was as good as Kelly had said
it was. Shannon ordered salmon in a balsamic vinegar
glaze and Reece had filet mignon napped with a shallot
and red wine sauce. No aspic, he said sadly, giving the
menu a disappointed look. It made her laugh and suddenly it seemed silly to be worrying about what the
end of the evening might bring. Whatever was going
to happen, it wouldn't happen without her consent.
Consent, hell, she admitted ruefully. If that kiss last
week was anything to go by, whatever happened was
likely to have her enthusiastic cooperation.

As it turned out, neither consent nor cooperation was
required. At the end of the evening, Reece took her
home, walked her up to her door in proper date fashion
and waited while she unlocked it. She turned to look
at him, her heart beating just a little too fast. She
waited, half-afraid that, whatever he wanted, whatever
he suggested, she was going to give him a breathy little

"yes" and melt like candle wax on a hot day. He studied her face for a moment, eyes dark and unreadable, and then his mouth quirked in a half smile. He brushed his fingertips across her cheekbone, murmured goodnight and turned and walked away.

Shannon stood in the half-open door, watching those long strides carry him over the damp, cracked concrete. For just a moment, a small unworthy moment, she hoped he'd trip over a crack, but he moved down the buckled walkway as easily as if it were broad daylight instead of misty darkness. She slipped into the house before he turned onto the sidewalk, shutting the door carefully, quietly and sliding the dead bolt into place before bouncing her forehead gently against the wood.

The next day, Thursday, Reece and Frank McKinnon arrived at the shop midafternoon, bringing sandwiches and coleslaw from Serenity Falls's one and only New York style deli, which happened to be run by a former Texan who'd never been farther east than Nebraska. But, whatever his antecedents, Willard Long knew his way around a pastrami sandwich. With rain pattering down on the street and dripping from the bright-striped awning out front and no customers in sight, they spread the food out on the classroom tables in the back of the shop and ate pastrami on rye and tangy coleslaw. Shannon tried not to notice how comfortable Reece was with her friends, how easily he fit into her life.

Friday evening, after the shop closed, Shannon rented a movie at the video store across the street. The owner was a middle-aged woman with a permanently harried expression and a teenage daughter whose sole purpose in life, according to her mother, was to turn her hair gray as quickly as possible. After dealing with the girl, who was currently handling the cash register, Shannon wouldn't have been surprised to see the woman's hair turn gray overnight.

Stitch—*Lacey is such a dork's name*—had pierced every conceivable body part so that silver rings and metal studs caught the light every time she moved. Not that she moved any more than she had to, preferring to point vaguely toward the possible location of any tape a customer might be seeking. Her only voluntary movement was the rhythmic up-and-down motion of her jaw as she chewed a never-ending wad of gum.

When Shannon brought up her selection of tapes, Stitch offered a running critique as she ran them across the scanner. The three tapes were, in no particular order, dismissed as dork-o-rific, total retro trash and a failed attempt to save the fading reputation of an overrated director. A more sensitive person might have been offended. Shannon found herself biting her lip to keep from laughing out loud and thinking how much she was going to enjoy telling Reece about this encounter.

Somewhere in the back of her mind, she wondered if she should be worried that he was the first person she thought of or maybe worried that she was renting movies with him in mind, thinking of whether he preferred drama or comedy, wondering if he liked the old Preston Sturges classics. Still, where was the harm in it? It wasn't as if they were involved. Or at least not "Involved" with a capital letter and all the complications that implied. He was her neighbor—her *temporary* neighbor—and she enjoyed his company. There was nothing complicated about it.

So, Friday night turned out to be movies and pop-corn and the discovery that they shared a taste for screwball comedy and diverged sharply on the importance of Mel Gibson's blue eyes for the success of a film.

Reece didn't kiss her good-night, didn't even look as if he were *thinking* about kissing her good-night, and that was perfectly all right because they weren't involved. Right?

Saturday Frank and Kelly invited both of them over for barbecued ribs, and Shannon felt a little uneasy at the thought that the McKinnons were seeing her and Reece as a couple, which they definitely weren't. They were just neighbors and—maybe—friends but Kelly's casual comment that, since Reece lived next door, they could drive over together made it clear that no one was seeing them as a couple, least of all Reece because, if he thought they were a couple, he'd want to kiss her again, right?

Barbecue plans had to be canceled when the rain made an abrupt reappearance late in the afternoon. The small party moved indoors, including three cats and one large and not terribly intelligent golden retriever named Mortimer. They ate take-out fried chicken—the humans did, anyway—and played Trivial Pursuit, with much squabbling over alleged cheating and Frank's accusations that only alien brain implants could explain his wife's uncanny knowledge in the science and nature category.

The game was declared a draw when Mortimer came over to see what all the fuss was about and swept a plumed tail across the coffee table, scattering playing pieces every which way. Kelly hinted darkly that Frank had signaled the dog to destroy the game in a craven attempt to avoid going down to humiliating defeat. Since Mortimer's sweet disposition was matched only by his obvious lack of intelligence, no one put much credence in that theory, and the evening ended with the four of them eating butter pecan ice cream and discussing the relative merits of the Marx Brothers versus the Three Stooges.

Reece drove Shannon home through a steady rain, the hiss of the tires on wet pavement and the rhythmic slap of the windshield wipers providing a backdrop for their conversation. The late-night streets were almost empty, the streetlights providing intermittent light, approaching through the darkness and then passing. It felt as if they were the only two people in the world, as if everyone else had just faded away.

And somewhere along the way, she realized she was talking about her marriage, telling him about Johnny, about how she'd been working as a waitress in Stockton and he'd been there visiting an elderly aunt, about how he'd come into the restaurant for breakfast and then come back for lunch and talked her into letting him take her out for dinner.

"He had a wonderful smile," she said, staring out into the darkness, and suddenly, for the first time in years, she could *see* that smile, could see his face clearly, see the laughter that always seemed to lurk in the back of his eyes.

Reece didn't say anything. He didn't have to. It was enough that he was there, large and warm and solid. Maybe it was the darkness and the rain and the laughter they'd shared earlier but the words were suddenly spilling from her, and as she talked, she realized that she hadn't forgotten, after all. She just hadn't let herself remember.

She hadn't let herself remember the whirlwind court-
ship, two weeks of dinners and movies and laughter
and the crazy exhilaration of driving to Vegas to marry
a man she barely knew, the nervous pleasure of realizing that she was really married, that she was the center of someone's life now, just as he was the center of
hers.

Sitting here in the dark, with the rain pattering
against the roof of the truck and the rest of the world
a distant, not quite real thing, the memories were suddenly sharp and real and the words were easy to find.
It felt good to talk about him, good to remember. And
when she thought about it, she realized that she
couldn't imagine talking to anyone else about this and
she knew that should probably worry her, but for now
it was enough to have the memories back, like a gift
Reece had given her without knowing it.

Sunday morning Reece appeared on Shannon's doorstep, empty coffee cup in hand, a pleading look on his
face. Laughing, she invited him in and poured him a
cup of coffee. They drank it in her kitchen, with rain
sliding down the windows and an occasional distant
mutter of thunder for accompaniment. When Shannon
mentioned breakfast, Reece's eyes widened in mock
fear and he quickly suggested brunch at a nearby bed-
and-breakfast, known for their blueberry muffins and
country-cured bacon.

Somehow, brunch drifted into a matinee of a new
film, which they both agreed had been highly overrated
and an early dinner at a café where they ate pot roast
so tender it fell apart at the touch of a fork and mashed
potatoes drowned in brown gravy.

And this time when Reece took her home, they stood

on her front porch, with a gentle rain hissing down around them, and he pulled her into his arms and melted her bones with a kiss. He pressed her up against the unlocked door, his big body hard and warm against hers, and she had a sudden image of him pushing the door open, taking her into the darkened house, into the softness of her bed. Her heart thudded with a mixture of fear and anticipation, but Reece was already easing back, his mouth softening on hers, his hands stroking gently up her arms until his palms cradled her face as he ended the kiss.

He stared down at her for a long moment, thumbs moving gently over her cheekbones. Shannon waited, hardly breathing. She wanted…she wasn't sure what she wanted. For him to kiss her again, for him to leave. She wanted to retreat into the safe little cocoon she'd spent the past three years building. She wanted to rip her way free of that cocoon and feel alive again. She was dizzy with the possibilities, scared and elated and terrified and eager.

Maybe Reece read something of that confusion in her eyes. Even in the dim glow from the porch light, she saw his expression change, soften. He lowered his mouth to hers, in a kiss as soft as a butterfly's wing, sweet as a baby's smile. And then he was stepping back, reaching past her to push the door open and nudging her gently inside, murmuring a good-night as he pulled the door shut behind her.

Shannon stood in the dark entryway, listening to the sound of his footsteps until they disappeared in the quiet hiss of the rain. Maybe, just maybe, she was in big trouble here.

The shrill ringing of the phone startled Reece out of a deep sleep. Heart pounding, he rolled out of bed, reaching automatically for the gun he no longer kept in the nightstand. By the second ring he was awake enough to realize he didn't need the gun, unless it was to shoot whoever was calling him at—he squinted at the clock—six o'clock in the damned morning.

Sitting on the side of the bed, feeling mildly light-headed from the adrenaline rush, he grabbed the receiver before the third ring. If this was some crazed telemarketer, he wasn't going to be responsible for his actions.

"Morgan," he snarled.

"Reece, it's Caroline."

The sound of his ex-wife's voice sent a fresh surge of adrenaline through him. *"Kyle."*

"He's fine," she said immediately. "Well, unless you count having no common sense and no consideration for anyone else as a *problem*," she added with bitter emphasis.

Recognizing the tone of voice, Reece scrubbed one hand over his face and tried to shake the remnants of sleep and adrenaline overload from his brain. One of Caroline's less endearing traits was a tendency to choose dramatic statements over clear communication, but if Kyle was hurt, she'd have said so.

"What did he do?" he asked. Since it was obvious that sleep was no longer an option, he stood up and reached for the jeans he'd worn the day before, tucking the phone against his shoulder as he pulled them up over his long legs. Offering up a fervent thanks to whoever had invented portable phones, he headed for the kitchen and the coffeemaker.

"What did he do?" she asked in a tone that suggested he should already know. "What do you think he did?"

"Shaved his head, got a nose ring, joined a rock band?" Reece reeled off possibilities as he groped for coffee in the semidark kitchen. He could have turned on a light, but that would have been an admission that he was really awake at this ungodly hour, awake and listening to his ex-wife's increasingly strident voice.

"Ha, ha. I suppose you think this is funny. You're the one who told him to do this. Don't think I don't know that you encouraged this whole thing."

"What whole thing?" He measured coffee into the filter.

"Don't play stupid with me, Reece Morgan," she snapped. "This is our son's future at stake here. Maybe you don't care what happens to him but I do and I'm not going to just sit here and let him throw his whole life away. I should have known better than to think you'd—"

He set the phone down and leaned against the counter as he filled the carafe with water. Picking the phone up again, he propped it on his shoulder while he poured water into the coffeemaker, listening with half an ear as Caroline expounded on his many faults, most of which seemed to circle back to an appalling lack of sensitivity. It was an old story, one he'd heard more times than he could count when they were married.

"—know my feelings don't matter but I'd think you'd give some thought to what's best for your son. He's—"

Squeezing his eyes shut, Reece reached for his patience, reminding himself that she wasn't really trying to drive him insane.

"—only nineteen and he's *ruining* his life, just ruining it and—"

"Caro, it's six o'clock in the morning on this side of the country," he said, cutting her off midrant. "Way too early to spend time going over a list of my faults, which I'm sure are epic. Just tell me what Kyle has or hasn't done."

There was a pause and he knew she was debating about hanging up on him. He didn't have to see her to know she was weighing the satisfaction of slamming the phone down against the likelihood that he wouldn't call back, which would mean she'd have to face the humiliation of calling him again if she wanted to continue haranguing him. There was a practical streak under the histrionics and he wasn't surprised when she chose explanations over a dramatic exit.

"He's quit school."

"He can't quit. He's already graduated."

"Not high school," she snapped. "College. He quit college. He came home for Thanksgiving break and said he wasn't going back."

Reece stared at the coffeemaker, willing it to drip faster. This conversation would be much easier to take with caffeine.

"Did he say why?"

"He said college wasn't what he wanted to do right now. Apparently, what he wants to do is become a Hell's Angel," she added with heavy sarcasm.

Reece had a dizzying flash of his son dressed in black leather, chains and tattoos and bit back a groan as he reached for the coffeepot. To hell with letting the cycle finish.

"What are you talking about?" He poured half a mug of fragrant liquid, ignoring the sizzle as the coffee continued to drip onto the warmer. Shoving the pot back into place he stuck the mug under the faucet and added a splash of cold water.

"I told you, Kyle's quit school and become a…a—" Three gulps of not-quite-scalding coffee and he could feel his brain coming online.

"Kyle bought a bike?" he guessed.

"Yes, and don't try to tell me that you didn't encourage him to do it. I know you told him about that motorcycle you used to have."

"Yes, but I didn't tell him to go out and buy one. What did he get?"

"What did he get?" Caroline's voice rose to a level that probably had every dog within a two-mile radius of her elegant home barking hysterically. "I tell you that he's gone off to kill himself on that…that *thing* and you want to know what it is?"

Reece leaned one hip against the counter and pinched the bridge of his nose. It was moments like this that reassured him of the wisdom of getting a divorce.

"Sorry," he muttered.

"You should be sorry you encouraged him to buy that thing in the first place."

"Caroline, could we just skip the blame game? Whatever it is, it's all my fault. I accept that. Now can we move on to what's going on with Kyle? Why did he quit school? What did he say? Why did he buy the bike and where the hell is he right now?"

In the silence that followed, he heard her breath hitch and felt his irritation fade. Caroline was always at her bitchiest when she was worried. The more worried she was, the nastier she got. Obviously, whatever Kyle was doing, he'd scared his mother to death. He sighed and reached for the coffeepot.

"Tell me what's going on, Caro," he said quietly.

It was pretty straightforward, really. He already knew that Kyle had only agreed to start college because it was what his mother wanted. Kyle had told him as much when Reece had taken him out to dinner a few days after he graduated from high school. Looking at his son had been like looking at himself at the same age. The restless need to be on the move, to be going and doing.

I've been in school since I was six years old, Kyle had said. *That's two-thirds of my life. Now, I'm supposed to sign up for another four or five years of classes and papers. When do I actually get to have a life?*

Reece understood what Kyle was feeling, but he also knew how his ex-wife felt about the importance of getting an education, and it wasn't as if he disagreed with her. So, he'd encouraged Kyle to give college a try.

You can always quit, he'd said. *It's not like you're sentenced to life with no hope of parole.*

Thinking of it now, he winced, wondering if maybe Caro was right, if maybe he *had* encouraged Kyle in making this decision.

Apparently, after two months of classes, Kyle had decided that making his mother happy wasn't reason enough to even finish out the semester. He'd quit school, bought a motorcycle—and Reece still wanted to know what kind but knew better than to ask—and said he was going to do some traveling, see the country a bit before deciding whether or not to go back to school. Caro had tried to talk him out of it. Had, from the sounds of it, talked nonstop since the day after

Thanksgiving, which was when Kyle had told her what he planned. But Kyle had stood firm and had left this morning.

"He's going to end up in a dead-end job working in a factory or parking cars at a restaurant somewhere." Caroline's voice was choked with tears. "And that's if he doesn't end up dead on the road somewhere."

Reece couldn't really see Kyle settling into life on an assembly line or parking cars, but he wasn't particularly crazy about the idea of his son being on the road alone.

"Kyle's sensible," he said, trying to reassure himself, as well as his ex. "He'll stick to decent roads, take precautions."

"What about at night? I keep thinking of him sleeping in some awful park or campground."

"Kyle?" Reece exaggerated his disbelief. "Are we talking about the same kid here? You remember the last time I tried to take him camping? He wanted me to lug a damned mattress to the lake so he wouldn't have to sleep on the ground. Trust me, Kyle's idea of camping out is doing without room service."

Caroline's chuckle was watery, but at least it wasn't more tears.

"It's not like he's broke. He'll be fine, Caro."

"Maybe." She sniffed. "You know, he's using the money you set aside for his education."

"I put the money in a trust for *Kyle. You're* the one who decided it was for his education, and you agreed with me when I suggested giving him control of it after he graduated."

"That was before I knew he was going to do something stupid with it."

"You mean before you knew he wasn't going to do

what you wanted him to?'' Reece asked dryly. He dumped the last couple of swallows of lukewarm coffee in the sink and poured a fresh cup.

''Education is important, Reece. What is he going to do with his life if he doesn't get an education?'' She didn't wait for an answer but continued, her voice edging perilously close to a whine. ''All his friends are going to college. I don't see why Kyle had to be different.''

''First of all, I never said education wasn't important. Or have you forgotten the years I spent going to school at night? Second, he's nineteen. Who says he has to decide what he wants to do with the rest of his life right now? Half the kids in college don't know what the hell they're doing there, anyway. They're just waiting to grow up. Maybe he wants to do his growing up somewhere else.''

Caroline started to interrupt but he talked over her. ''And thirdly, when has Kyle ever been anything *but* different? This is the kid who wanted to learn to tapdance when he was six and bloodied the nose of that obnoxious kid who lived next door for calling him a sissy.''

''Jimmy Karkowski,'' Caroline said immediately. ''He was a terrible bully and he was two years older than Kyle.'' Thirteen years after the incident, she still sounded indignant.

''And when Kyle was twelve and all his friends were riding skateboards or horses, he decided archery was the thing to do.''

''And you bought him that bow that was taller than he was,'' Caroline said reminiscently.

''He was sixteen when he decided not to play football and took up fencing instead and then added ballet

lessons because it improved his speed and control."
Reece paused to let the facts sink in. "Caro, the fact
that all his friends are going to college isn't going to
matter a whole hell of a lot to Kyle."

"No, I suppose not." Pride crept around the edges
of her lingering annoyance. "He gets that nonconform-
ist streak from you, you know."

"Yeah, right. I'm not the one who chained myself
to the gate of that ratty old house to keep the county
from tearing it down."

"That ratty old house was one of the few remaining
examples of Wilhelmina Matthewson's work. She just
happened to be one of the only nationally recognized
female architects at the turn of the century." She fired
up immediately, just as he'd known she would. "And
they were going to put up a concrete-block apartment
building."

Smiling into his coffee cup, Reece relaxed back
against the counter. Listening to her impassioned defense, he had a sudden image of her from the first year
of their marriage, curled up in a corner of the cheap
blue-and-gray-plaid sofa that had been one of their first
purchases as a couple, her light-brown hair caught up
in an untidy bun on top of her head, hands and mouth
moving a mile a minute as she explained how important her latest cause was and why he should take some
of his pathetically limited time away from work and
school to march in a picket line or put up posters or
attend a meeting in defense of whatever it was. He'd
viewed it as a challenge to see if he could distract her
from her current pet project, and he'd prided himself
on the fact that at least fifty percent of the time they'd
ended up in bed, which was the one place they'd been
completely compatible.

"You haven't heard a word I've said, have you?" The sharp question snapped him out of the past and into the present.

"Sure I have," he lied and grinned at the irritated little huff of breath that came over the line.

"I suppose you approve of Kyle throwing away his life like this." The words were sharp, but most of the edge was gone from her voice.

"Who says he's throwing away his life? Maybe he'll take a few months off, see the country a little and go back to school next fall."

"What if he doesn't?"

"Then that's his choice." He heard her draw a breath and continued before she could argue. "You raised him to make his own decisions, Caro. We agreed that that's what we wanted for him."

"But I didn't expect him to make a *stupid* decision like this," she complained, but the crisis was past. Nothing was going to make her approve of Kyle quitting school, but she was starting to become resigned to the reality of it.

"Stupid decisions are part of growing up. Kyle's a smart kid. He'll be okay." Privately he was wondering what kind of favors he could call in to have someone keep an eye out for the boy. Nineteen years old and hitting the road on a damned motorcycle. If he'd had Kyle in front of him, he'd be tempted to kick his butt up between his shoulder blades.

"He's just so young," Caroline sighed.

"Not that much younger than we were when we got married," he pointed out.

"And look how that turned out."

"I don't have any regrets. We had some good years and we ended up with Kyle."

"True." The silence that fell between them was easy, the kind that grew out of knowing each other for two decades, sharing a marriage, a child, going through a divorce and still managing to remember, most of the time, that they'd once loved each other.

"I suppose it's too late to ground him," Caroline said wistfully, and Reece laughed.

"You could give it a try."

"I'd have to track him down first." She sighed again. "I guess it's really early where you are, isn't it?" she said abruptly, as if it had just occurred to her.

That was so typically Caroline that Reece had to swallow a laugh. When she was focused on something, her concentration was so complete that everything else became background noise. He should count himself lucky that she hadn't called even earlier.

"Depends on what you consider early," he said amiably. "It's almost six-thirty. Some people might not consider that early at all."

"I guess I could have waited another hour or two to call," she said, sounding a little sheepish.

"That's okay. I had to wake up to answer the phone anyway."

She laughed and asked him how things were going with his grandfather's house, and he spent a few minutes filling her in on his cleanup efforts. Not that they'd been all that great, he admitted. He could have had the job done a couple of weeks ago if he'd put his mind to it.

"Are you thinking of staying there?" She sounded surprised. Not that he could blame her. His ex-wife knew how he felt about his grandfather. He'd lived in this town, in this house, longer than he'd lived anywhere else, but this had never been home. Coming back here had just been a stopover, a place to be while he decided what to do with the rest of his life. He certainly didn't want to stay here. Did he?

"I...don't know," he said at last. "Maybe."

He hadn't realized the idea was in the back of his mind until she mentioned it, but now that he thought about it, he realized that the idea held more appeal than he'd have believed possible a few weeks ago. He actually liked Serenity Falls, liked the combination of small-town nosiness and California indifference, the fake tile roofs and palm trees and architecturally barren strip malls cozying up with the occasional survivor from the Art Deco era. He liked picking up sushi, standing next to a farmer in dusty jeans and a gimme cap who was ordering California rolls and sashimi as comfortably as if it were burgers and fries. The mixture of down home and sophistication appealed to him.

And a certain long-legged redhead with pretty blue eyes appealed to him, too, he thought, letting his gaze slide out the kitchen window to the house next door. Shannon Devereux was high on Serenity Falls's list of positive attributes.

But that wasn't something he wanted to discuss with his ex-wife. He settled for telling her that the town wasn't the hellhole he'd remembered and admitting that the idea of settling down here had a certain appeal. When they hung up a few minutes later, they were back on comfortable terms with each other. He'd always thought it was ironic that it was only after the divorce that they'd learned to talk to each other. They were better friends now than they'd ever been when they were married.

He poured a fresh cup of coffee and contemplated Shannon's house. There was a light on in the kitchen.

He could see the golden glow through the curtains. She was probably making a pot of coffee, maybe popping a waffle in the toaster. The thought made him smile as he lifted his cup and took a slow sip.

They'd been dating for two weeks now, though he suspected Shannon would reject that description. But he didn't know what else you called it when a man and a woman saw each other every day, went out to lunch or dinner or sometimes both, went to the movies and generally spent most of their free time together. He wasn't sure where it was heading, but he knew where he wanted it to end up. He wanted it to end up with the two of them naked and horizontal on a nice soft surface. That would do for starters, but he was beginning to think that he wanted a lot more than just sex from his attractive neighbor.

"There's nothing wrong with having a relationship based on sex, as long as you both know that's what's going on." Kelly slid a stack of books into place and clipped a New sign to the rack in front of them. "There's no reason you can't have a blistering affair with Reece."

"Who said I wanted a blistering affair with him?" Shannon asked, trying—and failing—to concentrate on the invoices in front of her. Where were all the customers when you needed them?

"Oh, please," Kelly said, giving her a disgusted look. "What red-blooded woman between the ages of sixteen and ninety-six *wouldn't* want to have a blistering affair with that man? He's not only tall, dark and handsome, he's actually a nice guy. And I'd bet good money that he knows his way around a woman's body."

"Does Frank know you think things like this about other men?" Giving up on the invoices—she'd just have to hope her suppliers were both honest and accurate this week—Shannon lifted half a dozen bolts of fabric from the cutting table and carried them toward the back of the store.

"We have a don't-ask, don't-tell policy." Kelly picked up the remaining bolts and followed Shannon. "Look, you can tell me to mind my own business...."

"Mind your own business," Shannon said promptly.

"But the two of you practically sizzle when you're together." Kelly shoved a purple-and-green paisley onto the shelf. "You can't tell me you haven't given any thought to sleeping with the man."

"Thinking about it and doing it are two different things." Shannon found a spot for a sky-blue marble and slid it into place. She did think about it. She thought about it every time he kissed her at the end of one of their—they weren't *dates* exactly, though she knew it probably looked like that to other people. Whatever they were, they ended with a kiss. Or three. Long, slow kisses that left her heart pounding and her knees weak and then Reece would see her safely into her house and walk away. And she'd stand there, alone in the dimly lit entry and wonder what it would be like if he *didn't* walk away, if she invited him in for a nightcap. For a night of sizzling sex. "Reece is only here temporarily. He'll be leaving soon."

"So what?" The remaining bolts of fabric thudded onto one of the classroom tables. Kelly set her hands on her hips and fixed Shannon with a look of mixed affection and exasperation. "I'm not talking about a lifetime commitment here. So much the better if he's leaving. That will bring everything to a natural conclusion. No hurt feelings. No awkwardness.''

Shannon shoved the last three bolts onto the shelf at random. She felt pressured, not just by Kelly but by her own needs, desires.

"Why are you so determined to push me into bed with him?" she asked, exasperated.

"I'm not. I'm determined to push you out of that…that safety net of yours." Kelly lifted one small hand, cutting off Shannon's automatic protest. "Don't tell me you don't know what I'm talking about, Shannon Devereux. You haven't let yourself get really involved with anyone or anything except this shop, since Johnny died. I've introduced you to half a dozen perfectly nice men, and you haven't gone out on a single date with any of them. Now Reece Morgan comes along and the two of you are practically living in each other's pockets. He's gorgeous, he's nice, you enjoy his company and he'll be leaving, so you don't have to worry about anyone have expectations. Who better to have an affair with?"

The jangle of the bell over the front door saved Shannon from having to come up with a response. Ignoring her friend's irritated huff of breath at the interruption, she went to greet the elderly woman who'd entered. As she helped her pick out fabric to finish a quilt, she admitted to herself that Kelly's theory made a lot of sense. She had been wary of getting involved again, leery of where it might lead. But with Reece it wasn't going to lead anywhere, because he was only here for a short time. Maybe Kelly was right. Maybe a sizzling love affair would be a good thing.

Chapter 8

In typical southern California fashion, the weather had taken an abrupt turn from cool and damp to warm and dry. Reece's front door was open and Shannon heard the music coming through the screen door as she stepped onto the porch. The melody being picked out on the guitar was familiar but she couldn't quite place it. She cocked her head, listening, but the tune trailed off in a tangle of chords and a muttered curse and she realized it wasn't a CD she was hearing. Reece played guitar? The man was full of surprises.

She hovered on the edge of the porch, wondering if she should interrupt him and then wondered if she was hesitating out of consideration or out of cowardice. She'd never made plans to seduce someone before, and she was just a little nervous about the whole idea. But a plan was a plan and it had taken her a solid week to work herself up to this and she wasn't going to back out now. If her hand was not quite steady when she knocked on the door, no one else had to know.

She could see Reece through the screen. He was wearing a pair of jeans, old enough that the knees had faded to a soft, cloudy blue, and a gray sweatshirt with raveled cuffs. Sitting on the edge of the sofa, with the guitar resting on his knee and a lock of dark hair falling onto his forehead, he looked rumpled and sexy. And the way he smiled when he saw her... Shannon smiled helplessly in return.

"I didn't know you played guitar," she said as she pushed open the door.

"I haven't played in years. I gave my old guitar to my son five or six years ago when he wanted to learn to play. This was under my grandfather's bed. And as dead as these strings are, I'm not sure you can call what I'm doing playing." He plucked two strings. "They sound like old rubber bands."

"They sound okay to me." Shannon sat down on a worn leather hassock, elbows on her knees, hands clasped loosely together. "It's hard to picture your grandfather playing guitar," she said, thinking of the stern old man who'd offered her a brisk nod in greeting when their paths happened to cross and frowned disapprovingly at her haphazard landscaping efforts. "He wasn't exactly...folksy."

Reece grinned and shook his head. "Joe Morgan was about as unfolksy as it was possible to get. As far as he was concerned, 'The Star Spangled Banner' was the height of musical accomplishment. It was all downhill from there."

"Then, why the..." Shannon raised her eyebrows and nodded to the guitar.

"It was my dad's. His old Martin." He ran his fingers gently up and down the neck, his smile soft with affection. "This guitar has traveled more than most long-distance truckers. He lost it once in Buffalo, left it in some seedy little club and we didn't miss it until we were almost to Cleveland. He borrowed a guitar for that gig and then we drove all the way back to New York.

"I'm amazed the old man saved it, considering how he felt about Dad's music. I would have expected him to chop it up for kindling." Reece's hands cradled the guitar as if it were an infant. "The case was under his bed. Maybe he just forgot it was there."

"I take it your father was a musician?"

Reece looked suddenly self-conscious. "He and my mom cut some records in the sixties. Did pretty well with them. You might have heard their stuff on some of the oldies stations. Jonathan and Jennifer?"

"Your parents were Jonathan and Jennifer?" Shannon gaped at him in shock. "They were your parents? I love their stuff. I have their *Flowers in the Snow* album on CD."

"Do you?" Reece smiled, and picked out the first few chords of the title song. "Well, the little kid you hear singing very off-key at the end of 'All of You, All of Me' is yours truly."

"You're kidding."

"No. I was three years old. They had a baby-sitter all lined up, but she canceled at the last minute so they brought me into the studio while they were recording and told me I had to be very quiet. One of the engineers took a liking to me and gave me a mike to play with. I apparently sang along with Mom and Dad and he spliced it in on the end of the song." He saw her wide-eyed look and shrugged self-consciously. "Hey, it was the sixties. Peace and love and warmth and fuzziness breaking out all over.''

''So, you're practically a famous singer.''

''Yeah, well, my recording career pretty much began and ended with that ten-second bit.'' His fingers moved over the strings, drawing out a delicate melody.

Watching him, she tried to imagine him as a child, but she just couldn't transform six feet four inches of tall, dark and handsome into a chubby, dark-haired toddler.

''You were close to your parents?'' she asked, and then winced a little at the wistful sound of her own voice but Reece just nodded.

''Very close. We were on the road most of the time, playing clubs and festivals. We were never in one place very long so it was pretty much just the three of us.'' He picked out the opening to ''Scotch and Soda'' with absent-minded ease, the fingers of his left hand sliding up and down the neck of the guitar as he changed chords, while his right hand picked out the melody. ''We had a lot of friends on the road, though. I played cards with the Kingston Trio when we were all stuck in a snowstorm in Denver one time. Nick Reynolds was a demon at Old Maid. I sat in when my dad jammed with Pete Seeger and got to hear my mom sing harmony with Joan Baez.'' He looked up suddenly, his eyes bright in anticipation of her reaction. ''We went to Woodstock.''

Shannon's eyes widened. ''You're kidding. You were at Woodstock?''

''Me and half a million other people.'' His tone was dry, but his smile made it clear that he appreciated her reaction.

''Wow.'' Shannon drew her legs up under her, propping her chin on her knees as she watched him. "So, what was it really like? I mean, did you know it was a major cultural event?"

He shook his head, grinning. "Are you kidding? I was seven years old. I wouldn't have known a cultural event if it bit me on the nose."

"What do you remember about it?"

"Mud," he said promptly. "It rained, and there was mud everywhere. Way too many people and not enough bathrooms."

She shook her head, mouth pursed in disapproval. "Plebeian. You were witness to one of the great cultural events of the twentieth century and your only concern was whether or not there were enough bathrooms?"

Reece laughed and played a quick flourish of notes on the guitar. "By definition, all seven-year-old boys are plebeians. But, in my defense, no one who was there knew it was going to be a defining event for the Baby Boomer generation. It was just a concert, one that lasted for three days and had a lot of different artists. In the parlance of the time, it was a happening, man, but there was no way to know it was 'the' happening."

"I don't suppose you even remember any of the music," she said, looking disapproving.

"Not much," he admitted. "I remember Hendrix doing 'The Star Spangled Banner,' though. It was just about the last thing, and most of the crowd was gone by then." He plucked out a few chords, bending the strings a little to get a credible Hendrix-style whine.

"Was it amazing?"

"Well," he shrugged and looked self-conscious. "It was pretty noisy. Frankly, I thought something was wrong with the sound system."

Shannon flinched and moaned. "Oh, the waste, the waste. One of the great moments in American music and you thought it was a technical error."

"What can I say. I was a kid."

She laughed. It was easier to picture him as a tough seven-year-old, oblivious to the fact that history was being made all around him, than it had been to picture a sweet-faced toddler.

"It sounds like a fun way to grow up."

"It was." His smile took on a bittersweet edge and she knew he was thinking about his parents.

"How old were you when they died?" she asked softly.

"Ten." Reece didn't seem surprised that she'd followed his train of thought. "We were in Texas. They'd had a lot of rain. A *lot* of rain." His hands rested on the guitar but his eyes were distant, seeing thirty-year-old memories. "There was flooding, and some idiot had tried to cross a bridge that was closed. Moved the damned barriers out of the way and drove right out onto it. The car stalled halfway and the water was rising and, instead of getting out, trying to get back to shore, he kept trying to get the car started. Dad went out after him, slipped, lost his footing and went into the river. Mom went in after him. They pulled the bodies out a couple miles down river."

He ran his hand gently over the side of the guitar, rubbing it back and forth as if drawing warmth from the wood, his eyes on the idle movement.

Shannon let the silence stretch, not wanting to intrude on his memories, on his grief. She'd spent her childhood dreaming of having the kind of family he'd had. Now she had to wonder which was harder— dreaming and never having or having and then losing.

She thought of the Walkers, of their willingness to welcome her, to take her into their hearts, into their lives. What did it say about her that she could have everything she'd ever wanted, everything Reece had lost, and she was too scared to reach for it?

"What happened to the guy on the bridge?" she asked, seeking a distraction from her own thoughts.

Reece lifted his head and looked at her blankly, blinking like a man waking from a deep sleep. It seemed to take a moment for her question to sink in. "A cop got him out of the car. Turned out he was drunk and the bridge was the shortest route home. He couldn't figure out why anyone would have blocked it off." He stopped and shook his head, his mouth twisting with bitter humor. "He didn't even know Dad had tried to get to him, let alone that he'd been killed."

Shannon tried to think of something to say, some bit of wisdom, no matter how clichéd, to offer him but nothing came to mind.

"It must have been very hard on you, to go from living on the road like that, with your parents, to living here with your grandfather."

His sharp bark of laughter held little humor. "You could say that." He rested his forearm on top of the guitar, left hand wrapped around the neck. "My grandfather was career army. It was quite a jump from 'Give Peace a Chance' to calisthenics before breakfast."

"He did seem a little, ah, regimented," Shannon said, trying to think of something positive to say about the rigid, unfriendly old man she'd barely known.

"That's one way to put it," Reece said dryly. "He scheduled every minute of the day. Chores, homework, when I could see my friends, when I could watch television—educational programs only, of course."

"I gather you didn't get along."

"Not hardly." He shifted his grip on the guitar, fingers moving lightly over the strings, drawing out a bare whisper of sound. His eyes looked distant. "We fought like cats and dogs. I guess all that stuff about peace and love and living in harmony didn't sink in very deep with me," he said ruefully. "We butted heads over damned near everything. The older I got, the more he tried to control me and the harder I fought him. He wanted me to join the Boy Scouts and go to church. I wore my hair long, got my ear pierced and started smoking."

"You wore earrings?" she asked, laughing.

"Earring. Singular." Reece grinned self-consciously and reached up to tug his earlobe. "I was sixteen, and Rick McKinnon's girlfriend did it for me. Most of the time I wore a silver skull with red eyes but I had a gold hoop, too."

"I bet your grandfather loved that,' Shannon said, trying to picture him as a sixteen-year-old rebel with long hair and an earring.

"Oh, yeah." He laughed and shook his head. "He had a fit about the earrings, threw out some pretty ugly comments about men who wore earrings and cast serious aspersions on my masculinity. Said that between the long hair and the earrings, people were likely to mistake me for a girl."

Shannon stopped trying to tell herself that his grandfather had probably done the best he could. If the old man had been alive and standing in front of her, she wasn't sure she'd have been able to resist the urge to smack him. Hard.

"What did you do?"

"I bleached my hair blond and cut it short and spiky

so no one could miss the earring, and I started wearing eyeliner.''

''Eyeliner?'' Shannon gaped at him for a moment and then started to laugh. ''That must have really made his day.''

''Not so's you'd notice.'' Reece smiled but there was something dark in his eyes, an old and bitter anger. ''By that time I doubt if there was anything I could have done that would have pleased him. Not that I was trying. I was just marking time until I could get out.''

''It's hard, being on your own at that age,'' Shannon murmured, remembering how lost she'd felt after her father died. They hadn't been close, but he was all she'd had.

''It was easier than living with him. I had quite a bit of money from my parents. Apparently, there was a practical streak under the flowers and peace symbols. I got control of the money they left when I turned eighteen, a couple months before graduation. I only stayed until graduation because I knew he didn't expect me to stick it out, and I was damned if I'd give him the satisfaction of quitting. I already had my stuff in the car when I went to get my diploma, and I walked out of the auditorium, got in the car and left. I never talked to the old man again.'' He stroked his fingers across the strings, a discordant jangle of notes that made her flinch.

''But he left everything to you,'' she said, gesturing with one hand to indicate the house. ''He must have felt *something* or he would have left it to someone else or to a charity or something.''

''Yeah, go figure. Maybe he got sentimental in his old age.'' He lifted the guitar, turning it faceup and studying it for a moment before leaning over to set it in its case. He snapped the latches closed and set the case up against the wall next to the sofa. "Maybe he just forgot to change his will. Who knows?"

Shannon thought about that. She couldn't claim to have known Joe Morgan. A few nods and an occasional "nice weather today" didn't even really qualify as even an acquaintanceship, but she'd seen enough to know that he managed his life with military precision, a place for everything and everything in its place, everything done to a schedule. He didn't strike her as someone who would have forgotten to change his will. If he'd left all his worldly possessions to his grandson, it was because that was exactly what he'd meant to do. It seemed sad to think that Reece would never know why.

"The new Costner film is playing at the Rialto," he said, changing the subject. "I was going to give you a call and see if you wanted to go tonight."

Distracted by the unexpected look into his past, Shannon had temporarily forgotten her reason for coming over, but now it rushed back to her and she felt the color come up in her face. She rose, sliding her hands in the pockets of her loose khaki slacks.

"Actually, I came over to invite you over for dinner. At my house."

"Dinner?" Reece's brows rose in surprise.

"Yes. I, ah, thought it would be nice to eat at home. More or less. For a change."

"I thought you didn't cook."

"I don't, but I've got this recipe for stuffed flank steak that's pretty well foolproof."

"Dinner at your house, huh?" His tone was...odd, and Shannon reluctantly lifted her eyes to his face.

He knew.

Her breath caught in her throat. He knew exactly what the invitation meant, knew where she hoped the evening would end, and the hunger in his eyes had nothing to do with flank steak. No one had ever looked at her like that before, like they were starving and she was a banquet. It was exciting and a little terrifying.

''Dinner,'' he said, smiling slowly. ''Sounds good. What time?''

''Time?''

''What time is dinner?''

She flushed and dragged her eyes away from his. ''Seven,'' she said. ''Seven o'clock would be good.''

That gave her three hours to either prepare for a seduction or run like hell.

By the time Reece knocked on the door, Shannon had changed her clothes five times and put her hair up and taken it down—twice. She'd bobbled the mascara wand, giving herself a new and highly improbable third eyebrow. Pantyhose had been donned and then discarded when it occurred to her that the only thing more awkward than trying to put a pair of pantyhose on was trying to get them off with any sort of grace.

The realization that she was getting dressed with an eye to getting *un*dressed in front of Reece momentarily paralyzed her, and she sank down on the side of the bed, staring at the wreckage of her bedroom, and wondered if it was too late to run. At an average speed of sixty miles an hour, she could be at least forty miles away before Reece got here.

The fact that she was actually considering running away from her own home was absurd enough to restore her sanity. Just because she'd planned to sleep with Reece tonight, that didn't mean she *had* to. He wasn't going to push her into something she didn't want. The problem was, she was pretty sure that what scared her most was that she *did* want it. Wanted him.

By the time the doorbell rang, she'd settled on a silver-gray skirt that swirled softly around midcalf and a coral-colored blouse that managed to do nice things for her skin without clashing with her hair. She left her hair down, letting it tumble in soft waves down her back. One last look in the mirror, a deep breath for calm—or maybe for courage—and she went to answer the door.

Shannon had expected dinner to be awkward, conversation weighed down by awareness of where the evening was heading, but that wasn't the case. She'd set the table in the small, seldom-used dining room, using the pretty floral china that had belonged to the mother-in-law she'd never known and had turned the lights low. The meal turned out well and she offered up silent thank-yous to the patron saint of bad cooks and the inventor of the crockpot.

The conversation flowed easily, just as it always did between them. Reece told her he'd received a phone call from his son. She already knew about Kyle's cross-country trek and, though Reece hadn't said as much, she knew he worried about the boy, even as he admired his independence. Kyle was on his way to Albuquerque to visit his mother's sister and showed no signs of regretting his decision to try life on the open road. Shannon told him about her plans for the inventory-reduction sale after the first of the year, making him laugh with descriptions of quilters in a buying frenzy.

After dinner she made a fresh pot of coffee while Reece built a fire in the fireplace. The day had been warm but the temperature had dropped enough to make the added warmth of a fire pleasant. Not to mention how it added to the atmosphere, she thought, as she carried the tray into the living room. The fire had caught and flames were crackling through the smaller kindling, licking hungrily at the larger pieces of wood on top.

"Is there some sort of secret society that teaches men how to build fires?" She set the tray down on the coffee table and gave the fire a disgruntled look.

"It's part of our genetic code," he said solemnly. "Hardwired in right next to our inability to ask directions and refill ice cube trays."

"I thought that was just being pigheaded and lazy," Shannon said, handing him his coffee.

"A common misconception. Really, we're just victims of genetic programming."

"Aren't we all," she said dryly.

Reece had settled on the rug in front of the fireplace, and she joined him there, leaning back against the sofa, legs curled beneath her. For a little while, the only sound was the soft pop and hiss of the fire.

When his hand settled on her ankle, sliding beneath the soft fabric of her skirt to rest on her bare leg, Shannon released her breath in a soft little sigh and tilted her face up to his. *Yes.* She wasn't sure if she said it out loud or only thought it. This was what they'd been building up to over the past couple of weeks, maybe since that first moment when he'd opened the door, shirtless and barefoot and she'd felt her stomach clench with an instant of pure lust.

Yes.

Maybe she did say it out loud, because she could taste Reece's smile when he kissed her, taste his hunger in the heat of his mouth, in the wet warmth of his tongue as it slicked over hers. As they kissed, she felt the last traces of nervous tension fading away and a new feeling taking its place, something soft and languid and hungry, so hungry.

Long, slow, wet kisses, his hands warm and hard against her skin, his mouth tasting the pulse that beat frantically at the base of her throat. Shannon let her head drop back into the cradle of his palm. His other hand slid around her waist, faint roughness of calluses against her skin, and she realized that he'd pulled her blouse out of her skirt so his fingers were splayed against her lower back. She could feel the imprint of each finger separately, as if he were branding her with his touch. Her own fingers were curled around his upper arms, feeling the solid strength of muscles through the fabric of his shirt.

She whimpered a protest when he lifted his head. No, no, no. She didn't want him to stop, didn't ever want him to stop. Her eyelids felt weighted down, too heavy to lift. It took a conscious effort to open her eyes and look at him. His hair was rumpled into heavy waves, and she had a sudden tactile memory of running her fingers through it, feeling it curl like warm silk against her skin. And his eyes... Oh, God, his eyes. The heat in them warmed a still, cold place inside her she hadn't even known was there.

"I know making love in front of a fire is supposed to be romantic," Reece said, his voice low and raspy. "But I've got two words for you. Rug. Burn."

It took her lust-addled brain a moment to process that and then she startled herself by giggling. His quick grin did nothing to cool the heat in his eyes. He rose to his feet, pulling her with him, wrapping his hand in her hair and tilting her head back, his mouth coming down on hers in a long, drugging kiss that left her weak and clinging to him.

"Bedroom," he muttered against her mouth.

"Bedroom," she agreed.

The trip took a lot longer than it usually did. He wrapped his arms around her and kissed her in the living-room doorway, pressed her against the wall in the hallway—twice—held her against the doorjamb in the bedroom and tasted the taut line of her throat. And then they were finally in her bedroom, the door shut behind them, the soft golden glow of the bedside lamp painting shadowy patterns on the double-wedding-ring quilt that covered the bed.

Reece drew back, his eyes holding hers as his fingers reached for the buttons on her blouse, and Shannon thought again, *Yes.* This was what she'd been waiting for, what she'd wanted. It felt like forever since she'd let someone touch her, hold her. Her gaze steady on his, she brought her hands up to his chest, fingers not quite steady as she began to unbutton his shirt.

When she'd thought about this—and she could admit now that she'd thought about little else for the last couple of weeks—she'd pictured it one of two ways. Either every move had been as graceful as if choreographed, the whole scene washed in a romantic golden glow, or there'd been urgency and hunger and clothes pushed aside, the two of them almost struggling with each other.

Reality fell somewhere between the two. The hunger was there, but the urgency was banked, leaving time for touching and holding and learning the planes and angles of each other's bodies. There was a certain grace in the slow dance toward the bed, the soundless drift of clothes slipping to the floor, pauses for long, hungry kisses, the heated slide of hands against skin.

What she hadn't imagined was how right it would feel. Now that the moment had arrived, there was no hesitation, no last minute doubts.

Reece's palms cupped her breasts as if made to hold her, and Shannon let her head drop back, shuddering with the intensity of the sensation as his thumbs dragged across her nipples, teasing them into hard peaks. He bent over her, and she gasped at the feel of his lips on her, tongue laving her gently, then the sweet, drawing pleasure as his mouth closed over her. By the time he moved his attention to the other breast, her knees were barely keeping her upright and her breath was coming in shallow little pants.

"Please," she whispered, not at all sure what she was asking for. Reece lifted his head, and she caught just a glimpse of the blazing heat in his eyes before his mouth came down on hers, hard and demanding. His palm flattened against the small of her back, pressing her close, his mouth devouring hers. And suddenly they were out of time. The almost languid progression toward the bed was at an end and need was thrumming in the pit of her stomach.

She wasn't aware of moving until she felt the bed against the back of her legs. His mouth still on hers, Reece reached past her, throwing back the quilt and blanket and then he was pressing her down against the cool linens, his big body following her down, covering her. He was so much bigger than she was and, for just an instant, she felt overwhelmed by the sheer size of him, but the little flutter of feminine panic burned away in the sheer heat of their connection.

Contrast. It was all contrast. The flat, hard planes of

his chest and stomach pressed against the softer curves of her breast and belly. The fever-hot thickness of his erection pressed against her, lean hips settling into the soft, damp cradle of her thighs. *So close,* she thought. *So close.* Fingers digging into the heavy muscles of shoulders, she arched, wanting him closer, needing…something. Everything. She arched again, knees sliding up along the outside of his hips, and felt the blunt press of his arousal against her. He groaned, hips jerking in involuntary response. *Almost. Almost.* And then she felt him tense and he was pulling away.

"Damn," Reece muttered against her ear. "Wait. I've got to get…" He shifted toward the side of the bed.

"It's okay. I've got… I, ah…" Words failed her and she settled for pulling open the nightstand drawer. "In there."

Reece's brows climbed, and his grin took on a wicked edge as he pulled out a condom packet. "I like a woman who's prepared."

She wondered if she should confess that she'd driven thirty miles to the next town to buy the box of condoms, rather than risk having someone she knew see her make such an intimate purchase, and then decided that didn't exactly fit with the image of a grown woman making a mature decision to embark on an affair. Of course, neither did the fact that she blushed as she watched him tear open the packet and roll the condom on.

But then he was back against her, fingers slipping through her hair to cradle her head, his mouth coming down on hers as his hips eased forward, finding, entering that first tiny bit and then pausing until she whimpered, arching toward him. As if that were the permission he'd been seeking, Reece sheathed himself in her welcoming heat. Shannon cried out with shocked pleasure, the sound muffled against his mouth.

It was all heat and movement and tension that kept building inside, pulling her deeper and deeper until she was drowning in sensation and the only reality was the man above her, within her. The solid weight of his body, the rough hunger of his mouth, the rasp of his breathing, the slide of his hands over her skin. It was almost too much, pleasure so acute that it rode the knife edge of pain. Shannon's breath left her in sobbing gasps as she struggled to contain it, and then Reece shifted, one hand cupping her bottom, tilting her up to meet his thrusts. The pleasure peaked, driving the breath from her lungs on a thin cry.

"I've got you," he whispered roughly. "Let go. I've got you."

Trusting him to keep her safe, she did. She let the sensation take her, let it spin through her in thick waves until her entire body burned with the heat of it and a red haze blurred her vision. Dimly, through the pounding in her ears, she heard his guttural groan, felt the hot pulse of his release, his big body shuddering with the force of it.

She had no idea how much time passed before the world started to creep back around the edges of her consciousness. For long, endless moments, it was all she could do to remember to breathe. Slowly awareness filtered back. Reece was still over her, within her, though he'd shifted his weight to the side to avoid crushing her. There was a distant satisfaction in the knowledge that his breathing was as ragged as hers. She felt as if she'd just tumbled through the eye of a hurricane, but she hadn't taken the trip alone.

It took a major effort to lift her hand and rest it on

his damp shoulder. It was nearly as difficult to turn her face into the hollow of his throat. He smelled of sweat and sex. She'd never realized what a heady combination that was. Without thinking, her tongue came out to taste his skin. He shuddered, and his hands tightened almost painfully on her for an instant. His head came up slowly.

"Are you trying to kill me?" he asked.

"No. Just...tasting." She let her hands slide up his back, liking the feel of sweat damp muscles under her fingers.

"You know, I've read warnings about girls like you."

"Have you?" She shifted her hips slightly, smiling a little when she heard him groan. "What did they suggest?"

"Give them anything they want," he whispered against her mouth.

Chapter 9

If she'd thought about it, Shannon would have said that it was poor planning to start an affair on a worknight. No time for wallowing in the morning, no time to sit and ponder the night just past and either bask in the glow or worry that you'd made a terrible mistake. Definitely, starting an affair should be left for Saturday night or, in her case, Sunday night since the shop was closed on Monday. But she hadn't thought of that ahead of time and, as it turned out, seduction on a Friday night worked out just fine.

She woke alone to the smell of freshly brewed coffee. There was a half-opened rose on the pillow next to hers, and she smiled as she brought it to her nose and inhaled the light sweet scent. She knew for a fact that the slightly tattered blossom had come from the overgrown rosebush that sat at one corner of her front porch but the gesture was what counted, especially when she saw that he'd taken time to carefully trim the thorns away. The image of Reece robbing her rosebush in the early-morning hours made her smile widen.

There was a note by the coffeepot. If he'd stayed, he'd have made her very—underlined twice—late for work. He hoped she didn't mind that he'd made himself at home in her kitchen. He'd see her tonight. Dinner?

Not exactly a love note, but Shannon folded it and tucked it in the pocket of her robe, anyway. She wasn't looking for love notes, she reminded herself as she poured a cup of coffee. This was an affair between two consenting adults, not the romance of the century. Still, it had been sweet of him to make coffee. She brushed the rose against her cheek and allowed herself a dreamy smile.

She went through the routine of getting dressed, driving to work and opening up the shop on autopilot. As she stocked the cash register and sorted through the stack of messages Kelly had left for her the day before, she spared a moment's gratitude for the fact that the other woman wouldn't be coming in until tomorrow. Hopefully, by then she'd be able to get this dopey smile off her face. Otherwise, Kelly was going to take one look at her and know exactly how she'd spent the night, probably down to the number of times they'd made love.

There was a woman out front, clutching a quilt and looking hopeful. Shannon glanced at the clock and decided that opening ten minutes early wouldn't set a dangerous precedent. The look of gratitude on the woman's face as she unlocked the door made up for the fact that she then pulled out twenty bolts of fabric, looking for just the right binding. Or maybe a night of wild sex just put her in a particularly mellow frame of mind, Shannon thought as she reshelved the rejected prints.

Saturdays were usually busy but, unlike most retailers, December was generally a slow month for quilt shops. Most people were too busy to start new projects at this time of year and what time they had for quilting tended to go into finishing gift projects they'd already begun. Customers trickled in throughout the day, but they were mostly dazed refugees from the rigors of holiday shopping, looking to spend a few quiet moments petting fabric and looking through patterns. She chatted with the people who wanted to chat and left the others alone to recover their shattered nerves in peace.

It was one of those days where everything went right except the things that didn't go right and Shannon found she really didn't care about those. She beamed at cranky children, smiled when a customer knocked over a display of patterns, soothed a tearful new quilter who'd managed to sew several pieces together both upside down and backward.

Not even Edith Hacklemeyer's pinched expression could impinge on her good mood. She agreed with Edith that the holiday season got more commercial every year, nodded through her complaints about the excess of lights on a house down the block from the two of them and complimented her on the latest totally boring, utterly unoriginal log cabin quilt she'd made. By the time the older woman left, she was so disarmed by Shannon's amiable mood that she almost smiled. She caught herself in time, though, remembering that she really didn't approve of Shannon for several reasons, not least of which was her friendliness with that Morgan boy. A muttered warning about him was greeted with a smile so dazzling that Edith pocketed her change and left the store without saying another world.

Humming under her breath, Shannon waved through the door before flipping over the Closed sign. Tomorrow was Sunday, and the shop didn't open until noon, which meant that she could sleep in if she wanted. If she had a reason to sleep in.

And maybe someone to sleep in with.

Reece's truck was not in the driveway, and his house was dark. Shannon was surprised at how disappointed she was. It wasn't like she'd planned to run next door immediately. Had she? She felt a niggling little twinge of uneasiness as she pulled into her own driveway and slid out of the car. She didn't want to lose sight of what this was. Reece would be leaving soon. Just because he hadn't mentioned it, that didn't mean his plans had changed. He'd come to clean out his grandfather's house and to take stock of his own life. Sooner or later he'd be moving on. And that was a good thing, right? That was one of the reasons she'd decided to take this step, because an affair with him came with a built-in ending. No expectations, no hurt feelings.

Just the way she wanted it, she told herself as she unlocked her front door, and if the thought sounded a little hollow, it was just because she was still caught up in that whole middle-class myth that love and sex went hand in hand, at least for a woman. But there was nothing wrong with sex going hand in hand with more sex, especially when it was really amazing sex. The kind of sex that made her tingle all over just to remember it. The kind of sex she sincerely hoped was going to be repeated as often as possible between now and whenever Reece left.

Shannon changed into a pair of softly faded jeans and a soft gray sweater that clung in all the right places. If Reece had dinner plans that involved anything more elegant than a coffee shop, she could always change, she thought as she pulled on warm socks.

A peek out the kitchen window showed the house next door was still dark. Not that she was waiting for him, exactly. It was just that she wasn't sure what to do about dinner. Right. That was it. Shannon grimaced as she ran water into the teakettle and put it on the stove. Really, it would be nice if she could lie to herself at least occasionally.

She'd just poured water over a teabag when the phone rang. This time of night, it was likely to be a telemarketer trying to sell her the vacation package of a lifetime or offering her a chance to buy a condo she didn't want or magazines she wouldn't read. She thought about letting the answering machine get it, but there was something compelling about a ringing phone.

"Hello?"

"Shannon?" It was a woman's voice, pleasant but unfamiliar.

"Yes."

"This is your, ah… This is Rachel. Rachel Walker."

Shannon's stomach knotted instantly. She knew what the other woman had stumbled over. *This is your mother.* Which of course she was. Why couldn't it have been a telemarketer? At least she'd know what to say to someone who was trying to sell her something.

"How are you?" When all else failed, fall back on the basics.

"I'm fine. And you?" Shannon could hear the strain

in the other woman's voice. She felt guilty for putting it there, guilty that she couldn't open her heart to her newly discovered family as easily as they'd opened theirs to her.

Thank God for social niceties, she thought as they limped through the polite inquiries. Shannon asked about Rachel's family—*her* family. Rachel asked how the shop was doing. Had the rain caused any problems? The weather was good for another minute or two, speculation about whether or not this was likely to be a wet winter, agreement that it would be nice to get enough water to avoid drought conditions next summer but not enough to cause mud slides. Rachel was telling her that Gage had been injured in a mud slide in South America a couple of years back, when Shannon saw lights flash across the ceiling. Her heart gave a little thud.

Reece was home.

It took a conscious effort to keep her focus on the conversation.

"Everything worked out all right, thank heavens," Rachel was saying. "And he doesn't spend nearly as much time out of the country since he and Kelsey got married and had Lily."

"It must have been difficult for you, having him gone so much," Shannon said, her ears tuned for the sound of Reece's truck door slamming. Would he call or would he just come over?

"Yes, it was," Rachel said, and something in her tone made Shannon wonder if the other woman was thinking of all the years she'd waited and worried about another child, one who couldn't even have the decency to focus on their conversation right now.

A newly familiar guilt twisted in her stomach. What was wrong with her? Keefe was right. She was the one who'd gone looking for them. What had she thought was going to happen? A quick handshake and a nice-to-meet-you and that was the end of it?

"Actually, I had a reason for calling," Rachel said, breaking the awkward little pause before it stretched too far. "I was hoping you'd be able to spend Christmas with us. Of course, I understand if you have other plans," she added quickly. "I don't want you to feel pressured or obligated at all. It's just that…well, it's been a long time since we had all the family together for the holiday."

More than twenty years, Shannon thought. She leaned her forehead against the wall and closed her eyes. For the last two decades, she'd been a part of a family she hadn't even known existed. They'd kept her in their hearts, held her memory close. Not even her fantasies had come close to the reality of what they wanted to give her. Why was it so damned hard to accept?

"I'd like that," she said, trying to put real warmth in her acceptance.

"You'll come?" The open delight in Rachel's voice made her flinch. She wanted to feel a connection to this woman. Shouldn't there be some sort of instinctive recognition of the bond between them? "That's wonderful. Everyone will be so pleased."

Everyone. As in four brothers and their wives and children. Shannon suppressed a shudder of dread at the thought of finding herself alone in the midst of a Walker family gathering. Except maybe…

"Would it be all right if I brought someone?" she asked impulsively. Reece might have other plans, but if he didn't, maybe he wouldn't mind spending the holiday acting as a sort of shield between her and her family. "It's a friend of mine. My next-door neighbor, actually."

"The tall, dark and studly one?" Rachel asked, and Shannon's eyes popped open as her jaw dropped.

"What?" she wheezed.

Rachel laughed, a warm, inviting sound that made Shannon smile despite her shock. "Keefe said he'd stopped by to see you on Thanksgiving and he mentioned that your neighbor was there."

"*Keefe* said Reece was tall, dark and, uh…"

"Studly," Rachel said, when she had trouble finishing the description. "Actually, I think that was Tessa's contribution. Keefe didn't really offer much by way of description, though he did say that David liked your Reece and since Keefe thinks the sun rises and sets in that baby, I think that went a long way toward making up for the fact that Reece had some claim on his little sister."

There were so many things to protest about this speech that Shannon didn't know where to start. Did she protest that he wasn't "her" Reece, deny that he had any claim on her, or object to the idea that Keefe had any right to an opinion about it if he did? Before she could decide what, if anything, to say, Rachel was continuing.

"I was surprised when Keefe said he'd dropped by, actually. Serenity Falls isn't exactly on the way to the ranch," she said, confirming what Shannon had already suspected. "I hope he didn't put any pressure on you."

"Pressure?" Shannon said, stalling for time.

"I know Keefe can be rather ferocious when it comes to family. All the boys are like that. I hope he didn't suggest that you were *obligated* in any way. I mean, to spend time with us. We very much want a chance to get to know you, but family shouldn't be about obligation.''

No, it shouldn't, Shannon thought, closing her eyes against the sharp sting of tears. That was what she'd been to her father—an obligation. To his credit, he'd never shirked that obligation. No matter how much he'd regretted taking her away from her mother, he hadn't taken the easy way out and dumped her on Social Services in one of the many cities they'd lived in. She chose to take that as a sign that he'd loved her, even if he hadn't been able to show it, but all her growing-up years had been colored by the feeling that she was a duty to him.

''So, if Keefe said anything to you,'' Rachel was continuing hesitantly, ''about Christmas or anything else, I don't want you to feel like you have to spend the holidays with us.''

''He didn't say a word about Christmas,'' Shannon lied. ''He and Tessa just stopped by to say hello.''

''Good.'' There was no mistaking the relief in Rachel's voice. ''Wonderful as it is to have you back in our lives, I know it's not as…easy for you as it is for us. I mean, we always knew you were out there, somewhere, but we came as a bit of a shock to you. I don't want you to feel pressured.''

''No pressure,'' Shannon said, swallowing the lump in her throat. Why was it so hard to accept what the other woman was offering?

She was no closer to an answer when she hung up the phone a few minutes later. She'd spent her whole life wanting a family, and now she had one, a family so full of warmth and welcome that they made The Brady Bunch look like the Manson family and now all she wanted was... Well, she didn't know what she wanted. That was part of the problem.

When the phone rang again, she eyed it warily for a moment before picking it up. Her hello was more cautious than welcoming.

"Hey."

Just that one word, but she felt her knees weaken and her mouth curve in the goofy smile that had been sneaking up on her all day.

"Hey, yourself." She leaned back against the wall next to the phone and smiled at the refrigerator on the opposite wall.

"You have plans for dinner?" Reece asked.

"Well, someone had left me a note suggesting dinner, but they haven't followed up on it yet."

"I am now." His tone made the words seem intimate, and Shannon felt her skin heating.

"What did you have in mind?" Lord, was that her voice? She sounded like the bottom of a whiskey bottle, all husky and smooth.

"Nothing fancy. You. Me. Food." Reece's voice dropped dramatically on the last word, and Shannon grinned even as she felt a shiver run down her spine.

"Sounds...interesting. Did you have a particular time in mind?"

"How about right now?" The doorbell provided punctuation to the sentence, and Shannon's heart was suddenly beating much too fast.

"I don't know," she said, hearing the breathless tone of her own voice. "Someone's at the door. Maybe they'll have a better offer."

"I doubt it," he said in a voice that practically breathed sex. "Open the door, Shannon."

Heart thumping against her breastbone, she pulled

open the door. He was standing on the porch and his smile...his smile finished the melting job his voice had begun. Shannon wrapped her fingers around the edge of the door and held on, trying to will some stiffness back into her knees.

"Hey."

"Hey," she managed, wondering if it would be bad day-after protocol to jump on him and drag him into the house.

"The wonders of technology," he said, snapping the cell phone shut and dropping it in his shirt pocket. Shannon realized that she was still holding the phone to her ear. She shut it off and let her hand fall to her side.

Reece stepped inside, sliding one arm around her waist and nudging her back from the door so he could shut it. "You hungry?"

She shook her head, her mouth too dry to speak. Reece's smile took on a feral edge that made her pulse jump. Her hands came up to cling to his shoulders, and she realized she was still clutching the phone when it smacked against him. Reece reached up to take it from her, setting it on the little half-round table that sat against the wall at the same time he lowered his head to let his mouth take hers. You had to love a guy who could multitask.

It was the last coherent thought she had for several minutes. Reece didn't lift his head until he'd managed to melt every bone in her body and she was clinging to him like a shipwreck passenger holding onto a floating plank.

"I was going to take you out to dinner," he said, feathering soft kisses across her eyebrows, which she instantly decided were an erogenous zone.

''I've got frozen dinners in the freezer.'' She threaded her fingers through the dark-brown silk of his hair.

''No toaster waffles?'' He'd worked his way down to her ear, catching the lobe between his teeth and worrying it gently.

''Breakfast,'' she gasped, arching into his hold. ''We can have those for breakfast.''

''Sounds like a plan to me,'' he murmured against her mouth.

And that was the last thought either of them gave to food for quite some time.

If she'd known that having an affair would be this much fun, maybe she'd have embarked on one sooner, Shannon thought, watching Reece and Frank out on the patio. It was fifty degrees out and the sky was overcast, the air already smelling of rain, but Frank's Christmas present from his parents, an assortment of aged beef, had arrived the day before, and he was determined that the steaks had to be grilled over a mesquite fire, which was why he and Reece were huddled over the built-in barbecue, watching the steaks cook and slowly turning blue.

''Just like watching primitive man broil up a haunch of mastodon,'' Kelly said, pulling out the chair next to Shannon's at the kitchen table and sitting down.

''If primitive man had a gas barbecue and Gortex jackets.'' Shannon said dryly.

''Yeah, that does sort of take the man-against-nature element out of it, doesn't it?'' Kelly spooned sugar into the cup of tea she'd just made.

The kitchen smelled of the roasted garlic that had gone into the mashed potatoes and the earthy scent of steamed broccoli. Two of the cats were curled up on the cushioned window seat, and Mortimer slept in the corner, feet twitching as he dreamed of chasing rabbits.

"So, Reece is going to spend Christmas with your family." Kelly's tone was elaborately casual, and Shannon resisted the urge to sigh. It had been foolish to think that Kelly would be able to resist the urge to comment.

"That's the plan." She glanced out at the patio and saw that the first scattered drops of rain had begun to fall, grinned at the sight of Reece holding a red-and-black-plaid umbrella over the barbecue while Frank tended the steaks. "His son is spending the holiday in Albuquerque with his aunt, so Reece didn't have anything planned."

She thought she'd hit just the right casual note but she didn't really expect Kelly to let it go at that. For all her delicate appearance, she had the tenacity of a pit bull.

"I know I suggested that you have a wild affair with the man—and I haven't said a single word about the fact that you've obviously taken my advice," she added with a look of angelic pride that made Shannon snort and roll her eyes. "But don't you think that taking him home to meet the family is a little...I don't know. Commitment-y?"

"It's not a big deal." Shannon shrugged. "I'm not really taking him home to meet my family. I mean, they're my family but they're not..." She frowned and decided that trying to define what the Walkers were or weren't was just too confusing. "He didn't have any plans and I just thought spending the holiday at...well, with the Walkers would be better than spending it alone. No big deal."

Kelly look doubtful. ''I just don't want to see you get hurt.''

''That makes two of us,'' Shannon said lightly and tried not to look too desperately grateful when the door opened and Frank rushed in, cradling a platter of sizzling steaks as if it was a pot of gold dust.

She looked past him at Reece, who was shaking the rain off the umbrella before setting it outside the door. Kelly didn't need to worry about her. She wasn't going to get hurt. She knew exactly what she was doing. Didn't she?

Chapter 10

When Reece married Carolyn, he'd discovered he was also, to some degree, marrying her family, which consisted of two sisters and a mother. Caro's mother had thought her daughter was too young to get married—in retrospect, she'd had a point—and her sisters, both older than Caro, agreed. So, he was no stranger to suspicious, even downright hostile family gatherings. But three women with a niggling romantic streak didn't hold a candle to four large, protective older brothers.

Whatever hesitation Shannon might have about being part of the Walker family, it was obvious to Reece that they didn't share her doubts. She might have been taken from them and missing from their lives for twenty years but, in their minds, she'd remained a part of their family circle, and they were as protective of her as if they'd watched her grow up. The last time he'd been looked at so suspiciously had been by a band of terrorists, and he'd been trying to convince them that he really was a harmless American tourist. Well, at least he didn't have to worry about Shannon's brothers shooting him. Probably.

The other thing about the Walkers was that there were so *many* of them. When he and Shannon first arrived at her mother's house in Los Olivos, the phrase that came to mind was "a cast of thousands," but after introductions and a cold beer, he was able to sort it out to a little over a dozen people. Four brothers and their wives, three children, an infant, at least two cats and a dog the size of a Shetland pony, Rachel Walker, who was, he supposed, the matriarch but was too small and pretty for the word to fit, and a tall, older gentleman named Jason whose connection was easy enough to figure out once Reece saw the way he looked at Rachel.

The thing that struck him immediately—well, right after the deeply suspicious looks aimed in his direction—was that they all seemed to like each other. Not just love each other in that we're-family-so-we-have-to-care way but actually *like* each other. There was an easy camaraderie among the four brothers, and even the assorted wives and children all seemed to like each other.

His ex-wife's family had been much smaller, but the only thing they seemed to agree on was that they didn't trust him. The Walkers argued about everything from the proper way to build a bridge—one of them was a structural engineer but that didn't seem to stop his brothers from arguing with him—to whether or not cranberry sauce should be smooth or chunky—they seemed to split pretty evenly on that one. But under the squabbling, there was a sense that they were a unit, all of them against the world, if necessary.

It was clear that they considered Shannon a part of that tight-knit circle. It was equally clear that she saw herself as an outsider. Watching her uneasy interactions with the rest of her family, Reece was torn between the urge to shake her for being too scared to take what they were offering and the desire to pull her into his arms and hold her until the lost look was gone. Not that he was going to get much chance to do that. He wasn't sure which was most intimidating—the suspicious looks from her brothers or the open curiosity of their wives. Both had a definite dampening effect on the libido.

When Shannon had asked him if he'd like to spend Christmas with her family, it hadn't been hard to figure out that what she really wanted was a shield. He'd never thought of himself as a knight errant type but he was willing to give it a shot. Besides, two days and a night away sounded appealing.

In the two weeks since they'd become lovers, they spent at least part of every night together, but he couldn't quite shake the niggling feeling that they were doing something illicit. Maybe it was the knowledge that Edith Hacklemeyer was probably peering through her curtains, counting how much time he spent at Shannon's, making note of the exact hour of arrival and departure, though if she was noting his departure, she was keeping some pretty late hours. No matter how many times he told himself that Cacklemeyer was welcome to draw any conclusions she cared to, he still had to fight the urge to creep through the hedge like the straying husband in a bad farce. Two days away with Shannon would make a nice change. On the drive to Los Olivos, he indulged in visions of sleeping in and then waking up to make long, slow love in the morning.

Unfortunately, as it happened, any sleeping in he did was going to be at the whim of his roommate and, as he recalled, six-year-old boys were not big on sleeping late, especially on Christmas morning. He looked at the six-year-old boy in question and stifled a sigh. It should have occurred to him that, unless they stayed in a motel, there was no way he was going to be sharing a room with Shannon. So, here he was, at her brother's house, while she was ensconced in a spare bedroom at her mother's house, miles away.

"Sorry we don't have a real guest room," Gage Walker said, pushing open the door to his son's room and flipping on the light. "We talked about doing an addition last summer but Kelsey got a second greenhouse instead."

Contemplating the action-figure-strewn floor, the sports equipment propped in the corner and, more ominous than the rest, the bunk beds, Reece wondered if he could convince anyone that it was his lifelong ambition to sleep in a greenhouse.

"You can have the bottom bunk," Danny Walker offered, continuing before Reece could offer his heartfelt thanks. "It's harder for grown-ups to climb 'cuz they're old and stuff."

Catching Gage's wince out of the corner of his eye, Reece swallowed a grin. Yeah, these were the moments when parents reconsidered the joy of having children.

"Thanks, Danny. That's very considerate of you."

"Yeah, Mom said I should be 'specially nice 'cuz Dad and Uncle Sam and Uncle Cole and Uncle Keefe were pro'ly gonna give you grief." Oblivious to his father's strangled moan of protest, Danny eyed Reece speculatively. "Are you Aunt Shannon's boyfriend?"

"I…yeah, I guess I am." It had been a long time since he'd thought of himself as anyone's "boyfriend." The word conjured up images of high school proms and groping in the back seat.

"Do you kiss her and everything?"

Painfully aware of Gage's interested look, Reece coughed to clear his throat. "I, ah, kiss her," he admitted, leaving the question of "everything" out of it.

"Yuck." Danny screwed his face up in distaste. "Kissing's gross."

Reece and Gage exchanged an amused look. "You'll change your mind when you grow up," Gage told his son. He reached out to ruffle the boy's hair. "It's getting late, and I know you're going to be up early, tearing into your stocking. Go brush your teeth and get into your pajamas and tell your mom good-night."

"Aww, Dad." Danny caught his father's eye and swallowed the rest of his protest. Heaving a sigh, he pulled a pair of Spider-Man pajamas out from under his pillow and dragged his way out of the room.

"He's really good at the pathos thing," Reece commented after they heard the bathroom door shut.

"Yeah, if we could put that act on Broadway, we'd make a mint." Gage ran his fingers through his dark hair. "He'll keep you up all night if you let him. When he gets rolling, he can talk nonstop for hours, and he's wired because of the holiday. I don't know where he gets the energy. Kelsey says it's just because he's a kid, but I think he's battery powered." He looked at the bunk beds and sighed. "You can sleep on the couch if you'd rather, but I can tell you from personal experience, that's it's not really built for sleeping."

"I'll be fine." Reece sidestepped several small plastic bodies in varying states of undress, an exotic-looking space-age gun and a battered stuffed tiger, and tossed his overnight case on the lower bunk. "It's been a while since my son was this age, but I think I remember it well enough to hold my own."

"You've got kids?" Gage looked surprised, as if it was the first time he'd considered Reece apart from his relationship with Shannon.

"Just one. Kyle's nineteen and just quit college to take a cross-country trip on a motorcycle."

Gage moaned. "Oh, man, it's never going to end, is it? I mean, when I'm ninety, I'm still going to be worrying about him, aren't I?"

"Probably." Reece grinned. "I think it pretty much goes with the territory."

A thin wail came from the baby's room and Gage turned instantly toward it. "The master's voice," he muttered. He glanced back over his shoulder at Reece. "Kelsey made some incredible cinnamon rolls. They're supposed to be for tomorrow morning but I think you might get a special dispensation, being a guest and all. Let me see what Her Highness needs and I'll meet you in the kitchen."

"Am I supposed to steal the cinnamon rolls or talk her out of them?" Reece asked.

Gage stopped in the doorway to his daughter's room and looked back, blue eyes gleaming. "Whatever works."

Reece shook his head. He wondered if stealing cinnamon rolls qualified as some sort of male-bonding ritual. If so, it seemed a small enough price to pay to have at least one of Shannon's brothers looking at him

with something other than acute suspicion. Besides, it
had been years since he'd last tasted a homemade cinnamon roll.

When Shannon was growing up, Christmas had been
a modest celebration. There were gifts. Her father had
leaned toward the predictable: dolls in pretty dresses
giving way to bicycles and then, when she reached her
teens, gift certificates to the local mall so she could
buy herself something nice. He also expressed his appreciation of whatever she got him, whether it was
glue-smudged construction paper artwork or the lopsided ashtray for the cigarettes he didn't smoke. Like
Thanksgiving, Christmas dinner had generally been
eaten at a restaurant with the sound of piped-in carols
to fill any silences.

There was music at the Walkers', too. She caught
snatches of it now and again. Kermit the Frog alter-
nated with Garth Brooks and Tchaikovsky, reflecting
the taste of whoever happened to be closest to the CD
player when it came time to change the CD. She was
fairly sure the Tchaikovsky was courtesy of her oldest
brother's wife, Nikki, and Garth Brooks was Cole's
choice, but Kermit's serenade appeared suspiciously
soon after she saw Keefe near the stereo. The scary
thing was she wasn't sure he'd put it on for the children, and the idea that her large, tough brother was a
secret Muppets fan was mind-boggling, to put it mildly.

Then again, everything about this day was mind-
boggling. There was noise and laughter and food—
large quantities of all three. Children and animals
darted through the rooms of Rachel's modest home,
weaving in and out among the adults and furniture with
total disregard for life and limb. There was always an

adult hand nearby to slow a careening six-year-old or steady a wobbly toddler's steps.

There was no question of everyone being able to sit at the table so the meal was set up on the kitchen counters and served buffet style. It wasn't a meal with a recognizable beginning, middle and end. People served themselves, found a place to sit or stand and ate, then went back for seconds or thirds or, in the case of Cole and Gage's little boy, Danny, possibly fourths.

It was a classic American family Christmas, in all its chaotic glory, and Shannon felt like a little kid with her nose pressed up against the candy-store window, looking in on all that brightness and warmth. The fact that it was her choice that put her on the outside looking in didn't ease the feeling. They included her in their family so easily. Hell, they included *Reece* as comfortably as if they'd known him for years, and he seemed to fit right in. Why was it so hard for *her* to reciprocate?

''God, where did you find that?'' Shannon had been staring down at her eggnog, as if trying to find the meaning of life in the pattern of nutmeg sprinkles, but Sam's question, warm with amusement, made her look up.

Mary, Cole's daughter, had come into the room, clutching a guitar in her arms. The instrument was nearly as big as she was, and she had her arms wrapped around the body, the neck sticking up in front of her face, blocking her view so that she had to twist her head to one side to see where she was walking.

''It was in the closet in the little bedroom,'' she told her uncle. ''I found it yesterday and Grandma said I could get it out. She said you used to play it, Uncle Sam.''

"Yeah, about a thousand years ago." He took it from her when she handed it to him. He edged forward on the sofa and strummed his fingers across the strings. The sound that resulted was musical only by the very loosest of definitions. A chorus of moans was punctuated by a sharp, pained bark from the dog, and the fat black-and-white cat who'd been snoozing on Tessa's lap leaped to her feet with a startled hiss and shot from the room.

When the laughter died down, Mary patted the top of the guitar and gave her uncle a hopeful look. "Play something, Uncle Sam."

"Honey, I haven't played guitar in twenty years." Sam shook his head apologetically. "I wasn't very good even when I did play."

"Reece plays guitar." Shannon was a little startled to hear herself speak, and she bit her lip, giving Reece a quick, uncertain glance, not sure he was going to appreciate being volunteered like that. But he didn't seem to mind. He'd been leaning against the mantel—it was easier to digest standing up, he'd said—but on finding himself the recipient of hopeful looks from both Sam and Mary, he pushed away from the support and reached to take the guitar from Sam, who was more than eager to hand it over.

"Why don't you go get that stool I saw in the kitchen," he told Mary, "and I'll see if I can tune this thing."

Shannon saw Mary's father start to get up but his wife's hand closed over his arm. He looked at her and she shook her head warningly. He hesitated and then settled back into his seat, watching as Mary ran from the room with Danny close behind her. The silent exchange had taken only an instant but it reminded

Shannon that Mary had had heart surgery a few months ago. Rachel had called to tell her about it and she'd sent flowers and a box of candy, receiving a thank-you note back a few weeks later, written in a surprisingly neat childish print. At the time she'd told herself that she didn't want to intrude on the family but, in retrospect, it seemed incredibly thoughtless that she hadn't made more of an effort. They were trying so hard and she had given...nothing.

"Reece is practically a famous singer," she said, hoping he'd forgive her. "His parents were Jonathan and Jennifer, and he sang on one of their songs."

There were exclamations and Reece smiled and shrugged and explained how he'd come to be immortalized in song. By the time he was done, Mary and Danny were back with the stool. Reece thanked them and sat down, bracing the guitar on one knee, fingers twisting the tuning pegs as he brought the old strings into something approaching harmony with one another.

"I seem to be doomed to play guitars with rubber bands for strings." He looked up and smiled at Shannon and she smiled back, wondering if he was remembering the same thing she was, that the last time he'd complained about guitar strings, the first time she'd heard him play, had been just before they slept together for the first time.

Aware of the color creeping up her face, she looked down at her eggnog. Better not to think about that right now, not with her whole family looking on. She'd been surprised by how much she'd missed him last night. It hadn't even been two weeks, but she'd grown accustomed to the feel of him in the bed next to her, to falling asleep with her head on his shoulder. The narrow bed had felt large and empty, and that was maybe a little scary, considering the fact that this was supposed to be a temporary thing. It was the built-in temporaryness of it that had made it safe. But last night she'd been lonely without him, and that didn't seem to fit in with the whole "safe" thing.

Reece was playing a rather unique version of "Old MacDonald Had a Farm." At least Shannon didn't remember any emus in the version she'd learned. Not to mention aardvarks and antelope—contributions from Sam and Keefe. Mary and Danny were laughing, delighted with this unique vision of agrarian life. Little David, too young to know the difference between an aardvark and a Holstein, stood in the middle of the floor, rocking back and forth and clapping his hands to the rhythm of his own particular drummer.

Shannon was struck again by the realization that Reece was more at home with her family than she was. Then again, there was no pressure on him, no sense that, no matter how much they tried not to push, they were all watching her, hoping to see something of the child she'd been, the woman they'd hoped she'd become.

Suddenly restless, she set her glass down and stood up, slipping between her chair and Nikki's pretending not to see the other woman's questioning look, pretending not to notice the way Rachel's eyes shifted away from her grandchildren's happy faces. If she left the room, no one would come after her, but they'd wonder and they'd worry. Maybe she couldn't be whatever they'd hoped she'd be but she could at least avoid making herself even more of an outsider than she already was.

So, instead of fleeing out the door, out of the house and maybe just trotting her way back to Serenity Falls, she wandered along the outskirts of the room, as if that's what she'd intended all along, finally ending up near the piano. Old MacDonald was now raising sharks, which, according to Danny, make a growling noise that sounded a lot like the same noise his new Tonka truck had made earlier in the day.

Shannon risked a quick glance in that direction, half expecting to find everyone looking at her, but they were apparently absorbed in the impromptu concert. Relieved, she sank down on the piano bench. Obviously, her ego was running amuck. Or maybe it was paranoia spiraling out of control. Since when did she go around assuming that everyone was looking at her?

There were pictures on top of the piano, and she picked up a framed photo, studying the four solemn-faced boys and the little girl standing in front of them. She wished she could remember what it had been like to be a part of that obviously close-knit family. All she had were a few dim memories—a pink stuffed dog, the sound of her own giggles as someone swung her high in the air, hands picking her up and dusting her off when she fell down. Laughter and music, a lot like today, except…

"I remember someone playing piano," she said abruptly and then flushed when she realized she'd spoken out loud, interrupting the song. She started to apologize but Rachel spoke first.

"Gage used to play," she said quietly. "You liked to sit and draw pictures while he practiced. He was teaching you to play 'Chopsticks' when your…when you went away."

Shannon nodded, looking away from the almost painful look of hope on the other woman's face. Gage was watching her, something dark and…scared?…in his eyes. She smiled a little, wanting to take that look away.

"I still can't play 'Chopsticks,'" she admitted. Laughter greeted the comment, more than it deserved but it eased the sudden tension.

She wasn't sure how, because it hadn't been her suggestion and she knew it wasn't Gage's idea, she found herself the recipient of an impromptu piano lesson. It wasn't long before she had Danny on her lap and Mary crowded on the end of the bench next to her as both children tried their hand at pounding out the rhythmic little piece. It was mildly humiliating to find that they both picked it up faster than she did.

"Children learn easier," she said defensively when she hit the wrong keys yet again.

"Nah, you were always tone-deaf," Gage told her, grinning heartlessly at her outraged gasp.

"Maybe you're just a lousy teacher," she suggested with a dangerously sweet smile.

"Me and Mary learned okay," Danny pointed out, twisting his head to look up at her. "You've just got two left feet, Aunt Shannon."

"And both of them are on the keyboard," Gage murmured wickedly.

Shannon's offended glare was derailed when Mary patted her on the arm and said, "Don't feel bad, Aunt Shannon. I bet you're real good at lots of other stuff."

"Nonmusical stuff," Gage added helpfully, and Shannon lost the battle with her laughter.

A few minutes later, in answer to his niece's request for some "real music," Gage was making his way hesitantly through "Moonlight Sonata." Watching his long fingers skim over the keyboard and hearing his frustrated mutters as he stumbled over something that had obviously once been easy for him, it occurred to Shannon that, for a little while, she'd actually forgotten that Gage was her "brother" and had just enjoyed his company.

The idea was startling. She shifted her hold on Danny, whose head was starting to loll back against her shoulder as the day's excitement caught up with him. Maybe it wasn't the *Walkers'* expectations that were the problem. Maybe it was her own. Really, they hadn't asked for anything more than a chance to get to know her. She was the one who was hung up on the whole "family" label and what she *should* be feeling, which was stupid, really, because you couldn't force feelings.

It was amazing how much easier things were when she wasn't trying so hard, Shannon thought a few hours later as she stood on the front porch saying goodbye to her family. They even, almost, *felt* like family. Not that there had been some miraculous movie-musical-style moment of connection where bluebirds were singing and everyone was dancing with joy, but there was a tentative sense of *beginning*, a feeling that, given time, the connections would be there.

"Thank you so much for coming." Rachel Walker's smile was warm, her eyes just a little too bright. "It meant a lot to all of us."

"It meant a lot to me, too," Shannon said. "I...I really do want to get to know you." Her glance included her brothers. Their wives and children had already said their goodbyes and gone back inside. Reece was waiting in the truck.

"We want that, too." Rachel's voice was not quite steady. She hesitated a moment and then held out her arms. It wasn't the first time they'd hugged, but it was the first time Shannon had felt like she belonged. Her eyes were stinging when she pulled back, and she aimed a shaky smile at her brothers before turning away and hurrying down the dark pathway.

Reece had the truck running, and the interior of the cab was nice and warm. She felt him glance at her and was grateful of the darkness that hid her expression. Not that she was sure what it was since she wasn't sure what she was feeling but, whatever it was, she didn't want to talk about it. She'd had enough emotional dissection for one day. She didn't—

"As soon as we're out of sight of your four large and intimidating brothers, I'm going to pull the truck over in some secluded spot and ravish you."

Reece's tone was conversational, and it took her a moment to process what he'd said. When she did, her breath caught and her mind went perfectly blank for an instant before coming back online with a rush of need that left her flushed and breathless.

"I've never been ravished in a truck." Was that her voice? She sounded like she'd been smoking cigarettes and drinking whiskey for the last month. She sounded downright wanton.

"No?" In the light from a street lamp, she saw Reece's fingers flex on the wheel. "New experiences are supposed to expand the mind."

"I've heard that." She slid her hand across the seat and set it on his thigh, nothing overt, just her fingers resting lightly on him, feeling the flex of muscle and the heat of his skin through denim. "I'm always eager to learn."

He slanted her a look that had an almost palpable heat. "I'm counting on that."

Chapter 11

The week between Christmas and New Year's was gray and rainy, but New Year's Day dawned with bright sunshine and clear skies. The talking heads in Pasadena tried not to look too smug about the fact that, yet again, the sun was shining on the Rose Parade.

"I think someone's made a bargain with the dark side," Shannon said. "Only demon interference could explain why it never rains on the parade. Is that a bear?"

Reece squinted at the screen, trying to see through the fuzzy snow. "I think it's a dog. It rains on the Rose Parade."

She snorted. "Yeah, like twice in the past two hundred years. You can't tell me that's not a product of some hell world."

He eyed her speculatively as he reached for his coffee. "You've been watching too much *Buffy the Vampire Slayer*. Maybe it's just really good luck. Maybe

Pasadena-ites are just really deserving people and this is their reward. Besides, they weren't having the parade two hundred years ago.''

''Sure they were.'' She leaned forward to select a miniquiche from the platter on the coffee table and then pointed it at him. ''It's a little-known fact that the Californios held a parade right down Colorado Boulevard every year on New Year's Day. They decorated their, um, donkeys with native flowers and gave prizes for who had the most attractive...ass.''

Reece groaned and threw a crumpled-up napkin at her but she just grinned and popped the quiche in her mouth.

He still wasn't sure why they were sitting on his grandfather's ancient sofa, watching the Rose Parade in all its fuzzy glory and eating leftover hors d'oeuvres from last night's New Year's Eve party at the McKinnons'. Last night was the first time they'd ended up in his bed instead of hers, but that didn't mean they couldn't walk across the driveway to her more comfortable sofa and, if she wanted to watch a bunch of flower-bedecked floats, wouldn't it be nice if she could actually *see* them?

But watching the floats through a blizzard of bad reception apparently didn't bother her and neither did faded upholstery and springs that were prone to...spring in unexpected places.

When he'd awakened alone in bed, he'd assumed she'd gone back to her house. He crawled out of the tangled sheets and nearly tripped over a pillow, which he had a vague memory of having thrown out of the way sometime the night before. The memory was enough to put a smile on his face as he headed for the shower. They'd definitely started the new year off on a high note. With luck, they could continue on that same high note later this afternoon.

Now, two hours later, he was wondering if Shannon would be amenable to nudging that timetable up. She was curled up on one end of the sofa, her hair caught up in a messy knot on top of her head. She was wearing faded jeans and one of his blue workshirts, half-unbuttoned and knotted at the waist. He didn't need X-ray vision to know she wasn't wearing a bra. The soft, gentle sway of her breasts when she moved made his mouth water and made other body parts perk up with an eagerness that seemed downright greedy considering the previous night's activities.

She frowned and tilted her head as if hoping a different angle might clear up the picture on the screen.

"You know, if you want to actually *see* the parade, we could move this next door," Reece said, running his thumb over the top of her bare foot.

"We could," she agreed, but made no move to get up.

Reece shrugged mentally. It was her choice. His interest in the parade pretty much began and ended with... Well, actually, it never really began. He couldn't even remember the last time he'd seen it. Maybe when Kyle was little.

"Now, that's definitely a bear."

Reece turned his head obediently to look at the screen. "In a grass skirt?"

"It's a Hawaiian bear. They're very rare. They live in caves in the lava and only eat poi and moon pies."

"Did anyone ever tell you that you're a terrible liar?"

"I am not." She gave him an offended look. "I'm a very good liar."

"You know, liars never prosper." Reece's fingers closed around one slim ankle.

"I thought it was cheaters who never prospered." Shannon let him tug first one leg and then the other flat on the sofa, her eyes going wide and dark as he crawled up the length of her body. Her voice took on a breathless edge. "Liars are supposed to have flaming pants."

"Well, it was a relatively little lie. I don't think it's necessary to extract the full penalty." He hovered over her, weight braced on his elbows, hips nudging gently against hers, letting her feel his arousal. She smiled, a slow, feline curl of her lips that went straight to his groin.

"Maybe I could get some sort of dispensation for good behavior?"

Reece lowered himself slowly until his body pressed hers into the faded upholstery. "Depends on how good you are," he murmured, swallowing a groan when she shifted, sliding those sinfully long legs up alongside his hips so that he lay in the cradle of her thighs.

"Oh, I can be very...very...*very*...good." She brought her head up and caught his lower lip between her teeth, worrying it gently.

"You're missing the parade." He slid his hand upward, palming her breast and rubbing his thumb over the nipple, feeling it harden beneath the thin cotton of his shirt.

"What parade?" she whispered against his lips.

It was a slow, languid kiss, the heat between them banked with the knowledge that they had all the time in the world. Shannon opened her mouth to him, her tongue fencing teasingly with his, hands moving restlessly up and down his back, sliding over the thin cotton of his T-shirt.

Reece rocked his hips, teasing both of them with the feel of his trapped erection rubbing against her through two layers of denim. She moaned, a soft, hungry sound that cranked up the heat between them a notch. Urgency began to replace languor, lazy pleasure giving way to need. His hand slid between them, tugging at the knot she'd tied with the tails of his shirt. He needed to feel her skin against him, bare and warm and flushed with hunger.

It took a moment for Reece to figure out that the bell he was hearing wasn't part of the background mutter from the television.

"There's someone at the door," Shannon said, tilting her head to give his mouth better access to the sensitive skin under her ear.

"Probably someone selling something," he muttered, catching her earlobe between his teeth.

"At eight-thirty on New Year's morning?" Shannon's hands shifted, settled on his shoulders and pushed.

"They'll go away," he told her. He gave up on the knot and slid his hand under the shirt. She shuddered, body going boneless beneath him as his fingers closed over her bare breast.

The bell rang again, and her eyes popped open. Reece groaned and lowered his forehead to hers, admitting defeat.

"It might be something important," she whispered with a touch of apology.

"Yeah? Well, this is pretty damned important, too," he muttered. Reluctantly he slid his hand out from under her shirt and pushed himself up off the sofa. He took a few deep breaths, willing his arousal to subside to a point where he wasn't likely to be arrested for public indecency, and stalked to the door. Behind him, he heard Shannon shifting around, sitting up and probably putting herself back together. Dammit. Of course, that wasn't all bad. Getting her untidy again wasn't exactly a hardship. That thought might just be enough to save the life of whoever was ringing his doorbell. For the third time.

His expression less than welcoming, Reece yanked the door open. The young man on the other side of the screen grinned at him.

"Hi, Dad."

Chapter 12

There was nothing like being caught practically *in flagrante* very *delicto* by your lover's son to really kill the mood, Shannon thought. She glanced down to make sure everything was properly buttoned and tied. It was at least the tenth time she'd checked in the past fifteen minutes, but you couldn't be too careful. Not that she thought it likely that Reece's son didn't have a pretty good idea of what she and his father had been doing when he arrived, but there was no sense in making it obvious. Any *more* obvious.

When Reece introduced them, his eyes had skimmed over her, taking in the tousled mess of her hair, the man's shirt knotted at her waist and her bare feet before cutting to his father, also barefoot, rumpled and looking more than a little panic-stricken. Kyle's eyes flashed with speculative amusement but he didn't say anything, for which she was pathetically grateful.

Looking at him, Shannon thought she would have

known who he was, even if she'd met him in the middle of Times Square. The resemblance between him and his father was striking. Kyle matched Reece for height, but his body was leaner, still holding some of the lankiness of youth. He had the same thick dark hair and strong jaw, the same smile. It was like looking at a picture of Reece taken twenty years ago, except for the eyes. Where his father's eyes were dark brown, Kyle's were an unexpected clear, pale emerald. Shannon was willing to bet that he had girls trailing after him in hordes.

"Are you sure you want to cook?" Reece asked, eyeing her uneasily as she pulled a carton of eggs out of the refrigerator.

Breakfast had been her suggestion when it began to look like the three of them were going to stand in the living room forever. Reece had seized on the suggestion gratefully. It was obvious that his son's unexpected appearance at such a delicate moment had thrown him off balance. They'd moved into the kitchen, leaving the television muttering to itself, fuzzy images of pretty floats drifting past unseen. She'd poured a cup of coffee for Kyle and freshened her own cup and Reece's before poking through the refrigerator to see what the options were. Her suggestion of omelets had been met with enthusiasm on Kyle's part and cautious approval on Reece's.

She knew what he was thinking and couldn't resist teasing him. She gave him a sweet smile. "I'll make one of my special omelets."

"Special?" Reece asked warily. "What's in them?"

Kyle gave his father a surprised look. "Haven't you ever heard the saying about not looking a gift cook in the mouth?"

"Experience has taught me that it's better to be safe than sorry," Reece told him. He leaned back, bracing his hands against the edge of the counter and looked at his son. "The first morning I met her, she tried to feed me Froot Loops."

"That's not so bad," Kyle said. "I like—"

"And Pepsi," Reece added heavily.

"*On* the Froot Loops?" Kyle asked, his expression so exactly echoing his father's that Shannon nearly choked on a giggle.

"Not *on* them," she explained. "*With* them."

Kyle looked like he didn't think this was much of an improvement but was too polite to say so.

"And then, when I politely declined," Reece continued grimly, "she tried to feed me toaster waffles and grape jelly."

"It's a perfectly nutritious breakfast," Shannon protested. "The waffles provide a serving of grains and the jelly counts as a fruit."

Kyle eyed her with something approaching awe. "Did he eat them?"

"No." Shannon pursed her mouth into a prim line and slanted a laughing glance at Reece. "He made up some ridiculous story about being allergic to grape jelly."

Kyle cleared his throat and looked self-conscious. "Actually, it's a hereditary thing. I, ah…"

"Turn purple," Reece suggested, and Kyle seized on it gratefully.

"Yeah, I turn purple when I eat grape jelly. It's a very rare condition." He tried to look regretful. "So, if your special omelets have grape jelly in them, I'll have to pass."

"Grape jelly in an omelet?" Shannon's brows rose

in shock. "Don't be silly." She waited a beat and then gave them both a big, bright smile. "Everyone knows you always use orange marmalade in omelets."

Reece made breakfast. When Shannon offered to at least help, he instructed Kyle to keep her away from the stove, even if he had to use physical force. Laughing, Shannon began setting the table.

Conversation was easier than she might have expected. Kyle had his father's gift for telling a story, and his cross-country trip had given him plenty of those. He hadn't said anything about why he was here or how long he planned to stay, but, reading between the lines, Shannon had the distinct feeling that he was less than enchanted with life on the open road. She wondered if he'd come to Serenity Falls planning to spend time with his father and how that would fit in with Reece's plans. He hadn't said anything about leaving, but he hadn't said anything about staying, either.

She looked down at the remains of her omelet and wondered if the hollow feeling in the pit of her stomach was because she'd eaten too fast.

Shannon excused herself as soon as they were done eating, saying that she had some shop samples she wanted to finish up. She hadn't really planned on doing anything but spending the day with Reece, but she thought he and Kyle could probably use some time together and maybe it would be a good thing for her to spend some time alone, remind herself of how much she enjoyed being on her own.

When Reece got up to walk her to the door, Kyle made a point of the fact that he was going to clear the table. Shannon caught his eyes, saw the amused knowledge in them, and felt herself blush.

"I'll see you later today?" Reece asked, his hand settling on her lower back as they stood in the open doorway.

"Don't you think Kyle might want to have you to himself for a bit?"

"No." His hand slid up, nudging her gently closer. "He said he's planning on staying for a while. We'll get plenty of time together." He lowered his mouth to hers in a soft, quick kiss. "You know, it's great to see him, but his timing stinks."

Shannon felt the color come up in her cheeks, a mixture of desire and embarrassment. She lifted her hand to his face, tracing the solid line of his jaw. "It could have been worse," she murmured. "He could have shown up a few minutes later."

"God, yes." Reece laughed and dropped another, harder kiss on her mouth before she slipped out the door.

When Reece returned to the kitchen, Kyle had just finished rinsing the plates and stacking them in the drainer. He turned to look at his father, drying his hands on a red-and-white-checked towel.

"Nice neighbor." There was nothing suggestive in Kyle's tone but Reece felt himself flush.

"Yes. She's very…nice."

"Pretty, too," Kyle said mildly.

"Very." Reece fought the urge to shove his hands in his pockets like an erring child. Dammit, *he* was supposed to be the grown-up here.

"She the reason you've hung around here so long?" There was nothing but curiosity in Kyle's question.

"Part of it." It felt good to say it out loud and Reece

leaned back against the counter opposite Kyle and waited to see how his son would react to that.

Kyle nodded. "Yeah, I can see why. She's a hottie."

Reece laughed. "I hadn't thought of her that way, but I guess she is."

"Yeah." Kyle folded the towel and set it down before bracing both hands on the counter and leaning back against it in unconscious imitation of Reece's pose. "So, you *pissed* at me for quitting school? You didn't say much when we talked on the phone."

Reece shook his head. "I told you before that it was your decision and I'd support you whatever you decided to do."

"Yeah? Mom said pretty much the same thing but she just about had a cow when I told her I was quitting."

"She wants what's best for you," Reece said, choosing his words carefully. "And she's more…definite in her ideas of what's best."

"You mean she likes to run everyone's life," Kyle said dryly.

Reece started to defend his ex-wife, met his son's eyes and shrugged instead. "Your mother's a very strong-willed woman."

"Yeah." Kyle grinned and relaxed back against the counter. "Charles says she's pigheaded as a mule." Charles was his stepfather.

"Does he?" Reece let his mouth curve upward. "Well, I always did like Charles."

"Me, too. He's good for Mom because he only lets her manage him as long as she's pushing him to do what he wants to do."

"What did Charles say about you quitting school?"

"Said he thought I was an idiot, but everyone had a right to be an idiot when they were nineteen."

"Sounds reasonable." Reece cocked his head in question. "Are you sorry you quit?"

"No." Kyle's answer was prompt. "I may go back, but I just couldn't face another four or five years of school right now. It would be different if I had something I wanted to do, some career in mind, but I don't."

"Well, I guess you're entitled to take some time to decide what you want to be when you grow up," Reece said, and Kyle smiled, relieved.

"I thought I might hang around here awhile, maybe get a job. I mean, I've got plenty of money, thanks to what you've put away for me, but I don't want to use that just to live on. Besides, I figure working for a while might help me figure out what I want to do. If you don't mind me hanging around, that is."

"Well, it'll be a real hardship but I think I can bear up under the strain." The dry comment seemed to be the reassurance Kyle needed.

"I don't suppose Shannon has any younger sisters?" he asked, grinning.

"No, she's got four very large older brothers," Reece said, grimacing and Kyle laughed out loud.

"Man, you do like to live dangerously, don't you?"

Reece laughed, but he thought Shannon was likely to prove far more dangerous than her brothers.

Shannon hadn't planned on spending New Year's Day sewing samples for the shop but, since she found herself with the day unexpectedly free, she decided it wasn't a bad idea. Since getting involved with Reece, she hadn't spent much time sewing, and it was a pleasure to immerse herself in pattern and fabric. She'd always enjoyed sewing but, since buying the shop, there was the added challenge of trying to guess what was most likely to inspire her customers to part with a significant portion of their discretionary income.

Humming along to Chris Isaak's version of "Yellow Bird," she cut out brightly colored squares. She'd piece them together and then appliqué a pair of funky looking cats on the background, finishing up with a multicolored-stripe border that would pull in all the colors from the center of the quilt. She'd already ordered three bolts of the stripe, taking a chance that her customers would like the playful look of it as much as she did. It never hurt to show them how the fabric looked in an actual quilt.

Halfway through the afternoon, she stopped and went into the kitchen to make herself a cup of hot tea. She sat at the kitchen table and nibbled on a chocolate chip cookie while she waited for the water to boil. The wall hanging was coming along nicely. She just might get it done this evening. The stripe wasn't due in to the shop for another week or two, but it couldn't hurt to whet people's appetite ahead of time by hanging the sample up early. She'd done that last summer with a pretty little print featuring fairies riding bunnies and had sold two bolts of the fabric the afternoon it came into the shop.

The teakettle began to hiss and she got up to catch it before it started whistling. She'd just poured water over a tea bag when she heard someone tapping at the back door. Startled, she turned, her expression relaxing in a grin when she saw Reece looking through the window.

"What are you doing at the back door?" she asked as she unlocked it and let him in.

"I snuck through the hedge," he said, holding out his arm to display a thin scratch. "Damned thing bit me."

"It's a hedge. It's supposed to keep people out." She led him over to the sink, pulling a paper towel off the roll and dampening it before dabbing it against the scratch. "Should I even ask why you were going through the hedge?"

"Because I'm an idiot," he said, taking the paper towel from her and tossing it in the sink and then sliding his arms around her waist. "Because my nineteen-year-old son is staying with me and I'm suddenly feeling terribly wicked and dirty old manish."

"Did Kyle say something?" Shannon asked, frowning. She reached up to pluck a leaf from his hair. Kyle hadn't seemed upset by the idea that they were involved, but maybe he'd just been hiding his feelings.

"Kyle said he was going to go take a shower, then take a nap and if I had anything I wanted to do or anyplace I wanted to go, I didn't have to worry about him." Reece's smile was equal parts amusement and irritation. "He might as well have given me permission to go off and do illicit things. It was embarrassing as hell and he knew it, the brat."

"You could have thrown him off the scent by staying home," Shannon said. She hooked her fingers through his belt loops and tugged him closer, her pulse jumping at the feel of his arousal pressed against her belly.

"No, I couldn't. I don't have that much self-control." He bent to taste the sensitive skin under her ear and Shannon tilted her head to give him better access, her eyes fluttering shut.

"So why the back hedge?" she managed, sighing as his teeth closed over her earlobe.

"I don't know, it just seemed to fit in with the whole illicit affair thing. Sneaking through hedges in the dark of night."

"It's the middle of the afternoon." She turned her head to catch his mouth with hers.

"You've got to use your imagination." He slid one hand between them and began slipping open the buttons on her shirt—*his* shirt. "But next time, I'm bringing a chain saw."

Grinning, Shannon leaned back against his hold. He took advantage of the space between them and tugged the shirt open. She'd put on a bra since this morning and he frowned in mild disapproval before flicking the front catch open, baring her breasts.

"Now where were we?" he murmured, watching her with dark, hungry eyes. He cupped one soft mound, stroking his thumb across the peak.

"Right...right about there." It was difficult to talk when her brain felt like it was melting right along with her bones.

"Or maybe right...here?" The last word was a whisper against her breast. She shuddered as his tongue laved her nipple, painting it with quick little strokes that brought it to aching hardness. Her fingers curled into the solid muscles of his upper arm, and her head fell back as she arched, offering herself to him.

There was something deliciously wicked about standing here in the middle of her kitchen, bare to the waist, sunlight pouring through the back window—Sunlight. Window. Shannon's eyes popped open.

"Reece! The curtains are open."

"No one can see into your backyard," he murmured, licking a patch along her collarbone.

She shivered. He was right but...

"Someone could sneak into the yard," she said.

"Trust me, anyone who tries to sneak into your backyard is too busy trying to stop the bleeding from wounds inflicted by that hedge to have time to peer through the window." But he straightened and looked down at her, lust and exasperation mixed in his expression. "I'm trying to ravish you."

"I know." She slid her fingers through his hair, made her smile coaxing. "Have I ever mentioned that I have this fantasy about being ravished in my bed?"

He frowned. "That's sort of a boring fantasy, isn't it? What about the deck of a pirate ship or a treehouse in the jungle?"

"Splinters and mildew," she said, edging him toward the door.

"Splinters and mildew?" he repeated blankly.

"Pirate ship. Deck. Splinters," she clarified. "Jungle. Humidity. Mildew. And bugs." She shuddered. "Big bugs. Not my idea of a fun time."

"I think we need to work on your fantasy life," Reece said. Without waiting for a response, he bent to slide one hand under her knees and scooped her up into his arms.

Gasping, Shannon threw her arms around his neck, her pulse skittering with excitement.

"Is this where you carry me off to your jungle lair?" she asked breathlessly.

"I was thinking more along the lines of your bedroom." Reece angled her legs out the door and carried her down the hall. "Do you know how far it is to the nearest jungle? Not to mention the cost of renting a lair this time of year.''

He dropped her on the bed and followed her down, his mouth catching hers, swallowing her laughter. His hands caught hers, pinning them to the pillow beside her head. The soft cotton of his sweatshirt pressed against her bare breasts, abrading her nipples, and suddenly the playfulness vanished, burned away in the heat that flared between them.

She pulled her hands free, tugging at his shirt, needing to feel him against her, skin to skin. Reece released her mouth long enough to pull his sweatshirt off over his head, tossing it aside. He reached for her jeans at the same moment that she reached for his, and they rolled on the bed, her choked laughter mixing with his muttered imprecations as they struggled with the heavy denim. A seam ripped with a sibilant hiss, and then he was stripping her jeans down her legs, taking her peach-colored panties along with them. She arched into him, hands slipping on sweat-damp skin as he shoved his jeans down, urgency too great to take time to get them off. She could feel his hands shaking as he gripped her hips, fingers digging into her skin hard enough to leave bruises but she didn't care.

She cried out as he slid into her in one long, heavy thrust, filling her, completing her, making her whole. And then it was all heat and movement and sound. Her breath coming in panting gasps, his guttural groans, the soft, wet slap of flesh on flesh. It was too much, she thought, too much. Her body bucked as if to throw him off even as her legs tightened around his hips to pull him closer.

''Now,'' he whispered against her throat, against her ear. ''Now. Give it to me now.''

As if the words were all she'd needed, she felt herself spin out of control, her entire being concentrated on the spot where they were joined. The pleasure spiraled out, tighter, harder, hovering on the knife-edge of pain until it burst apart in a shower of lights and sparks, dancing red and gold under her eyelids. Her arms tightened around Reece and he shuddered and groaned against her.

Minutes or hours later she felt him stir. He'd shifted to one side and lay sprawled on his stomach, his knee bent, leg resting across her hips, one arm across her waist, face buried in the curve of shoulder and neck. His hand moved slowly, tracing a warm line up her side, finally curving around her breast in a casually possessive gesture that made her heart stumble with a mixture of pleasure and uneasiness. Maybe it wasn't a good thing for him to feel possessive. Maybe it was dangerous that she liked it so much.

But it was hard to worry about it when he lifted his head, giving her a smile that said he was unabashedly pleased with himself, with her and possibly with the world at large.

"Now, that's how to get the new year off to a good start."

There was really nothing to do but kiss him.

Shannon had never been a big believer in New Year's resolutions. She didn't believe there was anything mystical about January first. It was just an arbitrary number on a calendar invented by mankind to make it easier to keep track of things. It was also a busy time if you happened to own a quilt shop. With the holidays just past, every quilter on the planet seemed to be seized with a determination that *this* year, they were really going to make quilts for everyone they knew and they were going to start them all in January. It was also time for that annual rite of torture known as taking inventory and the big inventory reduction sale that preceded it.

As a general rule, the first part of January passed in a haze of long hours and hard work, and this year was no exception. But she had distractions this year that she hadn't had before. Well, one distraction. One large distraction. One large, very distracting distraction. It was a little frightening to realize how easily he'd fit into her life and what a large hole he was going to leave if he left. *When* he left, she reminded herself regularly. It wasn't a question of *if* he left. It was just a question of when.

And that probably seemed so depressing because she had some sort of low-level flu that she couldn't seem to shake. She must have gotten it from Kelly, who spent three days out sick right after the first of the year, but she hadn't gotten as bad a dose. She was never sick enough to stay home but she was tired all the time and vaguely queasy. It was the illness that was making her feel so vulnerable and…needy, because she'd known from the beginning that Reece was leaving, and she couldn't possibly have been stupid enough to fall in love with him.

Falling in love at forty wasn't all that much different from falling in love at twenty, Reece decided. There was still that nervous little jiggle in the pit of his stomach when he saw the object of his affections, still all those niggling uncertainties about whether or not she loved him in return and whether or not they could build a future together. He was planning on it. Definitely planning on it. He hadn't mentioned it to Shannon yet. She was…well, he wasn't sure what she was. Skittish? Wary? Either one fit. It was understandable, really. When you looked at her past history, there was nothing in it to encourage her to throw herself into emotional commitments.

Her father had taken her from her family and, though she hadn't exactly said as much, it was pretty clear that he'd been emotionally distant. Fear of being found out had kept him from settling anywhere for very long, and the frequent moves had meant that Shannon didn't get a chance to build long-lasting ties with anyone. And then, when she got married, her husband died just a few months later, leaving her alone again. It was no wonder she was having a hard time opening herself up to the Walkers, no wonder she always kept a little part of herself distant from him.

But things were changing. He knew she'd talked to her mother a couple of times in the month since Christmas. Maybe they were not yet to the point of having heart-to-heart, mother-daughter talks but Shannon seemed more at ease with the idea of having family, of having those ties. And, whether she admitted it or not, she'd let him in, too.

She loved him. He thought. Probably, she did. He hoped. God, he hoped so. Because he'd finally figured out what he wanted to be when he grew up and, much to his astonishment, he wanted to stay in Serenity Falls and build a life with Shannon Devereux. He wanted that a lot.

He wasn't going to push it, though. He didn't want to push her. They had plenty of time. He knew what he wanted. It was just a matter of getting her to admit that she wanted the same thing.

*   *   *

The way to a man's heart was supposed to be through his stomach. Reece had decided that, in these days of genderless thinking, the same could apply to a woman. In this case, he was hoping that the way to a coffee lover's heart was through a cup of Jamaican Blue Mountain coffee, freshly brewed and hand delivered. Considering what the beans cost, he was willing to bet they'd been hand delivered straight from Jamaica, one bean at a time.

Shannon was dressed for work when she opened the door. A loose ivory-colored sweater worn over a pair of rust-colored slacks, her hair tumbled around her shoulders in a spill of warm red-gold curls. A pair of scruffy blue slippers completed the outfit, and Reece grinned when he saw them.

"Nice shoes."

"Thanks," she said, offering him a vague smile, apparently accepting the compliment as if it had been sincere.

"I'd change them before you go to work," he suggested, poking one slipper with the toe of his running shoe. "Unless you're trying for the bag lady look."

"What?"

"The slippers?" he said gently. "Not exactly high fashion attire."

"Oh." Shannon looked down at her feet and nodded. "I guess you're right. I'll…change them."

"You okay?" he asked as he followed her into the house.

"Fine. I'm fine." She rubbed her fingers across her forehead. "I'm just a little distracted, I guess. Thinking about…stuff. Things. Thinking about things."

"You sleep okay?" He set the thermal pot down on the counter and slid one hand behind her neck, drawing her forward into his kiss. She pulled back a little and then seemed to almost collapse against him, sliding her arms around his waist.

"Pretty good," she mumbled into his shirt.

"Still got that flu bug?" he asked, brushing a kiss over the top of her head. "Maybe you should see a doctor."

She stiffened as if jabbed with a cattle prod, pulling out of his arms and taking a step back. "I'm fine." Her tone verged on snappish. "I've just got a lot on my mind. With the shop and everything."

"Okay." Reece lifted his hand, palm out, placating. "Just don't let yourself get too run down."

"I won't." Shannon looked away from him, pushing one hand through her hair. "I didn't mean to snap."

"That's okay." He pushed down his concern and smiled. "I come in peace and I come bearing gifts."

Shannon's smile didn't quite reach her eyes. "Isn't there some warning about 'Beware of Greeks bearing gifts'?"

Reece took two mugs off the hooks under the cupboard. "Yeah, but lucky for you, I'm not Greek and this isn't just any gift." He unscrewed the top on the thermal mug and the rich scent of coffee immediately wafted out. He inhaled deeply as he poured it into cups. "This is Jamaican Blue Mountain coffee, freshly ground, freshly brewed and freshly delivered."

Smiling, he turned and held a cup out to Shannon. She looked at it, looked at him, swallowed once, swallowed again. The color drained out of her face and she gave him a helpless look and clapped one hand over her mouth before turning and bolting for the bathroom.

Reece stood there, staring after her, coffee cup still extended. Through the door, he could hear the unmistakable sounds of her throwing up. Slowly he pulled his hand back, stared down at the cup for a moment and then turned to pour it back into the carafe, along with the cup he'd poured for himself. He tightened the lid on the carafe and rinsed both cups thoroughly and then opened the back door for good measure, letting in cold, clean air.

After several minutes he heard the water come on in the bathroom. Judging the smell thoroughly dissipated, he shut the back door and then leaned back against the counter, waiting. It was a long wait and he had plenty of time to think. He thought about how pale Shannon had been lately, how distracted she'd been the past few days. He thought about the fact that they'd been lovers for more than six weeks, had spent almost every night together and she hadn't once said anything about it being a bad time of the month for her. He thought about how careful they'd been. Most of the time. Almost all of the time. Almost.

He waited, hearing nothing but silence and wondering if she was on the other side of the door, hoping he'd go away. But he wasn't going to go anywhere until they'd talked, until he'd asked a few questions. He'd lead up to it gently. No sense jumping to conclusions. Maybe she just had the flu. That's probably all it was, and he didn't want to sound accusing.

The bathroom door finally opened, and Shannon came out, looking pale and hollow-eyed. Looking anywhere but at him. Flu, he told himself. The flu could really wipe a person out, make them throw up when they smelled coffee. That's all it was.

"Shannon?" He waited until she looked at him, saw the answer in her eyes even before he asked the question.

"Are you pregnant?"

Chapter 13

Shannon looked at him, not saying anything, not denying it.

Not. Denying. It.

Reece swallowed hard and fumbled for the back of a chair, pulling it out and sinking into it. The silence was so complete that he could hear the clock on the wall ticking the seconds away.

"Shannon?" It came out on a croak and he stopped, cleared his throat and tried again. "Are you...pregnant?"

Her eyes slid away from his, slid back for an instant and then away again. "Maybe," she said at last. "Probably. A little."

He stared at her blankly, his mind spinning back to Christmas night, driving back from her mother's house, pulling off the highway into a deserted rest stop, parking away from the lights. The two of them in his truck, risking hypothermia and breaking several public indecency laws. No condom. Not even a highly inadequate gesture of premature withdrawal. They hadn't talked about it, hadn't discussed it and made a logical, adult decision. There had been one frozen moment when they'd both realized what they were doing, the risk they were about to take.

She'd been sprawled on the seat beneath him, blouse pulled open, skirt pushed up around her waist, eyes glittering in the darkness, the wet heat of her pressed against him. So close, so close. And he'd waited, frozen, wishing he hadn't packed the condoms in his overnight case, which was in the back of the truck, knowing he should pull back. It was the right thing to do, the responsible thing to do. And then she'd arched against him, taking him inside that first tiny bit, and his breath had hissed between his teeth and he'd stopped thinking.

They hadn't talked about it afterward, either. Not really. Helping her pull her clothes back together, he'd said something about letting him know and she'd cut him off with a quick gesture of one hand and a blush that he could sense more than see. And that was the last thing either of them had said about it.

"A little?" he said finally. "I don't think you can be a little pregnant. It's sort of an either-or kind of thing." He tried to smile but couldn't quite manage it. "Have you been to a doctor. Are you all right?"

"No and yes." Seeing his blank look and apparently realizing that his brain was not exactly working at full speed, Shannon clarified. "No, I haven't seen a doctor yet. Yes, I'm all right."

"And you're sure you're..." He gestured vaguely toward her stomach.

"I did one of those home pregnancy tests. It...they're supposed to be pretty accurate."

"Yeah, I guess they are."

Silence descended again. Reece stared at the clock, watching the second hand make one full sweep around, trying to wrap his mind around this new information. He was going to be a father again. He and Shannon were having a baby. Shannon was having his baby. No matter how he phrased it, he couldn't make it seem real.

"You're feeling okay?" he asked. "Besides the coffee thing, I mean."

"It's not just coffee." Shannon was tracing aimless patterns on the table with the tip of one finger, her eyes on the movement. "But other than the fact that food is pretty disgusting, especially first thing in the morning, I seem to be fine. I've...got a doctor's appointment tomorrow actually."

"Good. That's good." A doctor's appointment. She'd made a doctor's appointment. She'd taken a home pregnancy test and made a doctor's appointment and she hadn't said a word to him.

"When did you plan on telling me?" he asked, and saw Shannon flinch away from the edge in his voice.

Her eyes shot up to his and then darted away. "Soon. I thought I might be...but I just... I did the test thingy this morning. I'm still sort of getting used to the idea myself."

Yeah, he could relate to that, Reece thought. He pushed down the annoyance, told himself it was stupid to feel like he was the last one to know. He wished she'd told him when she first suspected, but maybe that was unreasonable. If she'd needed a little time to deal with this on her own, that was her privilege. But if she thought she was going to *continue* dealing with it on her own, that was her mistake.

"We need to talk," he said.

"I know but I can't right now." She looked at the clock with poorly concealed relief. "I need to go open the shop." She stood up and pushed her chair under the table.

As if she was ending a damned board meeting, he thought irritably. The legs of his chair scraped across the floor as he rose. Her eyes widened, and she stepped back from the table as if afraid he was going to lunge across it and grab her. It was tempting.

"Shannon." Reece stopped, drew a breath and reminded himself to stay calm. "Can't Kelly do that for you this morning?" he said finally. "I really think this is important."

"It is." Shannon edged toward the door. "It's very important and I want to talk to you about…about this but it wouldn't be fair to call Kelly at the last minute like this. Saturdays are our busiest day and she's already scheduled to come in this afternoon. Besides, it's not like I'm sick." She flushed when Reece shot a pointed glance at the bathroom door behind her. "Not *sick* sick," she amended. "Just because I'm… Women in my condition work all the time, and if I'm going to be doing this for the next eight months, I'd better get used to it."

"The next eight months? So you're going to have the baby?"

Shannon was halfway out the door but his question made her stop and look at him, her eyes wide and startled. "What?"

"It's a simple question, Shannon. Are you planning on having the baby?"

"Yes. I'm sorry. I should have told you that right away. And I'm sorry if that's not what you wanted to hear but I want this child.'' Her voice wobbled and then steadied. ''I want it and I'm going to have it. You don't have to feel obligated to—''

''To hell with that,'' he snapped, cutting her off. He was around the table and reaching to catch her hands in his before she could move. ''Don't start telling me I'm not obligated, like it's a dinner check we agreed to split.'' She tugged on her hands but he tightened his grip, refusing to release her. ''Shannon, we need to talk about this. Call Kelly. Please.''

''No.'' She shook her head, looking down at their clasped hands. ''Please. I need... I can't do this right now.'' When she looked up at him, her eyes were full of tears and all his frustration slipped away, leaving only the need to comfort but, when he tried to draw her closer, she pulled back, shaking her head frantically. ''Please, Reece. I had this— I was going to tell you tonight. I had it all planned out. Dinner and...and everything. I didn't expect you to—'' She stopped and drew a deep breath, visibly grabbing hold of her composure. ''I can't do this now, Reece. I know it's not fair and I'm sorry but I just...can't.''

He couldn't ignore the plea in her eyes. His hands tightened over hers for an instant and then he released her. ''Okay. Tonight.'' That sounded almost like a threat, and he drew a deep breath, forcing back the urge to insist that they had to talk now. This minute. ''We'll talk tonight. We'll have dinner and we'll talk.''

''Thank you.'' Her obvious relief stung, but he told himself not to take it personally, which was pretty damned stupid, really, since it didn't get much more personal than this.

''No toaster waffles,'' he said, and she gave a wavery little laugh that made him want to grab her and hold her and never let her go. He settled for brushing his fingers over the curve of her cheek. "I'll bring dinner."

"Okay." She managed something approaching a real smile. "I've really got to get going."

He nodded and stepped back. "I'll see you tonight. And, Shannon?" She'd started to walk away but turned back to look at him. "Everything's going to be all right."

She hesitated and then gave him a jerky little nod. Reece turned and stared at the sunny kitchen. Twenty minutes ago he'd walked in here with nothing more on his mind than sharing a cup of coffee with the woman he loved, the woman he thought just might love him in return. Instead of a cozy cup of coffee and a few stolen kisses, he'd found out that he was going to be a father again, and all his plans for wooing and winning Shannon had just taken a sharp left turn into the unknown.

Reece had no idea how long he'd been standing in the middle of his grandfather's kitchen, staring blankly at the faded-print curtains while he tried to absorb the idea that he was about to become a father for the second time. He heard Kyle's bedroom door open and then the bathroom door close. A few minutes later his son shuffled into the kitchen, wearing holey gray sweatpants and an equally tattered black T-shirt, his dark hair sticking out in every direction.

"Hey." Kyle muttered, his attention focused on the coffeemaker. He frowned when he saw it was empty. "I thought I smelled coffee."

"Yeah."

Kyle turned to look at him, eyebrows raised. "So, you drank the whole pot already?"

"No." Reece shook his head, forced himself to focus. "It's in the thermos. I...took some over to Shannon's."

"Yeah?" Kyle got out a cup and reached for the thermal carafe. "I thought I heard you go out earlier."

He twisted off the lid, and Reece felt his stomach lurch as the rich, dark scent filled the room. God, was morning sickness catching? Kyle glanced at him, lifting the carafe and arching his brows in question. Reece swallowed and shook his head.

"No, thanks."

"More for me," Kyle said, grinning as he twisted the lid back on and picked up his cup. He closed his eyes in bliss as he took the first sip. "Oh, man, this is the good stuff, isn't it? That Moroccan Brown Trenches stuff."

"Jamaican Blue Mountain."

"Same difference."

"If you don't know the difference between Jamaica and Morocco and a trench and a mountain, maybe you really should go back to school," Reece said dryly.

Kyle's grin was unrepentant. "Geography never was my best subject."

"No kidding." Reece hesitated, debating about whether or not to tell Kyle about Shannon's morning bombshell but he was going to have to know sooner or later. "Look, I...I need to tell you something."

Kyle lowered his coffee mug, his expression concerned. "Are you okay? You're not sick or anything, are you?"

"I'm fine," Reece said quickly.

"Good." The sudden tension eased from Kyle's

shoulders. "Usually, when someone says they need to tell you something, it's bad news."

"It's not. Not bad news, I mean." He was half sorry he'd started this, but now that he had, he might as well finish it. It wasn't the sort of thing that could be kept a secret, even if he wanted to. "It's…I…" He saw the concern creeping back into his son's eyes and sighed. "Shannon's pregnant."

Kyle stared at him, looking almost as stunned as he'd felt when he first found out. Reece let the silence stretch, letting his son absorb the full impact of the news.

"Wow," Kyle said finally. He looked down at his coffee cup, lifted it partway to his mouth, then set it down on the counter with a sharp little click. "Wow, that's just… I take it you guys didn't plan this?"

"Hell, no, we didn't plan it." Reece shoved his fingers through his hair. "It just…happened."

"It just happened?" Kyle raised his eyebrows, his disapproval obvious. "What, like an act of God?"

"No. We…I didn't…" Reece felt himself flush under his son's disapproving look. "It was just one time, dammit."

"One time?" Kyle's mouth tightened in a way that was uncomfortably reminiscent of his mother. He jabbed his finger in Reece's direction. "*You're* the one who told me there was no excuse for carelessness. Right after you showed me what a condom was and how to use one."

He sounded angry, and Reece couldn't blame him. He'd been criminally careless and now…now…Jesus, he didn't know what happened now. He sank down on a kitchen chair, all but fell into it and scrubbed his hands over his face.

"It was stupid," he said tiredly. "Just…really stupid."

"Yeah, it was." Kyle was apparently not in the mood to cut him some slack. "What are you—What is Shannon going to do?"

"She wants to keep the baby." That much he was clear on. He had the feeling some of the details of their conversation were gone forever, lost in the buzz of panic and denial that had filled his head but he was sure of that. "She said I didn't have to feel obligated—"

Kyle's disgusted snort cut him off. "She doesn't know you very well, does she?"

"No." He sighed, relieved that his son *did* know him, knew him well enough to know he'd never walk away from his own child. Never *want* to walk away from his child.

He heard Kyle stirring around but didn't lift his head until a coffee cup appeared on the table next to his arm. "I'd add a shot of whiskey if I knew where it was."

"Don't have any." Reece picked up the cup, wrapping both hands around it.

"Maybe you should get some," Kyle said dryly, and Reece surprised himself by laughing. It only lasted a moment but it made him feel better. He sat up, straightening his shoulders as he lifted the cup and took a swallow of coffee.

Kyle pulled out the chair across from him and sat down, his expression serious as he looked at Reece. "Dad—"

Reece held up a hand to stop him. "Please, no lectures on safe sex. This whole conversation has way too much role reversal going on already."

Kyle grinned. "Oh, man, and I was just about to get all public service announcement on you."

"Yeah, well, don't." Reece looked across the table at his son and shook his head, his smile rueful. "No offense but I always figured that, if we ever had to have this conversation, I'd be on the other side of the fence."

"Hey, my dad really drummed the importance of safe sex into my head."

"Smart ass," Reece muttered.

"So, what are you going to do?" Kyle asked after a moment.

"Talk to Shannon." Reece set his cup on the table and cupped his fingers around it, drawing warmth from the thick porcelain. "She had to go open the shop, so we didn't get much chance to talk."

"She couldn't get somebody to cover for her?" Kyle asked, looking surprised.

"I don't think she wanted to," Reece admitted with a sigh. He leaned back in his chair, suddenly aware that he was as tired as if he'd been up for forty-eight hours straight instead of—he glanced at the clock— God, was it only ten o'clock in the morning? He caught his son's concerned look and forced a half smile. "She just found out for sure this morning. I think she needed a little time to get used to the idea."

"Yeah, I guess I can understand that." Kyle turned his coffee cup between his hands, keeping his eyes on the aimless movement. "What do you want to do? About the baby and Shannon, I mean?"

The answer came more easily than he'd expected. "I want to marry her."

"Because of the baby?" Kyle looked up at him, green eyes sharp and focused. "I've got to tell you, I don't think that's such a hot reason to get married. I mean, I know you're going to want to be involved with the kid and everything but there's more to marriage than just raising kids.''

"Yeah, I kind of figured that out about the time your mother and I split up," Reece said dryly. He stood and picked up his coffee cup to carry it to the sink, ruffling Kyle's hair on the way past. "I appreciate the sage advice, though.''

Kyle grinned and ducked away from his hand. "Yeah, not everyone is lucky enough to get the benefit of advice from someone who might have majored in psych if they'd stayed in college.''

"Psych? I thought you were planning on archeology. Get a fedora and go off in search of adventure.''

"I was thinking about it but then I found out that there's a severe shortage of four-star hotels on dig sites and you know how I feel about camping out. Nature Boy, I'm not." He'd turned in his chair to watch Reece rinse out his cup. "And don't think you're going to distract me from the subject at hand by bringing up my abandoned education.''

Reece shook his head as he set the cup in the drainer. "You get that pigheaded streak from your mother.''

"Yeah? She says I get it from you." Kyle pushed back his chair and stood up, jabbing his empty cup in his father's direction. "I'm not a kid anymore, Dad. I may not have your vast experience with relationships.'' He grinned and dodged the cuff Reece aimed at the side of his head. "But that doesn't mean I don't know a bad idea when I hear one. And marrying Shannon just because she's pregnant is a bad idea.''

"How about if I marry her because I love her?'' Reece rested his palms on the edge of the counter and leaned back, waiting for Kyle's reaction. It was the first time he'd said it out loud and it sounded surprisingly not-startling. It sounded…good. Right.

"Yeah?" Kyle tilted his head and gave his father a considering look.

"Are you okay with that idea?" Reece asked, suddenly worried that maybe he should have led up to it more gradually.

Kyle looked surprised. "Why wouldn't I be?"

"Well, you know, me getting involved with someone else, maybe getting remarried." He shrugged uncomfortably.

"You mean because I might have some lingering fantasies about you and Mom getting back together?" Kyle's tone was dry as dust and Reece grimaced.

"Okay, so forget it. It was just a thought."

"That's okay." Kyle gave him a patronizing pat on the shoulder as he rinsed out his cup and set it to drain. "Leave the psychological stuff to those of us who thought about taking classes."

"Smart ass."

"You're starting to repeat yourself." Kyle leaned one hip on the counter, arms crossed over his chest. "I think Shannon is great. She's nice and she's fun and what red-blooded American boy doesn't dream of having a gorgeous stepmother?"

His grin held an edge of mischief and, for just an instant, Reece saw the boy he'd once been. He felt a pang of nostalgia for the years gone by and then a sharp little jolt at the realization that he was going to get to watch another child grow up.

Kyle straightened away from the counter and looked at his father, his expression suddenly serious. "I think you guys are really good together. I think it would be great if you got married.''

Well, that made two of them, Reece thought. Now, all he had to do was convince Shannon that it was a great idea.

She was *not* running away from home, Shannon told herself. That would be childish and immature. She was simply taking a long drive to give herself a chance to think. A really long drive that had, so far, involved no thinking more complex than whether to leave the radio on or off. And there was nothing at all strange about the fact that she had started that drive in the middle of a busy Saturday, leaving the shop in the semicapable hands of two part-time employees.

Kelly had been coming in, she reminded herself, trying to soothe her guilt pangs. Actually, the fact that Kelly was due to arrive had been a driving factor in her decision to flee like the craven coward she apparently was.

Her fingers tightened on the steering wheel, and she released her breath on a long sigh. There. She'd admitted it. She was running away from home. She was running away because she knew Kelly would take one look at her and know something was wrong. Shannon wasn't up to deflecting her questions, she didn't want to lie and she wasn't ready to tell the truth.

Apparently, when it came to fight or flight, she ran like a jackrabbit.

But she couldn't run forever, and two hours of aimless driving was about her limit. Or maybe not so aimless, she thought as an exit sign loomed up in front of her. She felt a jolt as she realized where she was and, almost as if in a dream, she flipped on her turn signal and took the exit for Los Olivos.

Ten minutes later she was standing on Rachel Walker's front porch, watching the surprise in the older woman's eyes change to warm welcome.

Chapter 14

Shannon had heard it said that home was the place you could go where they had to take you in. She wasn't sure about the "had to" part of it, but there was certainly something wonderful about showing up on someone's doorstep and having them just...take you in. Rachel didn't ask any questions, didn't comment on her unexpected arrival. She just smiled and held the door open.

Shannon's eyes stung and she blinked hard. "I hope you don't mind me just dropping in like this." She laughed and hoped it didn't sound as thin to the other woman as it did to her. "I was in the neighborhood."

Rachel looked surprised. "I thought you'd decided to come after all."

"After all?" Shannon repeated blankly and saw a sudden flicker of concern in Rachel's eyes.

As soon as she stepped inside, she became aware of the dull roar of sound she'd come to associate with large numbers of Walkers gathered in one place. She heard someone laugh and a child's giggle. Obviously, most if not all of the family was here.

"I didn't—" With half-formed thoughts of retreat, she stepped back, but Rachel caught her arm and tugged her the rest of the way inside, shutting the door firmly behind her.

"Don't be silly. If you're not up for seeing everyone, we can sneak you through the kitchen. Sam and Nikki are staying in the big guest room but there's no one in the small spare room. I can stash you there." She was moving forward as she spoke. "The children wanted pizza so no one's cooking tonight. You should have heard the argument over what to order. Keefe can't stand pepperoni and Cole made gagging noises when Nikki said she liked anchovies. I suppose it's setting a terrible example for the children but, honestly, *anchovies?* So, then Danny wanted ham and pineapple but Kelsey says he doesn't actually like the pineapple, he just likes the *idea* of it."

Shannon let the words flow over her. No response seemed to be required, which was just as well. Somewhere in between the pepperoni and the pineapple, she'd remembered that this weekend was a joint birthday celebration for some combination of family members. Exactly who escaped her at the moment. Now that it was too late, it occurred to her that there had been a lot of cars parked out front. Rachel had invited her to join them and she'd said she'd try but weekends were a busy time at the shop. But not so busy, apparently, that she couldn't run like a rabbit at the first little problem, if you could call an unplanned pregnancy and a totally confused life a "little" problem.

Rachel led Shannon into the kitchen, bypassing the

crowded living room, but the kitchen wasn't entirely empty. Hippo, Rachel's enormous dog, lay sprawled in the middle of the room, taking up a large portion of the available floor space, and Sam stood in front of the open refrigerator door.

"So, was that Mrs. Klausman complaining about the— Hey, Shannon." His smile held the same easy welcome his—*their*—mother's had, and she wondered again why she'd found it so difficult to open her heart to these people. "How are you?"

"I'm fine." Her voice wobbled, surprising her. She saw Sam's eyes sharpen with sudden concern and felt her heart stutter. If he started asking questions, she was going to dissolve in a sobbing heap. Hormones, she thought. It had to be hormones.

Sam started to say something, caught his mother's eye and stopped. "Shannon's tired. I'm going to get her settled in the little bedroom," Rachel said.

"Sure." If he thought it was odd that a perfectly healthy young woman would be so exhausted by a two-hour drive that she had to lie down, he didn't say anything. "Pizza should be here in a half hour or so," he said. "If you feel up to joining us, I promise to fend the ravening hordes off long enough to make sure you get a piece."

"Thanks." She smiled, grateful enough for the questions he didn't ask to forgive him for making her stomach roll with the mention of pizza.

Rachel led the way down the back hall to the bedrooms. "I'll need to get some linens for the bed. Keefe, Tessa and the baby are staying at Gage and Kelsey's. With Lily there and Danny, they're already set up for children. Besides, Tessa's apparently been bitten by the green-thumb bug and I think she's hoping to convince

Keefe that what the ranch really needs is a greenhouse like Kelsey's.''

Shannon let the words flow over her in a pleasant wash of sound. She knew, though she didn't know how she knew, that Rachel didn't expect a response or even for her to really listen. It wasn't until she was standing in the small bedroom she'd occupied at Christmas, watching Rachel pull the duvet off the bed that something occurred to her.

"I didn't say anything about spending the night," she said, coming forward to take the duvet and drape it over the small armchair in the corner.

"Didn't you?" Rachel picked up a sheet from the stack she'd brought in from the linen closet. She spread it across the mattress with a quick snap of her wrists. Shannon moved automatically to tug it into place. "I guess I just figured that, since it was so late in the day, you weren't likely to be heading home tonight."

At the mention of home, Shannon flinched. Reece. She'd told him they'd have dinner together so they could discuss the situation. She glanced at the small alarm clock on the nightstand. "Could I use your phone?"

"Of course." Rachel finished smoothing the bottom sheet out before straightening up and fixing Shannon with a look that held concern but no demand. "You can use the one in my bedroom, if you like."

"Thanks." Shannon started toward the door, remembered the half-made bed and pivoted back. "Let me—"

"I'll get this." Rachel waved her hand at the door. "You go make your call." When Shannon hesitated, she arched both brows. "Go on."

Shannon went. For all her small size and gentle appearance, there was a certain air of authority about Rachel Walker that made it easy to imagine her raising four boys by herself.

Rachel's bedroom was painted a soft white and furnished with a light oak bed and dressers. The overall effect was both airy and restful. The phone was on the nightstand, and Shannon sank down on the edge of the bed, staring at it for several long moments before reaching for it. She had it all worked out, knew exactly what to say when Reece answered the phone. It all flew out the window when she heard Kyle's voice.

"Kyle? It's, ah, Shannon. Is your dad there?"

"Hi, Shannon. No, Dad went out to pick up some stuff for dinner. He should be back any minute now. Are you at home? 'Cause I think he was planning on cooking dinner here and then taking it over to your place."

"Actually, I'm not home." Shannon tried for casual and managed strained. She cleared her throat. "I...I was calling to tell him that I couldn't do dinner tonight after all. I decided to...visit my...family and I'm going to spend the night here."

"Are you okay?" The concern in Kyle's voice made Shannon's eyes sting.

"I'm fine. I just— It's my brother's birthday." She was almost positive it was Cole's birthday but she was probably going to go to hell for using it as an excuse like this. "I thought I should—"

"Dad told me about the baby."

"Oh." So much for polite lies. Shannon made a conscious effort to ease the tightness of her grip on the phone. "I, ah..."

"It's none of my business," Kyle said, interrupting her, which was just as well, since she had no idea what she was going to say. "I just wanted you to know that I'm okay with this." He laughed a little. "I mean, I'm not going to be overcome by a sudden attack of sibling rivalry or anything."

"That's good to know." *Sibling?* She closed her eyes while she absorbed that idea. She'd barely begun to deal with the idea that she was going to have a baby and now her child had a sibling. A brother. God. She drew a shaky breath. "I've got to go, Kyle. Tell your dad...tell him I'm sorry about dinner and I'll...I'll call him."

She barely waited for Kyle's goodbye before hanging up the phone. Sitting on the edge of Rachel's bed, she clasped her hands between her knees, shoulders hunched as she contemplated the pale-green carpet at her feet. She really needed to get a handle on this whole thing. The baby. Reece. Her life.

Sighing, she pushed herself to her feet and left the room. A muted clamor drifted from the living room, male voices, a childish giggle, a woman's laughter. She felt a brief, wistful urge to join them, let herself be absorbed in the noise and the warmth that seemed to be an integral part of any Walker family gathering. Sighing, she turned away.

"I'll find you something to sleep in later," Rachel said as Shannon entered the small bedroom. She smoothed one hand over the floral-print duvet and twitched a corner of a pillowcase into place. "I don't think you'll need it but there's an extra blanket in the closet, just in case."

"Thank you. It's very nice of you to take me in like this." Shannon managed a lopsided smile. "I don't usually show up on people's doorsteps like an orphan of the storm."

"You're always welcome here, Shannon. You know that." Rachel studied her a moment and then seemed to come to some decision. "I know it doesn't feel like it to you but we're your family and we're here for you. I'm here for you. I promised myself I wouldn't pry, but it's obvious that you're upset about something, and I just want you to know that if you want to talk, I'm a pretty good listener."

Shannon started to tell her that she appreciated the offer but really didn't want to talk but what came out was: "I'm pregnant."

The flat statement seemed to echo in the small room, as if she'd shouted it loud enough to ruffle the neat blue-and-white-striped curtains. Rachel drew in a quick, startled breath, her dark eyes widening in shock.

"I take you don't want to be pregnant?"

"No. I mean, I didn't plan on this but, now that I am, I...I want the baby." She was surprised by how much she wanted it. It seemed odd that a few weeks ago, motherhood had been nothing but a distant, maybe-someday possibility, but now that it was a reality, she couldn't remember a time when she *hadn't* wanted this.

"Reece doesn't want the baby?" Rachel probed gently.

"No. I...actually, I don't know." She hadn't really given him a chance to express any feelings one way or the other.

"You haven't told him?" Rachel looked surprised, and Shannon immediately felt defensive.

"I told him. I told him this morning."

"And what did he say?"

"Not much. I... Well, I sort of..."

"Come sit down," Rachel said, sitting on the edge

of the bed and patting the spot beside her. ''Tell me what happened.''

It was surprisingly easy. Shannon told her about Reece moving in next door, about how the fact that he was only there temporarily had been a *good* thing and then they'd…well, it was just one time but they'd been careless. She felt her face heat as she said it and was glad that she was sitting next to the other woman so she didn't have to meet her eyes. God, she couldn't believe she was telling her mother about her sex life. And then about the ''flu'' she couldn't seem to shake and how stupid she felt that the truth hadn't occurred to her sooner.

Rachel patted her hand. ''Well, you know, every now and again, you hear a news story about some woman who didn't know she was pregnant until she gave birth, so it could have been worse.''

That surprised Shannon into a choked laugh. ''I suppose that's some consolation. At least I figured it out before I went into labor.''

''So, tell me what Reece said when you told him,'' Rachel said, folding her fingers around Shannon's and squeezing a little. ''I liked him when he was here at Christmas. I'm going to be very disappointed if he was a jerk.''

''He wasn't.'' Shannon kept her eyes lowered, staring at their linked hands. There was comfort in that simple touch, a connection she hadn't realized she needed. ''He told me not to worry, that everything would be okay.''

''That's it? That's all he said?''

''I…didn't really give him a chance to say anything else,'' she admitted in a low voice. ''I'd just found out that I was…about the…'' She stopped, huffed out an exasperated breath. How was it possible that she could *be* pregnant and not be able to *say* the word? "I'd just found out about the baby." She got it out in a rush. "I wasn't ready to talk to him about it so I told him we'd have dinner and talk."

"Dinner tonight?"

Shannon nodded, her cheeks warming with a guilty flush.

"I don't understand," Rachel said slowly. "I would think you'd want to talk to Reece, want to find out what he's thinking. Are you afraid he won't take responsibility? Because, I have to say, he didn't strike me as the kind of man who would do that."

"No. No, I know he'll want to live up to his obligations." Shannon's hand tightened around her mother's, the fingers of her other hand plucking restlessly at the duvet. "He'll probably offer to marry me."

"And you don't want that?" Rachel asked gently. "Do you love him?"

Shannon opened her mouth, closed it without speaking and drew a shuddering breath. Straight to the heart of it. The question she'd been avoiding asking herself. But now that it was asked, the answer was obvious and devastating. That night in the truck, the night their child had been conceived, there had been one frozen moment when she could have stopped what was about to happen. A word, a hesitation, and Reece would have pulled back, would have ended it. She'd looked up at him, the hard planes of his face limned in moonlight and she'd had a sudden image of herself, belly rounded with the weight of his child and she'd wanted that with a fierce hunger she'd never felt before. It had been a deep visceral *need* inside to have his child, a part of him that would be hers to keep even when he was gone.

She'd never felt that way about anyone. She'd loved Johnny, and she'd mourned him deeply, but what she felt for Reece was so much more, so overwhelming.

Did she love him? So much it terrified her.

"That's not the point," she said carefully, and wondered if that sounded as much like an admission to Rachel as it did to her.

"I think it's very much the point, but I won't argue with you about it." Rachel squeezed her hand gently. "Why don't you tell me what you think the problem is?"

"I don't want him to feel obligated. Not to me or the baby."

"But why shouldn't he feel obligated? It's his child, too. His responsibility."

"No." The single word was sharp and hard. Shannon drew a shallow breath and repeated it more quietly. "No. I want more than that for my baby and for myself. I don't want Reece to feel *obligated*." Her tone made the word an epithet. "My father was *obligated* to take care of me. All my life, I knew that's what I was to him. A responsibility. An obligation. I didn't know why until I found out what he'd done, that he'd taken me away from you. He took care of me. I always had plenty to eat and a decent place to live but there was…" She shook her head, at a loss for the words to explain what had been missing. She'd never done without, and yet she hadn't had the most important things— love and warmth, a sense of belonging.

"I don't know why he didn't just leave me on somebody's doorstep somewhere, but maybe, after he took me away, he felt obligated to take care of me. I won't be an obligation to anyone ever again and neither will my child.''

There was a moment's silence before Rachel spoke, her voice thick with tears. ''Oh, Shannon. I'm so sorry.''

For the first time since they'd sat down, Shannon looked at her mother, saw the pain in her eyes. And the love. ''It wasn't your fault,'' she whispered.

''Maybe not.'' Rachel shook her head a little. ''I can't tell you how many times I asked myself if there wasn't something I could have done or said, if I shouldn't have realized somehow what he was going to do, that he was going to take you away from us.'' She lowered her eyes to their joined hands. ''It took me a long time to accept what had happened—at least as much as anyone could accept losing a child. I don't think I would have survived if it hadn't been for the boys. They needed me, but I needed them even more. Life went on, more or less, but there wasn't a single day went by that I didn't think about you, wonder where you were and if you were happy.''

Her voice broke on the last word, and Shannon felt tears start to her own eyes. After a moment Rachel cleared her throat and went on more briskly.

''I won't pretend to know what was in your father's mind, why he did what he did. It was not a good divorce.'' She lifted her head and met Shannon's eyes. ''It wasn't a good marriage and that was as much my fault as his. It was too soon after losing my first husband. I was scared and alone and scared of being alone. Your father and I were a poor match from the beginning and we should have ended things sooner. By the time I did end it, I was carrying you. I know every parent thinks their baby is perfect but you were so…wonderful. And all the harsh words and misery between your father and me just didn't matter anymore. It seemed so amazing that something so…perfect had come out of something so…flawed.''

Her expression tender, she reached up to brush Shannon's hair back from her face. ''You were such a happy little girl. Your brothers adored you. It was like you were our reward for all the bad things that had happened. You…completed the family somehow, as if we'd just been waiting for you.''

Shannon felt something dissolve inside at the love she saw in the other woman's eyes, some long-held barrier disappearing, taking a lifetime of loneliness with it.

''I don't know why he took you away. Maybe it was because he was afraid that, as long as you had us, you wouldn't need him. Maybe taking you was just an impulse and then, once it was done, he didn't know how to turn back. I'm not sure it matters anymore but I won't pretend to forgive him for it. Maybe if I were a better person I could, but I can't. What he did, what he took from us…from you…'' Rachel's eyes grew suddenly fierce, and her fingers tightened around her daughter's. ''You were *never* an obligation, Shannon. Not to me, not to your brothers. And I don't believe for a minute that either you or this baby are nothing but an obligation to Reece. Don't make decisions before you at least hear what he has to say.''

''I'm scared,'' Shannon whispered.

''Of what?'' Rachel stroked her hand over her daughter's bright hair.

''What if it doesn't work? What if he does want to marry me and we give it a try and it doesn't work or what if something happens to him? It hurt so much when I lost Johnny but what I feel for Reece is so much— It's more than I thought I could ever feel for anyone. It would kill me to lose him.''

"If you don't take the chance, you've already lost him," Rachel pointed out gently. "How are you going to feel if you turn him away now, shut him out of your life, out of the baby's life without ever seeing what you could have together?" She cupped her hands around Shannon's face, her eyes dark with love and compassion. "If you don't take the chance, honey, you'll spend the rest of your life wondering what you could have had. Maybe it won't work out. And maybe something will happen to him, maybe you'll lose him, but wouldn't you rather have a few months or years with him than no time at all?"

Shannon blinked against the sudden sting of tears. She was tired and confused and scared. Her whole life had been turned upside down and she didn't know what to do to put it right side up again. Her vision blurred and she blinked again, feeling the hot slide of a tear as it spilled over.

"I'm sorry," she whispered, bringing her hand up to press her fingers to her trembling lips. "I'm sorry."

"Hush." Rachel's arms were strong and warm around her, pulling her close, holding her tight. "Everything's going to be okay. Just let it out." She pressed her cheek against the top of Shannon's head. "Let it out, honey. I've got you."

And Shannon turned into the offered comfort, crying out all her fear and confusion on her mother's shoulder.

He'd given her twenty-four hours, Reece thought as he flipped on the turn signal and made the turn onto the street where Rachel Walker lived. If Shannon needed more time, she could tell him as much and he'd leave. Maybe he'd even be able to resist the urge to throw her over his shoulder and take her with him.

He considered himself a patient man. Contrary to the nonstop-action sequences so beloved of Hollywood, covert ops was largely a waiting game. Patience was a necessity if you wanted to grow old and die in bed. And he was a reasonable man. When Shannon had dropped the bombshell that he was about to become a father and then said she couldn't talk about it right then, he'd demonstrated both patience and reason. He hadn't insisted that they had to talk *now*. He'd accepted her need for a little time to come to terms with the changes this made in her life—in both their lives.

And last night when Kyle had given him Shannon's message that she wasn't safely next door, resting quietly the way any newly pregnant woman with an ounce of sense would be, but had instead, apparently, driven over a hundred miles by herself, he had again demonstrated his capacity for calm reason by not leaping into his truck and tracking her down. Okay, so Kyle had been instrumental in that decision, pointing out that showing up on her mother's doorstep and demanding to know what the hell she thought she was doing smacked of an overly possessive attitude at best and teetered on the edge of stalkerdom.

So, he'd done the reasonable thing and stayed home, charring the two filet mignons he'd bought to have with Shannon and overcooking the asparagus so badly that, when Kyle asked him what it was, it didn't even sound like sarcasm.

After a mostly sleepless night, he'd demonstrated yet more patience—not to mention good manners—by not calling Rachel's house at 5:00 a.m. when he finally gave up trying to sleep and got up. He'd only checked five times to make sure the phone was still working between then and eleven o'clock, which showed restraint. At noon, when she still hadn't called, he'd decided that patience and restraint could only take a man so far. Kyle had gone for a run, which made it the perfect time to leave since his son would probably have advised yet more patience and had, in fact, threatened to body tackle him when Reece hinted at driving to Los Olivos at six in the morning. Leaving while Kyle was gone prevented more arguments and possible physical violence.

Now here he was, and from the looks of it so was Shannon's entire family. Muttering a curse under his breath, Reece parked behind a truck he recognized as Keefe's and got out. Slamming the truck door did *not* suggest that his patience was running thin. It just slipped out of his hand. Really hard.

Somebody must have seen him coming, because the front door opened as he pushed open the front gate, and by the time he reached the porch, four large, male bodies stood between him and the house. Reece stopped at the bottom of the steps and looked at them. Patience and restraint, he reminded himself.

"I came to see Shannon." Well, it was stating the obvious but he had to start somewhere.

"Oh, yeah?" That was Cole, looking less than patient and restrained. "She didn't say anything about expecting you."

"I wanted to surprise her."

"Seems like you're just full of surprises," Keefe said, his tone so neutral it hovered on the edge of hostile.

Apparently, she'd told her family about the baby and

her brothers were laying the blame squarely at his feet.
Not that he blamed them. Reece felt himself flush but
he didn't say anything. He'd already endured a lecture
on safe sex from his son. He was damned if he was
going to start offering excuses to Shannon's brothers.

"Why don't you tell Shannon I'm here and she can
decide whether or not she wants to see me?"

"If she wanted to see you, she would have called,"
Cole said.

The logic was irrefutable, but Reece was not in the
mood for logic, and his store of patience and reason
was fast running out, too. He put his foot on the first
step and looked at the four of them steadily.

"If I have to go through all of you, I will."

Gage arched one brow and his mouth twitched with
something that looked like amusement. Cole looked as
if he was thinking about launching the first punch.
Keefe's eyes were steady, cool, his expression impos-
sible to read. Sam tilted his head a little, blue eyes
bright and interested.

"I think he means it," he commented.

"Good." Cole took a half step forward, and Reece
braced himself. Damn, this wasn't exactly the best way
to start off a relationship with what he hoped were his
future in-laws, and Shannon was not going to be happy
if he broke her brother's nose. He wasn't sure how
she'd feel if it was *his* nose that sustained the damage.
Either way, he had a feeling that a plea of "he started
it" was not going to cut it.

Sam's hand came down on Cole's shoulder. "Let's
not be hasty here." He looked at Reece. "At the risk
of sounding like a character out of a bad novel, you
mind telling us what your intentions are?"

Reece thought of telling him it was none of his

damned business, but that wouldn't get them anywhere. Besides, maybe they had the right to ask.

"I plan on marrying Shannon."

"Because of the baby?" Keefe asked.

"No. Because I'm in love with her." Reece could feel his patience thinning, fraying along the edges.

"Cut the guy some slack." That was Gage. He stepped back, using a shoulder to edge Keefe back with him. "Shannon's a big girl. If she doesn't want to see him, she'll say so and *then* we can throw him out."

It was said with a look of cheerful malice that startled Reece into a smile. "Bring help," was all he said as he came up the steps and shouldered his way past the four men.

"She's in the kitchen," Sam said as he pushed open the door, and Reece supposed that was as close to being given their blessing as he was going to get at the moment.

She was indeed in the kitchen. He stopped in the doorway, feeling a tightness he hadn't even realized was there suddenly ease in his chest. She was sitting at the kitchen table, wearing black leggings and a gray flannel shirt that was so much too big for her, it had to belong to one of her brothers. A ray of sunlight spilled through the window over the sink and caught in her hair, catching red-and-gold highlights in the thick waves.

She looked…perfect, and for a moment it was enough to just stand in the doorway and look at her. He would have stood there admiring the view for even longer, but Shannon wasn't alone. The entire distaff side of the Walker clan and their offspring were also crowded into the big kitchen, and he barely had time to draw a relieved breath before Addie saw him standing there.

"Oh, dear." Her voice was hardly more than a murmur, but with some sort of female sixth sense the other women immediately turned toward him. Finding himself suddenly the focus of so many pairs of eyes—even the children were looking at him—Reece fought the urge to check and make sure his fly was zipped. Ironically Shannon was the last one to register that something had changed. She was bent over the coloring book she was sharing with Cole's little girl, and it wasn't until Mary nudged her that she looked up and saw him.

"Reece." Her eyes widened into startled blue pools. He couldn't read either welcome or rejection in her expression, just surprise.

"Hi." As opening lines went, it wasn't exactly original. "I thought we should, ah, talk," he added, painfully aware of their audience, who made no attempt at a polite pretense of not listening.

All eyes swiveled to Shannon, waiting for her response, and Reece had no illusions about being able to either intimidate or persuade *this* batch of Walkers. If Shannon said she didn't want to talk to him, he might as well just turn around and go home. She hesitated, and he was surprised to see her eyes seek out Rachel's. The other woman gave her an encouraging smile, and Shannon flushed a little before looking at him and nodding.

"Okay."

As if on some prearranged signal, everyone was suddenly in motion. Reece stepped through the doorway and out of the way of the sudden exodus. He'd worked with military commanders who would have envied the efficiency with which the kitchen emptied, leaving him alone with Shannon and a silence so thick it was a tangible presence.

He moved closer to the table, his eyes devouring her. It was less than thirty-six hours since he'd seen her, but it seemed much longer. Yesterday morning he'd been reeling with the sudden knowledge that he was going to be a father. Now that he'd had a chance to get used to the idea, he found himself looking for some outward sign of the changes taking place inside her body.

"I was going to call you," she said. She was twisting a purple crayon back and forth between her thumb and forefinger, her eyes on the nervous movement. "I'm sorry about dinner last night."

"That's okay. Kyle enjoyed the steak. He would have enjoyed it more if I hadn't burned it, but then he wouldn't have had the pleasure of complaining about my cooking."

She smiled a little but didn't look up. Reece shrugged out of his denim jacket and draped it over the back of a chair. He pulled out another chair and sat down, facing her.

"So, why'd you run?" he asked conversationally.

"I didn't run," she said, her head jerking up and her eyes meeting his for the first time since that brief contact when she first saw him. "I...wanted to see... It was Cole's birthday."

"Uh-huh. And did you remember this before or after you got here and saw the whole family was already here?"

She held his gaze a moment longer, and then her eyes slid away. One shoulder lifted in a sheepish half shrug. "After," she muttered. "But I wasn't running away."

"You stick with that story," he said kindly, and was rewarded by a muffled snort of laughter. Still cautious, he reached out and closed his hand over hers, tugging until she turned to sit sideways on the chair, facing him but still not looking at him. She was apparently fascinated by the pattern on the floor. Still, she didn't pull her hand from his, and Reece figured he'd take his encouragement where he could find it.

"I had this all planned out. I was going to cook you a romantic dinner to impress you with my culinary skills and I was going to ply you with a reasonably adequate wine, because neither of us can taste the difference between that and a really good wine, and then, when I had you well fed and maybe just a teeny bit drunk, I was going to ask you to marry me." Her hand jerked convulsively in his, but he held on, refusing to let her pull away.

"When I found out about the baby, I had to rethink things a bit. The wine was out. I was going to go for the maximum cliché and propose on Valentine's Day but I had to move my timetable up a bit. I—"

"Wait." Shannon's hand was suddenly gripping his painfully tight. Her eyes were riveted to his face. "You were going to ask me to marry you *before* you found out about the baby?"

"That was the plan." He raised his eyebrows. "Is that why you ran away? Because you thought I was going to do the noble thing and offer to marry you just because you were pregnant?"

"I thought you might," she admitted. "And I didn't run away."

"You ran like a jackrabbit and why does everyone

think I only want to marry you because you're pregnant?''

"Who else thinks that?'' she asked, her eyes widening.

"Your brothers, who all look like they'd like to see my head part company with my body, by the way. And my son, who told me that getting married just because of the baby would be a mistake. That was right after he lectured me on safe sex.''

"Did he really?'' One corner of Shannon's mouth quirked up in a half smile.

"Smirk if you like but he was pretty upset. I expected to find myself grounded at any moment.''

"That must have been…interesting.''

"Let's just say I'm not anxious to repeat the experience,'' Reece said dryly. Shannon's eyes were bright with laughter, and Reece felt something unknot in his stomach. It was going to be okay. There were still things to say, questions to be asked, decisions to be made, but it was going to be okay. He reached for her other hand, and she didn't try to pull away this time.

"So, what do you think?''

"About what?''

"About marrying me but not because of the baby.'' His rubbed his thumbs over the back of her hands, watching her face.

"I think it's an…interesting idea,'' she admitted shyly. "Did you, um, have a *reason* for wanting to marry me before you found out about the baby?''

"Just the same reason I have now.'' He shifted closer so that their knees were touching. "I love you. I'm in love with you. I want to spend the rest of my life with you. Are those reasons good enough? Will you marry me?''

Shannon lifted her eyes to his face, her expression searching, worried. "I thought you were only going to stay until your grandfather's house was cleaned out."

"I could have had that done weeks ago."

"You hated Serenity Falls."

"When I was a kid." Reece nodded. "But it wasn't really the place. It was the circumstances. I was sort of thinking of starting a business. A bookstore, maybe, or a toaster-waffle franchise."

When she laughed, Reece decided he'd been cautious long enough and leaned forward to scoop her out of her chair and onto his lap. She gasped and clutched at his shoulders.

"Idiot." Since she was already curling into his hold, her head on his shoulder, Reece decided to take it as an endearment. He wrapped his arms around her and pressed his cheek against her bright hair.

"So, do you think I could get an answer here?"

"Yes." Shannon's voice was dreamy. Her fingers were toying with the buttons on his shirt, opening the top two so that she could slide her hand inside, pressing her palm over his heart.

"Yes? Yes what?" Reece prompted. He didn't really need an answer. She was giving him that now, lying in his arms like this, letting him hold her. Still, it would be nice to hear the words. "Do you love me? Are you going to marry me?"

"Yes to everything." She turned her head to press a kiss against his throat. "Yes, I'll marry you. Yes, I love you. Yes, I think you'd make a terrific bookstore owner or toaster-waffle king or anything else you want to do. Yes, I'm happy about the baby. Yes, I do believe in happily ever after."

"That's a lot of yeses." Reece swallowed to clear the sudden huskiness from his voice.

"Yes." He felt her mouth curve against his throat. "I'm feeling very agreeable. Enjoy it while you can. I'm told I may get very cranky in a few months."

"Oh, yeah?" Reece settled his hand over her flat stomach, imagining it was possible to feel the quick beat of the new life she carried. "Are you going to get cravings for pickles and ice cream?"

"Absolutely not." Shannon raised her head and looked at him with eyes so full of love that he felt it all the way to his soul. "I'm strictly a Froot Loops and Pepsi girl."

*   *   *   *   *

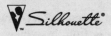

EXPLORE THE POSSIBILITIES OF LIFE—AND LOVE—
IN THIS GROUNDBREAKING ANTHOLOGY!

Turning Point

This is going to be our year.
Love, Your Secret Admirer

It was just a simple note, but for the three women
who received it, it has very different consequences....

For Kristie Samuels, a bouquet of roses on her desk can mean
only that her deadly admirer has gotten too close—and that
she needs to get even closer to protector Scott Wade,
in this provocative tale by **SHARON SALA**.

For Tia Kostas Hunter, her secret admirer seems a lot like the man
she once married—the man she *thought* she was getting a divorce
from!—in this emotional story by **PAULA DETMER RIGGS**.

For secretary Jamie Tyson, the mysterious gift means her romantic
dreams just might come true—and with the man she least
suspects—in this fun, sensuous story by **PEGGY MORELAND**.

Available this December at your favorite retail outlets!

Where love comes alive™

$ Saving Money $ Has Never Been This Easy!

Just fill out and send in this form from any October, November and December 2002 books and we will send you a coupon booklet worth a total savings of $20.00 off future purchases of Harlequin and Silhouette books in 2003.

Yes! It's that easy!

I accept your incredible offer!
Please send me a coupon booklet:

Name (PLEASE PRINT)

Address   Apt. #

City   State/Prov.   Zip/Postal Code

In a typical month, how many
Harlequin and Silhouette novels do you read?

❑ 0-2   ❑ 3+

097KJKDNC7   097KJKDNDP

Please send this form to:
    In the U.S.: Harlequin Books, P.O. Box 9071, Buffalo, NY 14269-9071
    In Canada: Harlequin Books, P.O. Box 609, Fort Erie, Ontario L2A 5X3

Allow 4-6 weeks for delivery. Limit one coupon booklet per household. Must be postmarked no later than January 15, 2003.

HARLEQUIN®
Makes any time special®

Silhouette®
Where love comes alive™

COMING NEXT MONTH

INTIMATE MOMENTS